REIGN OF PAIN

BOOK 3 OF THE *PAIN SERIES*

MICHAEL D'AMBROSIO

ISBN
978-1-963254-56-3 (Paperback)
978-1-963254-57-0 (eBook)
978-1-964982-25-0 (Hardcover)

REIGN OF PAIN

BOOK 3 OF THE PAIN SERIES

TABLE OF CONTENTS

CHAPTER 1

The *Reaper*, Marina's swift Calamaarian cruiser, was hidden under camouflaged netting, made from vines and fern leaves. Marina and Faust, her paramour and partner, sat outside the open hatch on primitive lounge chairs, made from bamboo. The heat and humidity that came with the summer season made Andros-5 quite tropical.

Marina, dressed comfortably in shorts, a sports bra, and a wide-brimmed hat, napped on one of the lounge chairs. Her long, dark hair was braided in six tails, similar to the wig she wore in the past, minus the flash grenade balls. Faust, well-tanned and muscular, wore shorts made from trousers, cut down for comfort. He sat on the edge of the hatch and tinkered with an electronic device.

Several beeps from the alarm system sounded and startled them. Marina awoke and scanned the perimeter warily. Faust rushed inside the ship and when he returned, he carried two pulse pistols and Marina's belt of daggers. He tossed the belt to her and disappeared into the trees. Marina strapped the belt to her thigh and rushed into the forest in a different direction.

Six armed mercenaries crept through the trees toward Marina's ship, dressed in Kronos Enterprise's black colors and armed with knives, pulse rifles and grenades. Marina laid low in the trees as they approached, sweat trickling down her nose from her forehead. She felt her ire return as she resented the trespassers who finally found her secret home and hunted her.

She took one of her four knives from the belt and was eager to attack. It had been a long time since she was involved in battle and she yearned for the feeling of conflict again. So long as things were quiet, she was content to stay in her temporary retirement but, once again, life would not allow her such a precious commodity.

When the last mercenary passed her, Marina leaped up and grabbed the man around his neck. As she slit his throat, two others turned and fired at her. She held her victim upright as a shield and retreated into the trees. The men immediately spread out to surround her. Two removed grenades from their belts and held them out, ready to throw.

"Take her alive," shouted one of the men. "She's worth a lot more that way."

"Nah. Too much trouble," another responded.

The two men reluctantly hooked the grenades back on their belts.

Marina dropped the corpse, no longer needing a shield, and lay across the mossy ground under large fern leaves, waiting patiently to strike again. The men briefly examined their dead comrade and moved on. Marina scurried to her feet and grabbed the next intruder from behind. With one quick motion, she jerked his head until his neck snapped, killing him instantly. The others were too far ahead to hear them as she dragged the corpse behind a tree. Now there were just four intruders left and Faust was waiting to ambush them.

The mercenaries grew nervous as they now realized that two of their team were gone and they hadn't even fired a shot. They huddled close together and approached the *Reaper*. Marina drew one of her daggers and fired it at the nearest man, striking him in the back, just below the neck. The man's eyes rolled up and he fell to the ground dead. The remaining three stood together with their backs to each other in a defensive formation. The sound of a branch snapping unnerved them. They fired in the direction of the sound, while screaming obscenities at Marina.

Marina watched from the opposite direction, amused by how gullible they were. She took another of the daggers from her belt and fired at one of the mercenaries. When the dagger struck the man in the neck, blood spurted from the ruptured artery onto the other men. One of them screamed in horror and stepped out of his defensive position, allowing Faust to fire a well-placed shot into his forehead. The man stared blankly with a smoking hole in his head and then fell to the ground. The last mercenary dropped his pulse rifle and raised his hands in surrender. Faust stepped out of the trees and ordered him to the ground. After searching him, he marched the man toward Marina's ship.

To show her disrespect for Kronos, Marina sat in her lounge chair and waited patiently for Faust to return with a prisoner to the clearing. When they arrived, Marina smiled innocently and inquired, "Were you looking for me?"

The man became red-faced with anger and balled his fists. Faust poked him in the back with his pistol and warned him to settle down. "We will keep coming for you until you are dead!" shouted the mercenary. "You pissed off the wrong people, lady."

Marina yawned and got up from her bamboo chair. She approached the man and touched his cheek in mock affection. Nonchalantly, she asked, "And who is it that little ol' me pissed off?"

The man spit on her and replied, "Kronos. You started a shit storm and it's coming for you."

Marina wiped the spit from her cheek and rubbed it on the man's nose. She smiled and then belted him with a left hook to the jaw. The mercenary was stunned by the impact from a woman, particularly a petite one like Marina. Marina belted him with a right hook to the other side of his jaw and staggered him. "You do know who I am. Don't you?" she questioned him sarcastically.

"Yeah, we know who you are," he responded arrogantly. "But out here, you have no one to protect you. You won't escape this time."

Marina punched him in the gut and kneed him in the head when he bent over. "Do I look like I need protection?" she taunted him.

The mercenary grew more uneasy as he knew she would kill him soon. She glanced at Faust and then questioned the man about Kronos. He refused to answer and then urged her to kill him. Marina shook her head disappointedly and requested, "Just give me one name. Who is the coward that feels the need to draw me out of my retirement?"

The man looked baffled by her words. "Retirement?" he replied.

"Look, asshole, isn't it obvious that no one has seen me in a long time?" she queried him cynically. "Why do you think that is?"

Faust joked, "I think they missed you, Marina."

"It's about Carl Klingman," the man blurted. "His girl Darra wants your head for killing Jack Klingman as well as someone dear to her. You must pay for what you did to their forces as well."

Marina laughed at him. The man became irate and stood up. Blood streamed over his lower lip and dripped off his chin. "They are coming for you. That's all I have to say."

"Thank you," Marina replied appreciatively and nodded to Faust. He fired a single red pulse into the man's chest, killing him instantly. "Time to move on. We've been compromised," complained Marina and then she sighed. This planet was her escape from the reality of war and now she had to abandon it.

Faust suggested that keeping Jack Klingman alive on Orpheus-2 might give them some leverage after all with his brother. Marina considered his words as they left the clearing. Together, they searched for the scout ship that the mercenaries arrived on.

When Marina and Faust located the ship by the river, they placed the intruders' weapons and corpses on board and then programmed the ship for 'autopilot'. Marina set a small box under the locator panel with a note that read 'bang'. Faust was amused that she still had an occasional sense of humor. They exited the ship and hurried back to the *Reaper*, while the scout ship departed Andros-5. Marina piloted her ship through one of the many valleys before departing the planet to avoid detection. Now that she was back in the game, she needed to find some old friends and the pirate haven on the planet Zim was the best place to start.

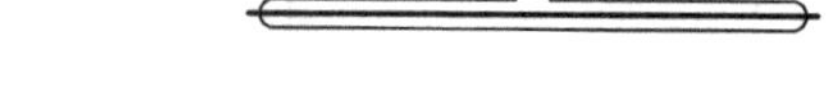

Marina's cruiser docked at Murgatroyd's Oasis in the end bay, furthest away from the other ships. She preferred to stay anonymous as much as possible and keeping her ship out of sight was part of her routine. The attack on her private residence on Andros-5 stoked feelings of anger that she had suppressed since the last war. She hoped to turn her command over to General Lennox and the rebel alliance but now she was drawn back into the middle of a new war.

Once the bay gates were sealed and the bay oxygenated, Marina and her partner Faust exited the ship and took the long walk to the pub. Marina wore a cloak with the hood up to hide her face. Faust dressed to blend in with loose-fitting pants and shirt. His turban and scimitar were the only unique features about him. He had often been to the pirate haven in the past and knew many of the black-market dealers who met there from their interactions on his former residence Magnus. Marina counted on Faust to handle any communication with their contacts while she remained silent and monitored their responses.

When they entered the pub, they were greeted by a young man named Stosh. He introduced himself as Korick's son and pledged himself as an ally to Marina. Faust requested that Stosh keep his presence there a secret for now. Unaware that Faust's partner was Marina, Stosh informed them that he had information that might mean something to Marina. He requested that they meet before Faust and his woman departed. Stosh then led them to a table in the back corner where they could view everyone entering and leaving the pub.

A young woman, Elspeth, greeted them and took their order for food and ale. When she left, Marina mentioned to Faust that Stosh could be a valuable ally for them in his position. He knew the clientele and was likely to hear things that were of value to her. Their other allies, Korick and Kellen, were involved in business transactions and unavailable.

Faust recognized two old friends and left Marina alone while he visited them. When Elspeth returned, she set down a pitcher of ale and two mugs. As she poured the ale into the mugs, she informed Marina that one of their people identified a Kronos field operative who arrived with three young children and was looking to sell them. Trafficking children was illegal at the station and likely to draw unwanted attention from Kronos or the Federation.

"Why are you telling me this?" questioned Marina.

Elspeth replied, "I recognized you from a prior visit."

"And who are you that I should be so trusting?"

"Your identity is safe with us. I am Stosh's sister, Elspeth," she explained. "We believe the children must belong to someone important and thought you would be interested in them." Convinced of her sincerity, Marina thanked Elspeth for her help. Elspeth glanced about the area for other customers to wait on and then left.

Marina sipped her ale and pondered if the children did belong to someone of importance. When Faust returned, she relayed the information to him and instructed him to investigate the children's origin after his meal. Elspeth returned with their food and whispered, "Second floor. Room nine. Fifteen minutes. You should be there." She set the food on the table and left with her tray.

"Sounds like you should eat fast," Marina commented. Faust nodded and hastily ate his sandwich.

Faust informed her that the leaders of the various groups selected a field general to lead the resistance in her absence. The general would delegate responsibilities and provide coordination of resources for the rebel alliance when it came time to confront Kronos again. Marina was pleased with the news. She preferred to work alone and having others to cover the obvious encounters made her life much easier – and safer. Marina instructed Faust to spread the word that the last Kronos base, when discovered, would be given to the general and his men to run as they saw fit with new possibilities for commerce after they defeat Kronos.

When Faust left to attend the bidding for the children, Marina noticed a big man in old military clothing with no emblems to indicate his loyalty. She caught him staring at her more than once and grew suspicious. Elspeth returned and filled Marina's mug. Marina questioned her about the patrons inside the pub at that time. Elspeth assured her that none were involved with Kronos other than the field operative with the children and she was upstairs for the bidding.

The scruffy man approached them and gestured for Elspeth to leave. He leaned across the table on his hands and stared Marina down. Marina suggested that he leave but the man reached for her hood. Instinctively, Marina grabbed his wrist and bent it backwards, forcing it down on the table. Wincing in pain, the man mocked her. "How dare you come here, pretending to be someone you're not," he chided.

Marina lowered her hood and grinned. Before he could speak again, she drew one of her daggers and stabbed his hand, pinning it to the table. As he reached for her with his other hand, she did the same, leaving him hunched over and vulnerable. Marina stood and walked behind him.

"That's enough," he begged. Marina then kicked the back of each of his knees. The man groaned in pain as he dropped to his knees on the floor, while his hands remained pinned to the table. Stosh gestured frantically from the bar for Marina to stop. Marina sensed that she couldn't trust the man and leaned on the table, nose-to-nose with him. Tears streamed down his cheeks and he pleaded for mercy. Marina glanced up at Stosh and sighed, an indication that she would comply. She retrieved her daggers from the man's hands and challenged, "Anything else you want to say?"

"No, ma'am. You made your point," he blurted, relieved to be free of the daggers. "I just assumed you were an imposter sent by Kronos to trap us." The man clenched his hands together to stem the flow of blood until Stosh returned with two bandages for him. Marina took her seat and drank from her mug of beer. Stosh whispered into the man's ear, urging him to leave them.

"Since you just exposed your identity to everyone in the pub," Stosh commented, "I guess it's safe to talk."

"Why the surprised looks on their faces?" Marina asked.

"It's been a long time since anyone saw or heard from you," Stosh admitted. "We presumed that you were dead or captured."

Marina gestured with her fingers to Elspeth for more ale. Stosh then informed her that the man she just abused was the primary organizer for her rebel group and the field general. Marina chuckled over the thought, seeing that he definitely wasn't the brightest client in the pub.

Stosh explained that the man had hoped to discuss a plan with her, once he was assured of her identity. "He obviously knows who I am now," Marina remarked.

Stosh revealed that the man, Tarsus, suspected that the children to be auctioned must belong to someone of importance at Kronos who was being punished for failure. He wondered if Marina knew who it might be and if they could use the children for leverage. Marina pondered if it could possibly be Antwan's children since he had suffered several setbacks already. She chose, however, to keep her thoughts to herself.

Elspeth returned with two pitchers of ale and another mug. She set them on the table. When Marina thanked her and gave her a gold coin, Elspeth eagerly stuffed it under her apron and left. Stosh filled her mug again and offered a toast to the rebellion.

Marina was curious as to what would happen to the children. Stosh assured her that Tarsus would take the children to someplace suitable and then question them. The Kronos agent would be given some compensation and then ordered to leave immediately after to prevent any suspicion of a rebel presence at the pirate haven. Stosh then questioned her about the resources available to her thus far and what they should expect from Kronos. Marina revealed that she hoped to rally several of the alien races before they take the war to Kronos, but she believed that she may have recently acquired an ally that would prove more valuable than all the others. She emphasized that this ally could be the turning point in the war but would have to be handled carefully as he was a volatile resource.

Faust was one of seven men who entered the dingy room for the bidding. A dozen chairs were positioned in front of a makeshift stage and the lighting was intentionally dim. Darra entered with three children, each with a sack over their heads and their mouths gagged. She marched them onto the stage and eyed her audience carefully for potential enemies. Faust was sure he had seen Darra on Magnus, a former base of operation once before, but could not place when or why.

Darra instructed the men to remain quiet and informed them that there was no negotiation. Each man was allowed one bid, no questions asked. The winner would take the children and leave immediately.

A dark-skinned man with long dreads bid five-thousand credits. A second man, oriental and well-dressed, offered six-thousand. Then Tarsus barged into the room, his hands bandaged, and reminded them that there would be no bidding for children. It was against the rules.

Before Darra could object, he informed her that the children would be confiscated and upon receiving non-negotiable compensation, she would immediately leave the station. She questioned what would be done with the children, wondering if this had anything to do with the intrusion. Tarsus stated that they would be turned over to the Federation as orphans and residences would be found for them. Darra reluctantly agreed and followed him to Stosh's office for payment.

Faust waited at the entrance to the pub for Tarsus to return so he could question him further. Tarsus escorted Darra past Faust to the personnel hatch at the bay entrance to ensure she left the premises. Once she entered the bay, the doors automatically locked to prevent her return.

Tarsus gestured for Faust to follow him to the second-floor office where they questioned the children. Faust conducted the questioning and led the children to believe that he wanted to find their parents and take them home. The young boy revealed that Antwan was their father and Tia was their mother. He also told them about how they were punished for Antwan's failures. After the questioning, Faust and Tarsus returned to the pub.

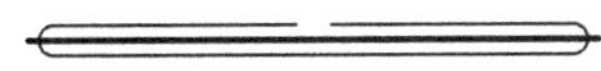

Marina was surprised when Faust and Tarsus both returned to the table and sat. Despite Tarsus' bandaged hands, he managed to hold a mug of ale in one of them. He did make it a point to keep his distance from Marina when he sat, though.

"I hope I didn't disappoint you," Marina commented. "Was I everything you expected?"

"I'll admit, I never thought I'd see the real Marina here," he replied. "I should have known better."

Marina assured him that she would make it up to him with a successful campaign against Kronos. Tarsus informed her that their plan to obtain the children without arousing suspicion from the other bidders worked well. "Do you know a woman named Darra?" he questioned her, curious.

Marina pondered a moment as she drank from her mug. "Should I?" she finally responded.

"Well, she has a vendetta against you and is determined to find you," he revealed to her. "She is offering a sizeable reward for any information that leads to your capture. It sounds personal."

Marina grinned and quipped, "Imagine that."

Tarsus then mentioned that the children belonged to a friend of hers – Antwan. Now, he had Marina's attention. Marina instructed him to send the children to her home planet Yord and turn them over to Katarina Tosci for protection. She believed that they could be used to leverage Antwan for information if they captured him. She then inquired as to the mother of the children, but he had no further information other than her name was Tia. Marina thanked him and promised not to injure him the next time they meet.

"Oh, there is one more thing, before you leave," he added. "You have some important visitors upstairs." Satisfied with their encounter, Tarsus left them and went to the bar. There he sat alone and drank from a mug of ale.

When Marina and Faust entered the corridor outside the pub, Elspeth met them and informed Marina that her visitors were adamant about speaking with her and were growing impatient. Marina looked concerned but Elspeth assured her that Tarsus vetted the visitors before admitting them to the facility. Reluctantly, Marina and Faust followed Elspeth to the stairwell where she left them to proceed alone. Marina kept her hands on her daggers underneath her cloak while Faust held the hilt of his scimitar, ready to draw if necessary. The two ascended the stairs, wary of an ambush but there was no one in the corridor.

Marina entered the office first and immediately recognized her visitors from the Taurus space station: Sara, the head of Galactic Security Services and Julian, the vice-president of Universal Shipping Services. Sara was dressed in her blue GSS uniform and Julian, bald and mustached, donned an expensive three-piece suit. Both sat at a table, looking uneasy. Marina took a seat across from them and expressed her surprise to see the two of them at the pirate haven.

Julian was direct with her and expressed their concerns over the stops that were assigned to the *Blue Eagle*, a vital long-distance hauler with advanced technology recently installed. He and his CEO Gemini feared that the stops were insignificant and presented unnecessary risks. Marina released her hold on the daggers. She glanced at Faust and indicated with a shift of her eyes for him to leave them.

"There is a reason for everything we do," she responded. "The resistance has grown and spread over a wide territory. We are getting closer to the day when we take Kronos down."

Sara expressed her appreciation for what Marina was able to accomplish in a short time but she, too, had concerns for the safety of the *Blue Eagle* and its crew. Marina revealed that plans were being prepared in various regions for the resistance through their allies. Then she commented that the *Blue Eagle* would provide valuable information to ensure the success of those plans. Julian warned her that the ship was vital to their business and not expendable for any reason. Sara then inquired as to what precautions were taken to protect the *Blue Eagle* should things go wrong.

Marina assured them that she had reliable forces in place to ensure the safety of the ship and crew. Sara requested that Marina keep them in the loop with anything to do with the *Blue Eagle*. Marina cautioned them that it was difficult to pass information along without risking it falling into the wrong hands. Frustrated, Sara and Julian stood to leave.

Marina reminded them that she was a liability for anyone caught speaking or traveling with her and because of that, she must avoid being seen. Thus, interaction with her had to be limited. As a consolation, she offered Faust to be their point of contact, whenever possible.

Faust returned to the office with Tarsus and Stosh. Marina invited them to stay a little longer so that Tarsus could fill them in on the rebel alliance's intentions for the *Blue Eagle*. Julian and Sara grew uneasy when Tarsus revealed that the *Blue Eagle* would be useful in drawing out high value targets in the area. Despite Marina's assurance that precautions were being taken, Julian and Sara were concerned. Julian repeated Sara's question regarding what kind of precautions could guarantee the safety of a unique ship with the latest technology installed on it.

Marina smiled and leaned forward on the table. "I am your guarantee," she informed them. "In addition, I have people who will be interacting with the ship's crew, particularly with one crewman named Mike Colby, to ensure their protection."

Julian mentioned that it took a while for the crew of the *Blue Eagle* to develop a chemistry and to overcome several personnel issues. He hoped that none of these interactions would affect that chemistry. Then he reminded her that the ship was a profitable part of their business and, for that reason, he insisted on knowing what risks the ship was exposed to. Marina promised that her partner Faust would report to them 'after' any missions were performed, for security reasons.

Elspeth entered and whispered something into Marina's ear. Marina became concerned and told her that she would handle it. Elspeth nodded and left them. Julian and Sara became anxious and questioned Marina if the news had something to do with the *Blue Eagle*.

Marina was amused by Julian's concern and, as a distraction, commented that Colby's love life would take care of itself. Then she revealed her concerns about Kronos' silence lately and that she needed to find something or someone who was linked to them. Julian glanced at Sara, wondering what Marina knew about Mike's personal life. Sensing their unease, Marina reminded them that Kronos would not go away and is likely planning something much bigger than before. Julian and Sara accepted her assurance and promised to support her. They ended their meeting and departed.

Inside the bay at the pirate haven, Darra boarded her ship and met with her five-man mercenary team. She instructed them to don environmental suits before her ship departed. They were to wait in the bay until the bay was secured and oxygenated once more and then enter the station through the personnel hatch. Once inside the station, they were to question pub clientele in search of information on Marina or where the three children would be taken. She also requested that they seek out any rebel supporters and attempt to obtain information on any planned rebel activity. The men promptly obeyed and dressed for their mission. *I love how money buys loyalty*, she thought to herself.

The men departed the ship and positioned themselves by the interior hatch, dressed in their environmental suits and oxygen tanks. Darra contacted the transport supervisor and requested he open the exterior gates. Once opened, she piloted her ship into space. When the exterior bay gates closed and the bay oxygenated, the interior hatch unlocked. The men removed their suits, hiding them in an air duct, and then entered the station.

Marina questioned Tarsus about who he could spare to infiltrate the crew of the *Blue Eagle* for her. "For what purpose?" he replied.

"I want to know at every stop what happens with that ship," she answered. "We need to keep the crew stable to make this work and we need to ensure we get them whatever protection they need."

Reluctant to spare any of his men, Tarsus pointed to a young couple at the other corner of the pub. "You can have them, if they are available," he informed her. "I've heard that they have done many missions for the rebel resistance."

Marina recognized the female as a good friend of hers from past missions and commented, "Then, I believe, they will do just fine." She requested that he bring them over for an introduction. Tarsus was surprised by her eagerness to meet them, but complied. Marina sipped from her mug and pondered how the *Blue Eagle* could be used effectively against Kronos without arousing their suspicion. She preferred cutting off pieces of the organization, one at a time, before going for the jugular. There was no telling how far Kronos' influence stretched and it would be fatal to underestimate them.

Tarsus brought the couple over and invited them to sit. The woman, Margot, and the man, Jonas, weren't intimidated by Marina and very relaxed. "Well, hello, Marina," said Margot pleasantly.

"It's been a while," Marina replied. "It's good to see you."

Margot nodded to her and responded, "And you as well. I hope you have something for me." Tarsus was surprised that they knew each other but said nothing.

Marina instructed them that their mission was to infiltrate the *Blue Eagle*'s crew when the time came. She then informed Tarsus that she would take Margot and Jonas to Parris-5 with her to protect the *Blue Eagle*, a very special freighter, and its crew. Taurus wasn't happy that Marina chose to handle the protection of the *Blue Eagle* alone and was taking two people that he knew little of to help her do it.

Marina explained that a recent failed attack against the freighter on Vega means that they can expect an attack on Parris-5 as well. Staring at Tarsus, she commented that someone revealed the *Blue Eagle's* itinerary and that person or persons needed to be identified. She reminded Tarsus that this operation needed to remain secret to minimize the resistance's exposure until they were ready to move on Kronos. With a surprised expression on his face, Tarsus assured her that he would find the leak and deal with those involved appropriately.

Then Tarsus inquired why she was so concerned with Vega and the freighter called the *Blue Eagle*. Marina informed him that allies from a distant location recovered a Scrat (alien) warship with significant battle damage. The plan was to restore it and use it for a deterrent against Kronos when the time was right. She hoped that Kronos would suspect that the Scrat, a militant alien force, was a new member of her alliance against them. This could force them to alter or postpone any planned attacks against her rebels for now. She mentioned that the importance of the *Blue Eagle* was to obtain critical components through the black market for repairs to the Scrat ship that were staged on Parris-5 for a pickup and she wanted no surprises.

Darra's five mercenaries entered the pub and split into two groups. One group entered the General area while the other approached the Arms area. Margot immediately noticed the outline of pulse pistols under their coats on their hips. She nudged Jonas and the two excused themselves from the table. Tarsus looked concerned by the presence of these new strangers and requested that Marina and Faust stay put. He left the table as well and exited the pub.

Faust suggested to Marina that they should leave immediately, but she was determined to see Margot and Jonas in action. Stosh approached and sat down at the table. He revealed that Darra left a team of five men to investigate the destination of the children and to coerce information on Marina from anyone they suspected of being a rebel. When Marina nodded toward the strangers in two locations, Stosh grew concerned.

"Relax," she said calmly. "It's under control."

Margot and Jonas efficiently disarmed and immobilized the mercenaries, while pub security ushered the unconscious men from the pub. Since no punches were thrown, the crowd had no interest in the arrest of the mercenaries and went about their business.

Marina was pleased that Darra's team was disarmed and taken into custody without anyone noticing. Tarsus returned and informed her that he would interrogate the men prior to their disposal. Satisfied with Margot and Jonas' competency, Marina informed Tarsus that he would join her on Parris-5. Tarsus assured her that they would be there to provide whatever support she needed. Marina thanked him and then departed with Faust. Margot and Jonas promptly followed them out of the pub. Tarsus punched the table, unhappy about taking orders from Marina. He believed that he should be running the rebel alliance and not her.

As they walked down the corridor to the end bay that housed the *Reaper*, Faust questioned Marina about what their next stop was. He was shocked to learn that she intended to meet with Golgar, the Calamaarian leader who already betrayed her in the battle for Orpheus-2 over a year ago. Surprised, Margot questioned the timing and importance of such a task. Marina explained that Golgar had to answer for his betrayal in their last conflict but, if there was a way to win his support, she would need to exercise restraint. Faust cringed, knowing that Golgar was dangerous and likely prepared to handle Marina differently after her last visit.

With the *Reaper* on autopilot, the four of them slept for the duration of the journey. One of the advantages of interstellar space travel was the ability to sleep for long periods of time with the aid of a simple cabin pressure adjustment. Whether it was healthy or not was another issue, but Marina was more than happy to take advantage of it.

When the ship approached Calamaar, the proximity alarm sounded and returned the ship to manual control. Marina stirred and awoke in her quarters. When she arrived on the flight deck, she was surprised to see Faust already at the controls. Faust indicated that the Calamaarians had just launched fighters. Marina, unconcerned, attempted to contact Golgar, the leader of Calamaar. When she received no response, she sent a warning that this wasn't a social call and she would not hesitate to handle things *her* way.

Margot and Jonas awoke and joined them on the flight deck. Margot noted the number of fighters on the monitor and wondered what Marina had in mind. Jonas stayed to the rear and was content to sit back and wait for orders. Margot studied Marina's actions, hoping to understand her thought process and maybe one day be a leader like her. Jonas was concerned by his sister's interest in Marina. He feared that she would get them involved in something dangerous and worse, one of them would be injured or killed.

There was still no response from Golgar as the Calamaarian fighters closed on them. Faust was silent, knowing that Marina had this under control. She took evasive action and then steered her cruiser directly at three of the fighters while three more chased after her from behind. As she directed her ship at the middle of the forward fighter formation, those behind her fired repeatedly. When she veered wide of the approaching fighters, two were crippled by friendly fire.

Marina piloted the cruiser into a U-turn and immediately targeted two of the fighters. Before they could respond, she had already fired several bursts and dropped beneath them. Both fighters exploded. With only two remaining, she targeted them, one at a time. Her cruiser incurred minor damage as her attackers failed to register a direct hit. Once the fighters were disposed of, the transmitter beeped, indicating an incoming transmission. Marina responded and chided Golgar, "What took you so long?"

A coughing, gurgling sound was heard from the transmitter as Golgar adjusted his interpreter box on his neck. "How dare you come here and attack my fighters?" he grumbled.

Marina snickered and responded, "Where's my invitation? I came all this way for some quality time with you. We need to talk."

"I will allow you access to my fortress, but you know the rules," he warned.

Marina laughed and terminated the transmission. With a pained expression, Faust covered his eyes. When Jonas inquired as to what the rules were, Faust related what happened the last time he and Marina visited Golgar. Despite her better judgment, Margot offered to accompany Marina but was refused.

The remaining twelve Calamaarian fighters circled from a distance but refrained from attacking, allowing Marina's ship the opportunity to approach the fortress and enter the transport bay. The fighters then followed one at a time and landed inside as well.

With the *Reaper* docked, a dozen Calamaarian soldiers waited at the hatch for Marina to exit. They were armed with pulse rifles and seemed anxious to use them. Marina was not a favorite among them for her prior antics and this latest embarrassment to their fighter pilots only fueled their disdain for her.

Marina instructed Margot and Jonas to wait inside the ship, but Margot would have none of that. "We have your back, no matter where you go," Margot stubbornly replied. Jonas nodded in agreement, but appeared less than enthusiastic. Marina appreciated her new team's loyalty. Faust advised Marina against any combat with Golgar or his soldiers, but he knew it was useless. Marina would do what she always does – fight to the death. Marina stepped off the ship first and entered the fortress. Faust nodded for Margot and Jonas to follow. He secured the hatch and then joined them. The soldiers split into two groups, one in front of Marina's team and the other behind them.

"I see Marina knows her way around here quite well," Margot commented. Faust affirmed her observation and mentioned that Marina had an uncanny knack for details when on enemy turf.

When they arrived in the main chamber, Golgar sat on his sculptured granite throne with a spiked, wooden club in his hand. He stood and grinned through his reptilian-like mouth, while displaying pointed teeth and onyx eyes on his snout-nosed, leather-skinned face. "So, Marina, we meet again," he remarked cynically.

"You betrayed me, Golgar," she responded. "I never took you for a coward, but obviously I misjudged you."

Golgar turned toward his throne, an attempt to deceive her into dropping her guard. He dropped the club but then took a short spear from a sheath on his leg. The spear had barbs on both ends and a handle-grip in the middle of the weapon. He turned and fired the spear at Marina, but she was ready. She pulled one of the soldiers in front of her for a shield and the spear penetrated his chest. The soldier groaned and fell to the floor, mortally wounded.

"Nice try, Golgar," Marina taunted. "So that's how it's going to be; no hugs or handshakes, huh?"

Golgar chuckled and inquired in a gruff alien tone, "What do you want?" He expected some form of entertainment from her and grew impatient. Margot and Jonas became uneasy. They studied the soldiers for any indication of an attack, fearing a confrontation would be fatal to them. Each placed a hand on their weapons, holstered at their hips. Faust gestured with his hand for them to refrain from interfering.

Marina informed him of the ongoing war with Kronos and how they would come for him if she and her forces failed to defeat them. She could tell by Golgar's silence that he already knew what she was going to ask. The two stared each other down, neither speaking for several moments, an intimidation tactic used by both. He paced about the room and then questioned Marina about what she expected from him if he agreed to her terms. He grew irate when she pressed him for an apology first for backing out on her in the battle for Orpheus-2 in an act of cowardice.

Faust, Margot, and Jonas were mortified by Marina's brazenness. Golgar's soldiers became anxious. Something was going to happen any second as the tension between the two mounted. Golgar approached a rubber block next to his throne and glanced back at Marina. Again, she knew what was coming and positioned herself in front of one of his soldiers. Golgar picked up the block, turned and fired it at Marina. She leaped sideways and landed face-first on the floor. The block struck the unsuspecting soldier and floored him. He lay in pain, badly injured with a crushed chest. Marina scurried to her feet and kept a watchful eye on Golgar. Golgar's soldiers were wary now of their exposure to the fight and stepped back.

Marina drew one of her daggers and stalked Golgar. He welcomed her approach and knelt on one knee, daring her to attack. When she did, he surprised her with a head-butt to her abdomen. She fell to the ground, gasping for air. Margot looked to Faust for direction, but again he gestured for her to refrain from interfering.

Golgar raised his fist to pummel Marina's face and as he struck at her, she rolled out. Golgar's fist slammed into the floor, causing him great pain. He groaned and shook his clawed hand several times. Marina stood quickly and delivered a karate-kick to the side of Golgar's head, leaving him stunned and wobbly. She then struck him behind his knee with another kick. Golgar fell to one knee and cursed her.

Sensing his weakened condition, she circled him, considering her next attack. When she lunged at his head from the side and reached for his neck, he pounded her face with a short but powerful jab. Marina lay motionless on the ground. Faust, Margot and Jonas were horrified, fearing her injury was serious.

Golgar perched over her and, sensing victory, taunted her. While on her back, Marina curled her legs up and double-kicked him in the face. Golgar staggered backward, dazed and off-balanced. Marina stood and lunged at him again. The two fell to the floor with Marina on top. She drew her second dagger and held both against Golgar's throat.

"Enough," he pleaded. Marina got off him and was supported on her feet by Faust. Two of Golgar's soldiers assisted Golgar to his feet. He barely made it to his throne and sat with a thud.

"So, what's it going to be, Golgar?" Marina asked. "Are you with me or against me?"

Golgar gestured for her and her friends to leave. "I will be there when the time comes," he responded weakly. "You have my word."

Marina thanked him and then left the chamber. Faust nudged Margot and Jonas ahead of him and they returned to the *Reaper*. None of them spoke a word to Marina, despite their concern for her condition. The right side of her face was swollen and her right eye had a small cut over it. She labored when she walked and wheezed when she breathed.

Once on board, Faust took charge of piloting the ship and recommended Marina rest. Marina instructed him to take them to Parris-5 immediately where they would rendezvous with Tarsus' group. When she left the flight deck, Margot followed her to her quarters and treated her wounds. Jonas took the copilot's seat and questioned Faust, "Does she take a beating like this often?"

Faust frowned and replied, "Not often. Every time. It's the only way she knows." Jonas shook his head in disbelief, wondering what he and Margot got themselves into.

When they reached the half-way point of their journey, Marina briefed Margot and Jonas about the *Blue Eagle* and a former Special Forces mercenary named Mike Colby. Familiar with the name, Margot mentioned that Colby was a hero for the attack on the Scrat that ended their war. Even more so, he did it with only two partners. Marina expressed her concern that she didn't need a "cowboy" waging his own private war with Kronos right now and she was counting on Margot to keep Colby under control when the time came. Margot was amused by the idea of working with her idol and wondered in what capacity they would interact.

Curious, Jonas inquired if Marina had met the man before. Marina chuckled and nodded. Jonas and Margot waited anxiously for her to continue. Reluctant to relate the whole story, she only responded that she had to recalibrate Colby over their difference in opinion about galactic warfare and hopefully he has seen the light. Faust interrupted playfully from the pilot's seat that, in simple terms, Marina kicked his ass. Margot was stunned as she and Jonas were former Galactic Special Forces as well. That meant he was well-trained to fight and for Marina to defeat him was impressive on her part.

Margot felt a certain respect for Colby even though they never met. Her unit was deployed to another part of the universe when Colby took down the Scrat command and their weapons factories. Sensing Margot's apprehension, Marina assured her that Colby was a big boy and got over it.

Curious, Margot inquired as to what she was specifically expected to do to keep Colby in line. Marina smiled at her and suggested that her charm should be enough to subdue him. Jonas and Faust realized that this just became a conversation for the women and stayed silent. Margot blushed and responded, "I'm not an escort for hire, Marina. While I appreciate the compliment, there is a limit to what I will do for the job."

"I expect no less and no more from you," Marina replied. "I'm sure you'll handle him just fine."

Marina moved to the front of the flight deck and took the copilot's seat. She accessed the ship's database and brought up the engineering plans for Parris-5. After reviewing them, she recommended that Margot and Jonas do the same. With a distant look in her eyes, Margot pondered about what her encounter with Colby would be like. Marina could already tell where this was headed and considered it an advantage if Margot's relationship with Mike Colby developed into something more than just acquaintances.

Polaris, a planet located in the outer fringes of the galaxy, was a prehistoric domain for wildlife not seen in ages around the galaxy. There was one exception, though. On a majestic mountain peak on an island amid a vast ocean was a futuristic facility with a transport center that could accommodate ships of all sizes. At first glance, the facility appeared abandoned, but upon closer inspection, there were towers erected among the trees with sensors, both long and short range.

Inside the facility, the Kronos leader Carl Klingman hosted a meeting with ten of his senior scientists from Base Five to discuss his projects. Carl's first item of interest was a cyborg assassin, created as an experiment. He was anxious to know how the assassin's performance rated.

A woman named Dr. Sianni Kepler stood and waited for an indication from him to speak. Sianni was tall, blonde and had the innocent look of a young school girl. She informed him that the test subject's first five assignments had been very successful with no issues. Sianni mentioned as an example that their assassin, known as Borath, coerced the surrender of a powerful shipping corporation called Aurora without a single shot being fired, although there were numerous fatalities of corporate employees.

"Marvelous!" exclaimed Carl. "Have you begun the mass production of these fine specimens?"

Sianni beamed proudly over his approval and responded, "We have initiated the assembly line along with its integration lab. Our forty volunteers for the project have been very compliant."

"And what does that translate to?" he inquired, curious.

"I expect a total of forty cyborg soldiers by the end of the month. Future assembly lines along with the required volunteers will allow us greater production capability and should generate fifteen subjects per month per line," she explained. "These additional assembly lines should be operational in six months."

Carl nodded to her with a smile. She bowed and took her seat. Carl then inquired as to the delivery system for the cyborg army. Another woman, Dr. Kimo Stylus, stood and requested permission to speak. Kimo was dark-skinned with long, braided hair, and Oriental with a certain allure to her. Carl liked his scientists young, beautiful and, of course, very intelligent. He motioned to her that the floor was hers.

Kimo announced that their fleet of thirty-five drones was nearly complete. She was quick to emphasize that the drones would not only deliver the cyborg army, but provide cover for them as well during their attacks.

Carl was pleased and nodded for her to sit. He paced the floor behind each of them. "I am pleased with the progress that this team has made, but I do have one more question."

The scientists grew uneasy by his remark. Carl returned to the head of the table and leaned on it with his palms. "Have we addressed the travel time to place our new army prior to attack? The galaxy is a big place and time is not a luxury that we have a lot of."

No one spoke as this was a difficult issue for them to resolve. Finally, a young, dark-skinned man at the back end of the table raised his hand to speak. Carl ogled the man and seemed smitten with him. "And you are?" he asked.

"Corbin, sir," he replied.

"And what do you have to tell me, Corbin?"

Carl noticed that three of the scientists subtly shook their heads at Corbin, but Corbin was confident. He explained how they had spent many resources trying to duplicate the mystery transport module that was never recovered from a mercenary named Colby and that their attempts to create portals with their current designs also failed. Carl showed his growing impatience with folded arms, while looking down. Many of the scientists covered their faces, fearing what was about to unfold.

"I took the initiative to establish a contact on Orpheus-2 to obtain the latest technology developed by the Federation for creating portals," he announced. "Why reinvent the wheel when it already exists? Why not just take it from them?" The other scientists were shocked as they had no idea that he pursued that route for a solution.

"And how did that work out?" Carl inquired.

"I have the contact committed to helping us in return for asylum," Corbin announced proudly. "The Federation is in the final testing stage and should be completed within the next two weeks. Once it is completed and deemed successful, my contact with arrange for a pickup of three critical components for the new portal generation system. Those components will allow our portal generation system to function successfully."

Carl walked around the table and stood behind Corbin. He placed his hands on his shoulders and pressed himself against the young man. "You will join me for dinner and then a late evening, Corbin," he whispered. "I will reward you for your ambition."

Corbin placed his left hand on Carl's and smiled. Carl removed his hands from Corbin's shoulders and returned to the head of the table. "Keep up the good work, everyone," he announced and then departed the conference room.

Kimo fumed at Corbin and shouted obscenities at him. "You threaten all our safety with your recklessness!" she chided him. The other scientists were mortified and said nothing.

Sianni approached him and poked her finger against his nose. "If you screw this up, Klingman won't be the only one fucking you," she warned. "I guarantee you won't like what we do to you." Corbin forced a smile, knowing the risk he just took.

The other scientists frowned at him. All left the room leaving Corbin alone to ponder his fortune or misfortune, should he fail. Their flight back to Base Five was a quiet one.

CHAPTER 2

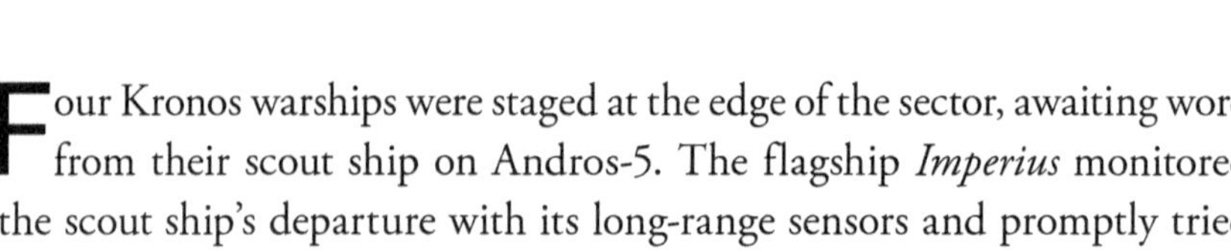

Four Kronos warships were staged at the edge of the sector, awaiting word from their scout ship on Andros-5. The flagship *Imperius* monitored the scout ship's departure with its long-range sensors and promptly tried to communicate with it. When they failed to get a response, Commander Jacque Horan suspected that they may have captured Marina but perhaps she got loose and damaged the ship's comm/nav panel in a scuffle. He ordered his pilot to lock onto the scout ship and bring it in manually using their tractor beam.

Darra, middle-aged with long, black hair and a well-sculptured body, approached the commander. He seemed annoyed by her presence and reluctantly turned to her. "What is it now, Darra?" he asked impatiently.

"I want to board that ship!" she demanded. "If Marina's on it, I want her first."

"Your impulsiveness will cost us one day," he chided. "I warned you about that before."

Darra got in his face and repeated her demand. Horan was angered by her disrespect and threw her to the ground. He immediately placed his boot against her neck and warned, "If you ever show such disrespect again, I will end your life at that very moment. Are we clear?"

Darra realized she overstepped her limits and became apologetic. Horan removed his boot from her throat and focused on the monitor with the comm/nav technician. Darra got to her feet slowly and waited for a further response from Horan. Finally, he grew tired of her presence and replied, "You will join the security detail and board the scout ship when it's secured."

Darra thanked him but before she could leave, he warned her, "If you screw this up, you are finished. Understand?" Darra nodded and hurried off the bridge.

Horan contacted his security officer and instructed him to keep an eye on her. He grumbled as he took his seat in the center of the bridge. Two beeps were heard, indicating an incoming message. The technician answered the call and listened for several seconds before deferring the call to the commander. "Sir, it's headquarters," he announced.

"I'll take it in my quarters," he replied and left the bridge.

The scout ship was drawn into the cargo bay and secured. Darra anxiously led the security detail to the hatch. They waited uneasily for their team to exit but the hatch didn't open. The security officer warned her, "It could be a trap. Don't do anything stupid."

Darra sneered at him and opened the hatch from the external access panel. She rushed in with her pulse pistol drawn, ready to fire. Once inside, she realized she was duped. The bodies were stacked neatly in front of her.

The security detail entered and waited for orders. The security officer stood next to her and suggested she wait outside while they searched the rest of the ship for explosives. Darra disregarded his request and rushed to the flight deck. The officer followed her and warned her not to touch anything. Darra eagerly activated the locator panel to see where the ship had been on Andros-5. The officer quickly took cover outside the hatch when the screen failed to illuminate.

Darra punched the panel and then considered that Marina sabotaged it so they couldn't find her. She knelt in front of the panel and reached underneath. The officer peered in and shouted, "What the hell are you doing?"

"I know exactly what I'm doing. Marina is playing us," she barked sarcastically and removed the box from underneath the panel. The screen illuminated and showed an image of Andros-5. "See, I told you," she boasted.

The officer approached her and took the box. He opened it and showed her the note. It read "Bang! Next time you're dead." Also inside was a magnet, placed there to interrupt the display. "You could have killed us all," he chastised her. "You're more dangerous than Marina is." He tossed the box to her and suggested sarcastically that she keep it as a reminder of her astute intuition. When he departed, Darra cursed the man and threw the box across the flight deck. The box shattered, sending shards of plastic across the floor. The security team departed the scout ship, leaving Darra to savor her moment of incompetence.

The security officer returned to the bridge and met with Commander Horan. He informed him of the scout ship's status, the casualties and Darra's recklessness. Horan immediately requested her presence on the bridge. He then revealed to the security officer that headquarters will send additional support if needed, to make sure Marina becomes a non-issue.

"Perhaps we should have left her alone," the officer suggested. She hasn't bothered us in quite a while."

"And I considered that," he replied. "That stupid bitch Darra is screwing somebody at headquarters. She obviously convinced them that this was worth the effort."

Darra arrived on the bridge and approached them. Horan scolded her for her recklessness and then instructed the security officer to lock her up. Darra was appalled by her treatment, thinking that she was privileged in the hunt for Marina. A security detail was summoned and took her away, her wrists cuffed together in front of her. Commander Horan then instructed his comm/nav technician to contact Marina. He knew better than to expect a response but thought it worth the try.

On board the *Reaper*, Marina and Faust were seated on the flight deck. The transmitter beeped twice for an incoming message. Marina commented cynically, "I wonder who this could be?" She acknowledged the signal and waited for the sender to speak. Commander Horan's voice, hoarse and raspy, surprised her as she expected someone a little more subtle. The commander introduced himself and inquired as to what Marina's intentions were. She shook her head in disbelief and replied, "You sent a patrol to hunt and kill me. Hmm, what do you think they are?"

Commander Horan attempted to explain the situation. He suggested that Marina go back into 'hibernation' and he would inform his superiors that she was terminated on Andros-5. Marina liked the idea but requested some time to think about it. Before she would trust them, she wanted to see if they retreated to a nonaggressive position away from Andros-5. Horan agreed to give her time and would wait for her to contact him with an answer. Marina terminated the transmission and turned to Faust for his opinion.

"I'm not sure I like it," he responded. "This is too easy."

"Perhaps, he's cutting his losses," she suggested. "Or this Darra is the only one interested in finding me."

"So, who is Darra?" inquired Faust, knowing he wouldn't get a straight answer from her.

Marina leaned back in her seat and considered who she might have pissed off in the recent past. Faust chuckled over her smug grin and then focused on their flight path. The two of them discussed what Kronos' plans might be and if they could be a significant threat to Yord. Marina then concluded that they needed to know more but in a subtle manner.

Darra descended the stairs ahead of the two security officers. She knew they had their pulse pistols trained on her from behind and were lax since she was cuffed. Three steps from the bottom, she stumbled and fell. Faking an injury to her knee, she writhed on the steel floor. The two officers rushed to her aid and knelt next to her. The first man extended her leg gently and felt for the source of her pain. The second man rested her head on his thigh. She touched his thigh with both hands as if seeking support, and then retrieved his pistol from his hip holster. Before either could react, she fired a pulse of energy into each one, leaving smoking holes in their chests. Darra chuckled as she tried several codes to unlock the cuffs. The code was a four digit number so it didn't take her long to figure out the obvious combination. Once free, she dragged the corpses to her intended cell.

Three technicians maintained the Ordinates Inventory Compartment in the lower midsection of the ship. Darra barged in and approached them. "I need three able-bodied men to take out some traitors," she announced. "Can I count on you?"

The men were surprised by her request. One inquired, "What's this all about? We haven't been informed of any security issues."

Darra informed the men that their commander was conspiring with the assassin Marina to destroy the other ships. The men were concerned as everyone knew of Marina's success against Kronos and the number of their peers that she killed. Then she tossed a bag containing a dozen valuable gems on the table in front of them. One of the men picked up the bag and took out one of the gems. He held it up for his peers to see and smiled. "What do you need us to do?" asked the senior member of the team, pleased by her offer.

Darra instructed them to load two of the tactical nuclear torpedoes onto the scout ship and stage a third one in the power distribution compartment. The first two torpedoes were transferred from the rotating rack by the men onto a portable lifting device. Two of the men moved the third torpedo a short distance down the corridor to the next compartment.

Darra followed them and opened the torpedo's panel. She diverted several wires to the guidance system from the control panel on the wall. The screen on the control box displayed several menus. She scrolled through them and programmed the torpedo for 'manual control' and 'instantaneous' detonation. "This will fix that rat bastard," she uttered to herself. Once preparations were completed, she boarded the scout ship with her three accomplices and departed the *Imperius*.

Commander Horan waited uneasily. He knew Marina's history of success against Kronos and was reluctant to become another casualty. She was a worthy adversary – almost too worthy in his mind. His security officer suggested he discuss the situation with headquarters but he knew better. Horan informed the other ships to back off until further notice, aware that any suggestion of treason would lead him to be relieved of his command.

An alarm sounded and startled them. The security officer then responded to a call on his transmitter. Two of his security detail were found dead in a cell in corridor H and Darra was missing. Horan was irate when he heard the news. "Find her and kill her!" he shouted. "She's crossed the line for the last time."

The security officer rushed from the bridge, leaving Horan with the comm/nav tech and the pilot. Horan requested that the pilot search for Darra's location through the ship's surveillance system. The comm/nav technician then received an incoming message. It was Marina.

Horan took the message without concern for discretion this time. Marina informed him that she wasn't comfortable with their position in relation to Andros-5, but agreed to his offer out of 'trust'. Before Horan could respond, the security officer burst onto the bridge and informed him that Darra escaped in the scout ship with two of their tactical nuclear torpedoes. Horan muted the open line to Marina and ordered the pilot to target the scout ship. He then turned his attention back to Marina.

Marina noted to Horan that she was aware of a ship headed toward Andros-5 and warned of the consequences. The security officer then received a message from one of his team. A third torpedo was missing from inventory but scanners showed it was not on board the scout ship. Horan broke a sweat and informed Marina that a renegade officer escaped the ship and would be destroyed promptly. Marina grew suspicious and ended the transmission, curiously awaiting the outcome.

On board the scout ship, Darra monitored the transmission between Horan and Marina. She immediately presumed that Marina was still on Andros-5. She and three of her followers programmed the two torpedoes in the launch tubes. These torpedoes were harmless until a proximity timer in the guidance system activated and directed lasers into the torpedo's plasma chamber, thus arming it. At that point, three lasers of intense power would pummel the plasma for five seconds, releasing intense power. The heat from this reaction would then generate additional plasma in the warhead, creating a growing sphere of energy that made it lethal to large ships, space stations and small planets.

Darra contacted Commander Horan and mocked him for his inability to take action against Marina. Horan immediately looked to his comm/nav tech and ordered him to fire at the scout ship. When the weapons officer attempted to fire, the missing torpedo in the power distribution compartment exploded and created a cascading explosion that engulfed the ship in a brief ball of fire. Marina and Faust watched the images from the long-range sensors displayed on the monitor. They were perplexed as to what they just witnessed.

Meanwhile, Darra informed the other warships that Marina was responsible for the loss of the *Imperius* and that she was acting against Andros-5 to avenge her peers. Grinning deviously, she nodded to the senior tech. He eagerly operated the weapons control panel and launched both torpedoes toward Andros-5.

Marina and Faust were horrified when the small planet erupted into a huge fireball and vanished, leaving not a trace. "If this is the war they want, they just got it!' screamed Marina in a rage. Faust cringed as he knew Marina was now in 'kill' mode and not very cooperative when in that frame of mind.

Darra danced around the scout ship and high-fived her three accomplices. She felt confident that Marina was gone and revealed her plans to deal with her superiors. The men agreed with her plan and that the other commanders would be convinced that Marina was behind the loss of their command ship.

Marina guided the *Reaper* at full speed toward the scout ship. Faust cautioned her that it could be a trap, but she was in her 'zone.' She ordered Faust to lock onto the scout ship with their pulse cannons and fire as soon as they were within range. Faust turned and grabbed her by both arms. "They think you're dead," he emphatically stated. "Don't blow your cover. You'll need it later."

Darra noticed the *Reaper* approaching at a high rate of speed. She swore as she realized they were no match for the cruiser. The officers panicked and questioned her as to whether it was Marina or someone else. Darra ignored them and sent an SOS to the three remaining warships. They promptly responded and headed toward the *Reaper*.

Faust warned Marina of the approaching ships and urged her to turn back. Marina ignored him and continued until they were within range of the scout ship. She fired the cruiser's cannons in a spread pattern to trap the scout ship. Several pulses of energy streaked toward the scout ship from the *Reaper*. Immediately, Marina turned her cruiser away and fled toward the Aegis asteroid belt for protection.

Two of the pulses struck the scout ship and crippled it, while the others served their purpose and prevented the scout ship from dodging them. Inside, sparks shot across the cabin and covered the injured personnel. Darra was unconscious at the controls while her men writhed in pain. One of the forward panels burst into flames and fragments from the displays ejected, inflicting multiple lacerations on her face.

The first warship, the *Celestial Queen*, arrived and recovered the scout ship. They promptly boarded and took Darra and her team to their infirmary for medical attention. Darra, despite her injuries, was elated and exclaimed, "I got her! She's dead. Marina is dead!"

When she was treated and stronger, Darra instructed Commander Zhi to relay the news to headquarters that she avenged her ship, her commander, and her crew for Marina's assault. Commander Zhi complied but was suspicious of Darra's version of the events. He questioned Darra about who piloted the ship that attacked her. She assured him that it was one of Marina's cohorts.

Marina was visibly upset with the turn of events. Andros-5 was her haven of peace and held the precious memory of the reunion of her father and mother during the Weevil War. She debated the destruction of the *Imperius* with Faust and why an officer would destroy his or her own ship. Regardless, they would pay for Andros-5. Marina frequently monitored the long-range sensors to make sure no one followed them.

Margot and Jonas were stunned by the turn of events, staying out of the way and silent. Even more so, there were three Kronos warships still in their vicinity. The two waited for Marina to brief them but she left the flight deck and went to her quarters.

Marina slept while Faust piloted the *Reaper* toward Magnus. Marina dreamed of her first encounter with Kat there. She remembered how helpless she felt under Kat's spell until she discovered the thin strips that Kat used on her lips, laced with a hallucinogenic drug to control Marina. Their relationship was a strange one. Sometimes Marina viewed herself as being violated, while other times she felt as though it a consensual attraction.

Kat really was a witch in control of black magic, but she seemed to really care about Marina. Kat often reminded her, "Our fates are intertwined." Marina awoke in a sweat. She pondered if this was a dream or if Kat was reading her thoughts from far away. Then she wondered, *What did Kat mean anyway? Their fates are intertwined. Why and how?*

Marina returned to the flight deck and sat quietly next to Faust. He knew something bothered her besides the recent events but knew not to ask. She placed her hand on his knee and thanked him for not asking questions right now. He briefly placed his hand affectionately on her cheek and then focused on the controls. Marina was a complicated person that no one would ever understand – not even him. She turned her attention to Margot and Jonas. "Are the two of you okay?"

"We're… just great," muttered Jonas.

"A little surprised by the excitement," added Margot. "Just tell us what you need us to do and we'll handle it." Marina appreciated Margot's steadfast support. Margot knew not to question her but welcomed any intel that Marina chose to share with her. Faust interrupted and informed them that they would arrive on Magnus shortly.

Magnus was once Kat's base of operation in her black-market business and the place where Marina first encountered her as a courier making a delivery. It was abandoned when Kronos raided her clientele and left the station damaged beyond repair. Kat and Faust had fled to Yord as refugees to join Marina in her war against Kronos.

When they approached Magnus, Marina performed a scan of the station and noticed on the monitor that there were seven active devices placed in various locations. She questioned Faust about the condition of Magnus when he and Kat fled the Kronos raid. Faust informed her that the power to the station was shut down to prevent a fire or an explosion after the evacuation in case they decided to return one day. There was no reason for active devices to be detected, which concerned them.

The short-range monitor showed that the outer bay gates were open and there was no sign that the station was functional. It sustained significant damage at the forward control section as well as the cargo area. Those were the two critical sections that were required to survive on the station.

Marina instructed Faust to halt their approach and monitor for any trailing ships, while she checked for any missed incoming messages. He immediately noticed that one of the Kronos warships followed but kept its distance at the edge of their sensor's range. Marina then instructed him to circle the station and depart the region from the back side. Curious of her intentions, Faust obeyed.

Margot and Jonas watched, eager to see what strategy she employed. Marina programmed one torpedo for low-yield plasma and launched it toward one of the open bays. As soon as the torpedo passed the open gate, the seven devices detonated, destroying what remained of the station.

The low-yield torpedo burst into an explosion of its own, seconds after the initial blast.

On board the Kronos warship, the commander and his staff observed the station's destruction. One officer pointed out the second, smaller explosion to the commander and indicated that it was consistent with a ship exploding within the station after the devices detonated. The officers felt confident that the *Reaper* was gone and departed the area.

Marina instructed Faust to take them past a small station called Vega by way of the Aegis asteroid belt. It was a much longer route but it would likely convince Kronos that she and her crew were eliminated. Meanwhile, Marina was interested in how things went with her potential asset Colby and his ship the *Blue Eagle* on Vega, since she arranged the stop for them to pick up vital components for a battle-damaged Scrat ship that they had in their possession. The Scrat ship would be a great advantage in battle for her people and she needed to do whatever she could to help her friends on Taurus to make the repairs to the ship.

Ecstatic, Margot praised her for her brilliance in dodging the Kronos ships and hugged her. Marina beamed proudly and promised not to keep her in suspense anymore. Margot was pleased to have earned Marina's trust and understood that things move fast with Marina and often without a plan. Meanwhile, Jonas said nothing until Marina questioned him on his silence.

Jonas replied, "Margot speaks enough for the both of us." Everyone laughed and Marina hugged him as well. This was a rare moment for her to show such positive emotion.

During the trip from Magnus to Vega, Marina spent time with Margot and Jonas, getting to know them on a more personal level. Faust hoped that Marina's new friends would help calm her in her quest for vengeance against Kronos.

Eager to know more about her target Mike Colby, Margot inquired as to what Marina knew about her new asset and why he was so important. Marina related that they only met twice and he pissed her off both times with his cowboy antics. Margot then questioned her as to why she felt he was an asset if he was reckless. Marina revealed that it was his commitment to take down Kronos that convinced her he could be a valuable ally, despite his flaws.

Margot mentioned that she had hoped to be part of the mission taking the war to the Scrat on their own worlds but her unit was deployed elsewhere. She admitted that she looked upon Colby as an epic hero when she heard the stories about how he took down the Scrat singlehandedly with no backup. She paused with a saddened expression and then asked Marina what happened to him after that mission. Marina was surprised by her question and confessed that she knew nothing about his life other than the rumors. Margot wondered aloud why a hero would be allowed to just disappear with no regard for his well-being after such a victory.

"Sometimes heroes prefer their solitude," Marina explained, curious of Margot's interest in Colby.

Faust navigated the *Reaper* toward Vega and activated the short-range sensors. The front of the small station displayed four significantly damaged gates with armed freighters trapped inside. Workers could be seen in their environmental suits with welding torches, cutting away at the damaged frames. Faust interrupted Marina's conversation and summoned her to the flight deck. When she arrived, she immediately saw the damage to the station on the monitor.

"Any sign of a Newton-class freighter in those bays?" she inquired, referring to the *Blue Eagle*.

Faust maneuvered the sensors for a closer look and shook his head. "Those four ships in the bays are newer models. I already checked their identification symbols in the database. They are private couriers, most likely mercenaries or pirates."

Marina was impressed that the vessels were trapped until the gate frames could be removed from their path. She wondered how the crew of Colby's ship were able to recognize the ambush and escape.

"Any sign of Tarsus' team?" Marina inquired. "He was supposed to be here for backup."

Faust did a long-range scan that produced nothing. "No sign of them," he replied, growing concerned that they were betrayed.

Margot and Jonas peered over Marina's shoulder and were amazed at the damage. "Colby's team did that?" questioned Margot.

"Sure looks like it," Marina answered.

Marina then instructed Faust to get them to Parris-5 in a hurry. Faust queried her as to what she expected to find at their next stop. She wasn't sure but feared that the *Blue Eagle* was exposed with no protection.

"What is this *Blue Eagle*?" inquired Jonas, curious. "I keep hearing its name come up."

Marina explained that the *Blue Eagle* was an obsolete class ship that was upgraded with special technology, which made it quite the asset. Then she mentioned the one thing that really stunned them. "Colby has in his possession a module that allows him to teleport his ship over vast distances in a blink of an eye," she revealed. "This is the same technology that allowed the Scrat to come here from the other side of the galaxy."

"And it's up to us to make sure that no one else gets it?" questioned Margot.

"That's right. Colby has a knack for finding things out, but he takes risks," Marina admitted. "I need the two of you to keep him grounded."

"We were special forces, just like him," Margot pointed out. "That should carry some weight with him." Marina was happy to have the two of them, but grew more interested in Margot's interest in Colby. Margot grew confident and assured Marina that she could handle him. Marina patted her arm in appreciation.

The *Reaper* approached Parris-5 and was soon contacted by the transport supervisor. He inquired if the ship was a five-seven-three model. Faust recognized the code which was a request to speak with Marina. He responded that they were a five-one-one model, the appropriate response, and for the speaker to stand by. Marina took a seat next to him and spoke to the man.

"What do you have for me today, Guillen?" she asked.

"The target is here along with fourteen helpers," he replied. "No actions taken yet."

Marina thanked him for the information and requested an isolated bay to maintain their secrecy. Guillen granted them the last bay which gave them a space of seven empty bays between their ship and the next one. He then mentioned that a certain ship, a friendly of vital interest, was docked in the third bay. Marina knew he meant the *Blue Eagle*, her asset's ship, and expressed her appreciation for his discretion. Marina donned a hooded cloak from a locker and strapped her daggers to her thigh.

Faust docked the *Reaper* and remained on board while Marina, Margot and Jonas departed the ship for the *Blue Eagle*. Margot asked what instructions Marina had for them when they arrived at Bay 3.

"You'll know what to do when the time comes," Marina responded, unconcerned. "This is how I work, unfortunately."

In the main corridor at the personnel hatch to bay three, were fourteen men in dark uniforms, just like the Kronos' agents she encountered in the past, with no identifying patches on their attire. Marina gestured with her hand for Margot and Jonas to stop. They observed the men, while plotting their next move.

The personnel hatch opened and a man stepped out from the bay. Muscular and clean-cut, he wore a tee-shirt and jeans with a baseball cap. Two of the men bull-rushed him and shoved him back inside. One of the men held him at gunpoint, while the other tied him up. The first man spoke into his transmitter and announced that they had Colby in custody.

Marina pointed to a crawler, a mechanical device for moving cargo. She instructed Margot and Jonas to take it into the bay. Sensing an escalation in the situation, Marina contacted Guillen and requested immediate support.

Margot and Jonas operated the crawler and took it toward the main hatch. Jonas used a magnetic key to override the pass-code device and pressed the 'open' knob. The key was military issue and used by Special Forces to gain access through any digital locking device that was pass-code protected.

The inner bay cargo hatch opened and the crawler was brought into the bay toward the *Blue Eagle*. Margot and Jonas saw the men tie Mike Colby up and approached to question their actions. One of the men ordered them to mind their own business and leave. Margot informed them that they were the ones who needed to leave immediately, drawing a laugh from the men.

Colby was grateful for the help, but realized that neither Margot nor Jonas were armed nor physically capable of taking on his burly assailants. This wasn't going to end well in his mind.

The remaining twelve men in dark uniforms entered the bay through the personnel hatch. Four surrounded Jonas and Margot, while the others approached the *Blue Eagle*. Colby panicked as he had no way to warn his crew on board the ship. Then Marina entered the bay, disguised in her hooded cloak. Undaunted, she called out to the sentries and warned them to stay away from the *Blue Eagle*. Now, Colby was really baffled. None of this made sense. Fourteen of these mercenaries against him and three unarmed strangers.

Margot taunted the closest men, warning them that they should have heeded her warning and left while they had the chance. The leader of the sentries ordered one of his men to close the inner bay cargo hatch to ensure no one witnessed what was about to happen. The mercenary left, but never returned. A dozen armed men and women in plain clothes then entered the bay and gunned down the mercenaries nearest the ship with pulse fire.

Marina hurled two daggers at the men closest to Colby. They fell to the ground, one dead and one badly wounded. Margot untied Colby and escorted him to Marina. Jonas joined the others and assisted in removing the mercenaries' bodies from the bay for identification. The personnel hatch on the *Blue Eagle* opened. The ship's captain, Tisch, and one of the crewmen appeared, surprised by the corpses and the strangers.

"Thanks so much for helping me out," Colby said appreciatively and shook hands with Margot. She smiled coyly and gestured toward Marina, who was responsible for his rescue. Marina dragged the wounded survivor to them and dropped him on the floor. A dagger was embedded in his chest, just above his heart.

"One twist and you die," warned Marina. The man was frightened as he suspected who she was. Only the infamous Marina could throw a dagger with that kind of accuracy. Mike, meanwhile, still had no idea who she was, under the cloak.

Tisch demanded an explanation for what had just occurred. Margot again pointed toward Marina and introduced her as the leader of the rebel alliance. Marina slid the hood back and removed her cloak. Colby was stunned to see her again in her black leather pants and bodice, a daunting reminder of his past experiences with her.

"I need to interrogate my prisoner," Marina announced to them.

Embarrassed, Tisch offered the use of the flight deck or her quarters for the interrogation. Marina accepted her offer, but paused to stare down Colby. "Well, Mr. Colby," she remarked. "It seems we meet again."

Humbly, Colby requested a private conversation with Marina. The two stepped aside from the others. Marina inquired if he still wanted to go another round with her like he claimed during their past meeting. Colby surprised her with an apology for his poor judgment at the pirate haven on Zim. He admitted that he was now aware that this was far from a one-man operation against Kronos and he wanted to pledge his loyalty to her.

Marina was pleased to hear that he understood her situation and then inquired if he would have a problem taking on a mission with Margot. He was interested, but expressed his concern about leaving his position on the crew. Marina's plan was to have Jonas take his place on board the *Blue Eagle*, while he and Margot would lead an effort to kidnap someone of importance. Mike was eager to help and was happy to leave the *Blue Eagle* on a temporary assignment. He mentioned that he needed to discuss it with his captain before committing.

"We can help with that," replied Margot.

On the bridge of the *Blue Eagle*, Marina and Margot performed the interrogation of their prisoner. Colby was amused as Margot grabbed the man's wrist with one hand and gripped his shoulder near his neck with the other while twisting the wrist. The man screamed in pain and wasted no time revealing their purpose on Parris-5. "We were sent to kill Colby and some courier from the fringes. Now please stop!" he blurted.

"I want more," Margot demanded as she now placed both her hands against the prisoner's head and squeezed the temple area. The man cried out, "Someone from Empire put out a bounty on Colby and his ship. We saw an opportunity to collect and thought it would be easy."

Margot turned her attention to Marina and suggested she do the honors. Marina kicked the man behind his left knee, staggering him. She then slammed him to the ground on his back. She placed her boot on the man's groin and threatened to crush his manhood if he didn't continue his cooperation. "Where is Antwan?" she inquired.

The man refused to answer until she increased the pressure on his groin. His eyes grew wide and he pleaded for mercy. "Do I hear something of value," she taunted and twisted the man's leg. "Antwan's going to Archimedes-9 to make sure Colby is dead and the *Blue Eagle* is in his possession!" he cried out. "Please stop!"

Colby saw the opportunity to intercede and get answers to his questions. "What is Kronos to Empire?" he demanded to know, while pressing both man's temples, as Margot had done. Tisch was appalled at the techniques used by all three on the mercenary, but said nothing.

"Empire is a subsidiary of Kronos!" he shouted and squirmed desperately. "Kronos runs everything!"

"Where do we find Kronos," Colby asked.

"We don't know that information," answered the prisoner.

Colby glanced at Marina and Margot for their next move. "I believe he's spilled everything he knows," Margot relented.

"When you cross Kronos, you usually end up dead," the prisoner warned, weakened by the abuse he received.

Colby commented to Marina, "Kronos probably already knows what happened here. They have eyes and ears everywhere."

Marina informed Mike that they were to pick up a high-value prisoner on Archimedes-9 and deliver him to Murgatroyd's Oasis for transport elsewhere. Mike waited for her to say more, but she just stared back at him, stone-faced and silent. Mike frowned as he knew this was all he would get from her. He exited the ship and stood by the personnel hatch to the bay.

Margot exited the ship and hurried to catch him. "We've heard that your ship is special and is designed for long-distance hauls," she mentioned.

"And what else have you heard?" Colby inquired, suspicious. "I sense you know more than you're letting on."

"I know Kronos has deep pockets and that's one hefty bounty they put on you. It got Marina's attention for sure."

"So, what's to keep you from killing me and claiming the bounty?" Colby asked cynically. Margot surprised him and held her pistol to the back of his head. "I should have known," he grumbled.

Margot stepped in front of him and stowed her pistol. "If I was after the bounty, you'd already be dead," she chided. "And then I'd take your ship for the bonus money."

Jonas introduced himself and Margot to Colby. Colby then introduced himself as Mike. He recalled the ass-whooping he got from Marina on Zim and asked why he should trust them. Jonas reminded him that they didn't have to interfere with the Kronos mercenaries and that they weren't for hire. Then Margot surprised him when she mentioned, "We still have our integrity and you are one of our own."

One of our own. Mike pondered her comment as he considered they might have once been Special Forces. He kidded her about her relationship with Jonas. "You two come as a package or something?"

"We're siblings," replied Margot playfully.

"I was thinking more of your background – military, mercenary, or whatever."

"You ask a lot of questions, Mr. Colby. Be patient," she suggested.

"Please, call me Mike," he requested. Mike folded his arms and studied the two of them. They seemed harmless, but he knew better. If they worked with Marina, then they can fight.

Jonas left them and boarded the *Blue Eagle* for his introduction to the crew. Margot invited Mike to join her at the pub to get acquainted. As if on cue, Marina exited the *Blue Eagle* and departed the bay, again without a word. Mike was baffled, thinking that she was going with them. Margot reminded him that Marina had much to do in preparing the alliance for their big move on Kronos and couldn't risk being seen with them. Disappointed, Mike hoped that he would have learned more about this alliance from Marina.

Marina returned to her ship and sat next to Faust. She was pleased with how things were proceeding. Margot and Jonas were now on board the *Blue Eagle*, giving her eyes, ears, and muscle to protect the crew and the ship. Even better, her new asset, Mike Colby, had pledged his loyalty to her and seemed to have become a team player. Marina instructed Faust to set a course for Urthos for her meeting with Emperor Rethos and Empress Attilena. She promptly left the flight deck for her quarters.

Once the ship was programmed and set to autopilot, Faust joined Marina in her quarters. Marina sat naked on the bed with her hands folded on her knees. "I wondered how long it would take you to join me," she teased. "You are responsible to fulfill my needs, you know."

"And other things," he added as he undressed. Marina slid under the covers and he joined her. The two made love and then rested for much of the journey.

Faust piloted the *Reaper* into Urthonian space and attempted to make contact. Marina awoke and joined him on the flight deck. Faust took notice of her pleasant demeanor and commented, "Things must be going well for you. You actually smiled while we made love."

Marina revealed how she was learning to delegate duties to others. She admitted being tired of the war but felt a renewed desire for battle when Kronos destroyed her small world. Faust commented that Margot and Jonas seemed like good people. He questioned Marina about her past experiences with the two. She knew little of Jonas but had worked with Margot many times in the past. The two had an uncanny knack for knowing the other's intentions without speaking.

Marina admitted that she already missed Margot. Margot seemed to have the one thing Marina felt that she lacked – compassion. Marina always saw the weaknesses and flaws in others while Margot seemed to see the good in them as she displayed with her comments about Mike Colby.

"Will we see them again?" questioned Faust.

"I certainly hope so," Marina responded. "If not, we have big problems."

A response from Urthos interrupted their conversation and requested what their intentions were. Marina responded that she wanted to speak with the Emperor and Empress regarding their alliance. After a brief delay, the speaker gave them permission to land in their transport bay. Marina nodded to Faust for him to continue.

Marina found it strange that there were no guards to greet them. Even more strange, no fighters were sent to intercept them prior to their communications. Sensing her unease, Faust pointed out that there were no vessels in the area and no evidence of an attack on Urthos. Faust docked the *Reaper* and was prepared to follow Marina off the ship.

"Stay here, Faust," Marina ordered. Disappointed, he obeyed.

Marina followed the long, dark corridor to the royal chambers and hesitated outside the door. She had a bad feeling that she wasn't going to like what she found. Then she felt her mind being probed and was more at ease. Empress Attilena recognized her and invited her to enter.

The royal chamber was simply a stone chamber with two banana-shaped thrones opposite the entrance. There was no one else but the two of them. At almost seven feet tall, Attilena appeared much larger with her sickle-like arms. She was a muscular creature with insect limbs and a plain, elongated face. Her skin was more like a shell and was colored dark green and black. Marina approached Attilena and knelt before her. Attilena gestured for her to rise.

"Marina, it has been a long time," Attilena spoke weakly. "I feared you were killed in the aftermath of the war."

Marina was concerned by the Empress's frail state and drew closer to her. "Where is the Emperor?" she inquired.

Attilena lowered her head and then responded, "Rethus passed away recently from wounds he received during the battle for Orpheus-2. He never quite recovered and now is gone."

Marina expressed her sympathies to Attilena and reminded her of the rewards of their victory, as bittersweet as it was. Attilena understood and assured Marina that there were no hard feelings over it and that Rethus died an honorable death. The two then discussed the current events unfolding with Kronos and the new threat that Marina feared was coming.

"I will offer you what little I have left," responded Attilena. "We lost our technicians and our facilities during the war so we haven't been able to restore our fleet."

Marina was shocked and realized that the Urthonians would be of little help, if any. When Attilena pledged to help with whatever resources she had left, Marina was reluctant to ask her to sacrifice more than she already had. She offered to assist her in any way possible in rebuilding her kingdom and assured her that their friendship was lasting. Attilena was thankful for her offer and suggested that they speak again after Kronos is defeated. With that, Marina departed.

When Marina boarded the *Reaper*, Faust could tell by her demeanor that her visit didn't go well. Marina related the sad state of the Urthonian forces and Rethus' passing. Then she stunned Faust by requesting he take her to the planet Fentho to meet with the Andoran leader. Faust urged her not to involve them as their history with humans was shaky at best, but she insisted. He sensed that she was falling into a depressed state of mind and fretted that it would affect her judgment.

Faust grew concerned when Marina went to her cabin and remained there for the duration of the trip. Several times he knocked but got no response. He feared that her depression might drive her to do something foolish or even dangerous.

CHAPTER 3

Darra approached the security office on Kronos Base Four, one of the five that housed Kronos' fighting forces. With one arm in a sling and her bruised face with several stitches over her eye, she looked like hell. Her hands exhibited redness from the flames on her scout ship and she limped slightly. She carried a backpack with her and set it on the floor nearby.

A Kronos sentry gestured for her to stop for identification but, despite her handicap, she twisted his arm until he fell to his knees and the arm snapped. The sentry fell against the wall, wailing in pain. Darra held his good hand to the palm reader and shoved his face against the retinal scanner. The door slid open, giving her access. When she entered, the injured sentry triggered the alarm on the wall and drew his pistol. He hobbled into the room after her.

When Darra entered, the senior officer leaped out of his seat and held a pistol to her head. The injured sentry attempted to strike her in the back of the head with his pistol but she turned and punched him in the bridge of his nose, knocking him unconscious. The senior officer slammed her in the side of the head and staggered her. He warned her to cease her aggressive action or he would shoot her. A dozen sentries arrived and surrounded her. Darra wasn't at all fazed by their presence. The officer instructed her to have a seat at the table while he contacted his superiors. He promptly sent out a coded signal and waited.

"I want to speak with Klingman, either one," demanded Darra.

An elder female officer's face appeared on the monitor and questioned the reason for the unscheduled contact. Darra pushed the officer out of the way and positioned herself in front of the monitor. The officer raised his hand to strike her but the female officer on the monitor ordered him to stand down.

"You have a lot of nerve, Darra," the woman warned. "Your lack of respect for authority will be the end of you."

Undaunted, Darra responded, "Save your speech, General. I want to speak with either Klingman – now!"

"You don't make demands to us, you horrible, little troll," responded the female officer, who then moved away from the screen.

Darra waited impatiently as the senior officer stared her down. She threatened to cut his eyes out of he didn't back off. The officer smiled at her and took a knife from the sheath on his belt. He picked residue from under his finger nails and flicked the detritus at her as a sign of blatant disrespect toward her. Darra hacked up a glob of phlegm and spit it on the table in front of him. He shook his head in disgust and left the table.

Carl Klingman's face appeared on the monitor, capturing her attention. "Well, Darra, I hope you have something important for me that was worth disrespecting my officers for," he commented. "You look like you came out on the short end of a gangbang, my dear."

"Save the pleasantries, Jack," Darra responded. "The job is done."

"Are you sure?" he asked, surprised.

"Of course, I am. Now, I expect to be rewarded for my success."

Carl studied her face briefly and then asked, "What happened to the *Imperius?*"

Darra was surprised that he already knew about it. "Its captain attempted to strike a deal with Marina," she explained. "He and his crew got what they deserved, compliments of Marina."

"That's an interesting story," he responded. "Antwan's woman is yours as promised and your bounty will be credited to your account immediately."

Darra smiled and stood to leave. Carl commented, "I'd be careful if I were you, Darra. You're playing a dangerous game."

Stunned by his words, Darra was about to reply but thought better of it. She glanced at him briefly and then left the office. Klingman instructed the officer to keep an eye on her and, if she steps out of line, then he should terminate her. The officer thanked Klingman and ended the transmission.

Darra boarded a scout ship and departed the base. She contacted Tia at her apartment and informed her that she would investigate the location of her children as a reward for her loyalty. Grateful, Tia thanked her. Darra assured her that she would be back soon and ended the transmission. Pleased with her results, she placed the ship on autopilot and retrieved a bottle of whiskey from her knapsack.

Pondering her next move, Darra considered the chance that maybe Marina was alive and tricked her into thinking that she succeeded. She would have to be wary of that possibility and, if it was true, then she needed to terminate Marina before anyone, especially Klingman, found out.

After a search on the data base for assassin activities under Kronos employment, she saw that an old friend, Borath, was hired by Antwan for three kills and a ship. Fascinated, she probed further into the text and discovered that the ship was the *Blue Eagle* and the three names on the kill order were Marina, Mike Colby and Gemini, the CEO of Universal Shipping. Darra weighed joining the hunt, but then considered the consequences of pissing off Borath by taking the bounty. *Perhaps*, she thought, *I'll save that decision until the time comes.*

Feeling the effects of the whiskey, she laid on the cot and, with her hand in her pants, pleasured herself. She glanced at the near empty bottle and imagined what she might do with it in her own perverted way. Darra and her two sisters were raised in a slum town outside of the palace district of Yord. Her father had gambling debts and often used his daughters to settle those debts, thus turning them into whores at an early age. It was survival for the girls and they accepted it. Her mother died when the girls were young. She recalled very little of her except that she was subservient to her father and never stood up to him. Darra's only interest in life revolved around herself. No one else mattered.

When the *Reaper* entered the Andoran region, Marina made several attempts to contact the Andoran leadership but failed. Faust awoke and sat up attentively. A lone Andoran fighter finally approached and responded to her request. "Who are you and what do you want?" the gruff voice inquired through an interpreter box.

"I am Marina, Queen of Yord," Marina responded. "I need to speak with the Andoran leader."

"I am Pirwa, the Andoran supreme commander," he replied. "What do you want?" His fighter circled Marina's cruiser and came to a stop, indicating a willingness to talk.

"I am summoning allies in my battle against Kronos," she informed Pirwa. "I hoped that you would be willing to help us in our efforts to defeat them."

Pirwa responded, "Kronos sent an emissary to speak with us already. We were warned that if we interfered, we would be annihilated. They guaranteed that we would be left alone if we stayed out of their war with you."

Marina chuckled at his response. "And you believed them? That's funny," she chided.

"We already committed to stay neutral," he informed her. "Perhaps if the situation changes, we would be inclined to change our position."

"Well, thanks for nothing, Pirwa. I hope you don't need our support when they turn on you. We might be committed to neutrality at that time, unfortunately for you." Marina started the *Reaper's* engines and darted off. She cussed and punched the control console.

"Now what?" questioned Faust.

Marina smirked and then contacted Tarsus on Zim. "Have you sent support for the *Blue Eagle* on Archimedes-9?" she inquired.

"Negative, Marina. Three Kronos command ships are nearby. They seem to be waiting for something to happen."

"Damn it!" blurted Marina. "We can't lose that ship in an ambush!"

"I understand, but we are no match for three command ships," he reminded her.

"I guess I'll have to handle this myself," she complained. Tarsus attempted to explain their situation further but Marina had no time for excuses. She ended the transmission and set a course for Archimedes-9. Faust grew nervous when she stared at him and he responded, "Yes, boss?"

"My quarters now," she ordered. "I need something from you and I need it bad." She then departed the flight deck and entered her quarters. Faust cringed and set the ship on autopilot.

When Faust entered, Marina wrapped her arms around him and kissed him hungrily. "You know what I need right now," she whispered and undressed him. She was on top of him like a wildcat, eager to satisfy her hunger. Sex with Faust was her therapy for overcoming her addiction to the Stardust drug and to control her anger issues. Marina never engaged in sex for love; only to tame her needs for the drug and for blood-thirsty violence.

Later, the two lay close together in the small bed. Worried by her silence, Faust questioned her about what bothered her. Marina revealed that she was concerned about the lack of support from her allies. She knew she couldn't count on Golgar and Attilena's forces were of no use to her. Even the Andorans were reluctant to help.

"What do you propose to do about it?" inquired Faust.

Marina shook her head and responded, "Kronos is cutting off my resources. I only have myself and few others to count on against them."

Faust suggested that perhaps it's time for Marina to let others fight for their freedom or at least take some responsibility for their own defense. Marina considered his advice and wondered if he was right. She then related her experiences with her new asset Colby and his partner Margot. Her renewed optimism got Faust's attention.

"This man, Mike Colby, seems a lot like you," he mentioned.

"He's not nearly as good as me, Faust," she replied. "But we do have a lot in common and I intend to use that to my advantage."

"Be careful," he warned. "His recklessness could be your downfall."

Marina kissed his cheek and assured him that she would be careful. He then requested some time to rest, as she exhausted him.

"Faust, you're becoming soft," she teased.

"Only after I serve you my queen," he responded playfully and rolled over to sleep. Marina slapped his ass and left her quarters.

On the flight deck, Marina studied the monitor for any unexpected craft but there was nothing within range of the sensors. She sent a message to Archimedes-9 to her partner Rebecca. After speaking with the communications technician, she waited while he summoned Rebecca. Rebecca oversaw Archimedes-9 and was Marina's eyes and ears in that part of the galaxy. She controlled everything that happened on the station as well as any interaction with outside groups involving it.

Rebecca's voice startled her as her mind drifted to the issue of her allies. "Well, look who finally remembered to call," Rebecca teased.

Marina apologized for not staying in touch and then updated her on the problems with her allies. Rebecca mentioned that a friend of hers, Mike Colby, was up to some interesting things and might have a breakthrough soon. Marina pressed her for more and was surprised to learn that Colby was working on a plan to bring the Scrat into their fold.

"Now, how the hell is Colby going to do that?" questioned Marina.

"Colby is like a kid in a candy shop with no supervision," Rebecca kidded. "He is always getting into something he probably shouldn't, yet he always comes out smelling like a rose."

Marina assured her that she would come for a visit as soon as she resolved some other issues affecting her alliance. Rebecca promised to contact her as soon as she had more information on Colby's success and then ended the transmission.

Marina stared at the stars on the port side monitor and became teary-eyed. She and Rebecca had become so close at one time, especially during Rebecca's pregnancy. Marina was there to support her all the way up to the birth of her daughter. Everything was so good, but then she felt the need to go out on her own again. She feared getting too close and feeling like part of a family. The pain of losing a family member was something she tried hard to avoid. She summoned Faust after the birth of Rebecca's daughter and they disappeared on Andros-5 for what became her temporary retirement.

Marina contacted Kat and spoke with her for several minutes. Kat was concerned about Marina's disposition and requested that she return to Yord to spend some time with her friends. She assured Marina that she would be happy with the progress of the Seers. Eager to visit her young Seers, Marina agreed to come soon. The two women bade each other goodbye and ended the transmission.

Marina slept in the copilot's seat while Faust piloted the *Reaper* toward Yord. An incoming message from Korick on Zim interrupted her moment of peace. Korick informed her that an assassin named Borath had just arrived at his facility with twenty mercenaries. She was relieved to learn that there was no attack from them on the pirate haven, but she knew why they were there. They wanted the *Blue Eagle* and Mike Colby. *But how did they know?* she pondered, concerned about a spy having access to her orders she sent to Taurus. No one else would have known the *Blue Eagle's* additional stops that she gave to Gemini's people.

Faust questioned her about the risks to the *Blue Eagle* and if she might be over-reacting. Marina reminded him that she swore to protect the ship with what resources she had available and Tarsus already failed her. Feeling the pressure that was mounting on her, Marina took control of the ship from Faust and raced toward Archimedes-9. She needed to head off Colby and Margot before they departed for Zim. Yord would have to wait. Margot and Colby would have Antwan in their custody and would be at risk on the *Blue Eagle* without Tarsus' team to back them up. She already had doubts about Tarsus and needed to be sure the *Blue Eagle* was safe.

Faust warned her about Borath, who was part cyborg and a very expensive hire who never failed. Marina shook her head and admitted her fear that she would one day have to confront Borath. After pondering the circumstances, she complained that her alliance was falling apart and she would go down with it.

Faust reminded her that she was the baddest bitch in the galaxy with a unique team around her. He suggested that she didn't need allies; only her team. Marina laughed cynically and asked, "What team would that be?"

"Colby seems to handle confrontation well, after what we saw on Vega," he answered. "Margot and Jonas also know how to handle themselves and are reliable."

"But Borath is a different story!" Marina snapped.

"Then let's come up with a plan to trap him," Faust responded. "You always outwit your opponents."

Marina considered his words and then thought about Colby. Perhaps she could count on him to handle things on his own after all. He may prove to be more reliable than Tarsus and the other rebels, who seem content to sit on the sidelines and watch. "Maybe Colby isn't as reckless as I thought," she commented. "Perhaps he can plan on the fly like I do."

"Why do you say that?" questioned Faust.

"Because Britt thought I was reckless and, for that, he didn't trust me. Perhaps I need to trust Colby. Besides, Margot will back him up."

"And Jonas?" asked Faust.

"Jonas can fight but is reluctant," replied Marina. "That can get you killed."

"But he will defend his sister, if necessary."

"I'm counting on it," she answered in a somber tone.

Marina then considered that it was time to go small against Kronos, just like before. She couldn't rely on an army but, using a small team or two, they might be able to find the snake and cut off its head. She knew that she needed Kat to join them and instructed Faust to go to her home planet of Yord and bring her back. Another incoming message interrupted her thoughts. It was Rebecca.

Rebecca informed her that Antwan and his mercenaries attempted to trap the *Blue Eagle* and Colby. She revealed how Colby turned the trap back on the terrorists and succeeded. Then she informed her that Colby and Margot were badly injured during the evolution. Marina requested that they remain there but it was too late. Rebecca explained that her friends had recovered somewhat and were on their way to Zim with Antwan in their custody. Marina thanked her and ended the transmission.

Marina stood and paced frantically. "Get us to Zim as fast as you can," she ordered Faust.

Faust offered to contact the *Blue Eagle* for a status on her friends but Marina feared it would give both their positions away. "This shit never ends," she grumbled to herself. Faust reminded Marina that her friends did capture Antwan, but that did little to allay her fears.

Once again, the *Blue Eagle* was hung out to dry with no backup or support. "We have to get ahead of this and fast, Faust," she uttered, nearly in a panic. "We're always playing catch up and it's going to cost us big time if we lose that ship."

"Forget a plan," Faust suggested. "Let's just go in and do what we do best – wing it."

Marina agreed and departed the flight deck. She returned to her cabin and donned her battle attire; her leather bodice with daggers strapped to her thigh and a pulse pistol tucked in her back side, under the belt for her leather pants. It was time for the old Marina to return; ready to take on anyone, anytime.

When they arrived on Zim, Marina instructed Faust to stay put. She would have Antwan transported on board and then Faust would return with him to Yord. There he would pick up Kat and return to the pirate haven to meet up with her.

When she exited the bay and entered the main corridor, five men, dressed in black, approached her. Marina knew better than to expect a welcoming party of friends, although, she wondered how they knew she would come. When they closed on her, Marina drew two daggers and fired them at two of the mercenaries. The daggers found their marks in their throats and took two of the mercenaries out of the battle. One of the remaining three mercenaries drew a pistol while the others rushed at her. Marina drew another dagger and fired at the mercenary with the pistol. He never got a shot off before the dagger embedded in his left eye socket. The man fell to the ground with a thud and died.

Now with only two coming at her, Marina resorted to hand-to-hand combat and relied on her martial arts skills. She easily disposed of the two after inflicting numerous wounds to their limbs and abdomen areas. Marina felt the rush of adrenalin that she grew accustomed to in her younger years when she toyed with her victims, just to see them suffer. It was her calling card to others not to screw with her. Then came the news she dreaded. Faust arrived and relayed a message from Korick that Colby and Margot had an encounter with Borath. "How bad?" she asked, fearing the worst.

"You'd best go up to his office immediately," Faust advised her. Marina karate-kicked one of the wounded mercenaries in the jaw and the loud cracking sound indicated that she broke it completely. The mercenary looked at her, pleading for mercy and could only whimper. Annoyed, Faust fired a shot into his head and killed him.

Marina became teary-eyed that Margot and Colby might die while fighting her battle. Faust warned her that Borath might still be in the facility. If so, he would surely come for her. Marina wiped her eyes and regained her composure. Faust returned to the ship while she hurried to Korick's office on the second level.

When she entered the office, she was horrified by the condition of her friends. Colby and Margot both lay on a table; their bodies battered and bloody. Borath had carved the left side of Margot's face until the flesh dangled with blood still dripping onto the table. Both appeared unconscious. Oddly, nearby was a drum labeled 'peanut oil' that caught her attention. Korick, the owner of the pirate haven, and Kellen, a friend of theirs, stood somberly by the table.

The doctor stitched Margot's face back together, while the others watched, devastated by her injuries. Marina informed the doctor that they were her most valuable assets and she needed him to save them. He confessed that, other than the stitching, there was little he could do and their prognosis was grim. Marina paced the floor and then questioned Korick, "How did they get here? Is the *Blue Eagle* here?"

Korick looked befuddled and replied, "I don't know how they got here. No ships arrived; not even for a brief stop."

Marina was baffled. "And what about Borath?" she inquired uneasily.

"Dead," responded Korick. "I don't know how they did it but they got him good."

"And Antwan?"

Korick shrugged his shoulders. Marina paced the room and feared that this was another setback that she couldn't afford. She kicked the drum in anger. It made an odd sound that wasn't liquid, but she disregarded it. Korick lifted the cover off the drum and pointed inside. Marina peered inside and was relieved to see Antwan's limp body.

"Damn he's good!" Marina blurted as Korick put the lid back on. "Colby saved us from a very bad day."

Korick's men were relieved as well, fearing that they lost a high-value target in their own facility – a rebel stronghold, no less. Marina gestured for them to wait outside. When the door closed and she had privacy with Colby and Margot, Marina leaned over Margot and squeezed her hand affectionately. She cried when Margot remained unresponsive.

Then she turned her attention to Colby. She held his hand in hers but he was unresponsive as well. "Colby, you son of a bitch, I didn't give you enough credit," Marina uttered. "If you can hear me, I need to know how you got here."

Marina sat on the edge of the table and grew teary-eyed. The two people that became her greatest asset against Kronos were dying and, for once, she cared. Then she heard Colby mutter something. She leaned closer to him and asked softly, "What is it, Mike?"

Mike smiled when she called him by his first name. "Bay Seven," he spoke, barely coherent. "Cloaked."

Marina's eyes widened and she shouted for Korick to stay with them. Seeing her full of hope, he knew something had happened. She rushed past him and down to the transport bays. If Colby was right, then there was a chance that things were turning around in a hurry.

The bay appeared empty when Marina entered. She trembled as she feared the ship wasn't there after all and that Colby was delirious. Ten steps in and she was relieved to feel the invisible ship. "Out-friggin'-standing!" she exclaimed to herself. She felt along the side until she found the manual release for the hatch. Anxiously, she opened the hatch to be sure she wasn't imagining it. The hatch opened and the inside of the shuttle was visible. Marina immediately closed the hatch and hurried back to Korick's office.

When she arrived in the office, the others backed away from the table, granting her privacy with her friends. Korick asked if she found what she was looking for. She nodded and ordered them to move Colby and Margot down to Bay Seven.

Korick was baffled by her mention of Bay Seven. "Do I want to know why?" he asked.

"No!" she shouted. "Just do it fast." Korick summoned several of his men to carry out Marina's orders.

Marina instructed Kellen that he was to come with her. They went down to the station morgue and inspected the body of Borath. Marina was amazed at the damage that Colby was able to inflict on Borath. Amazingly, the exposed areas around several of his wounds showed that he was more cyborg than human. More so, she was anxious to know how Colby survived to defeat the cyborg assassin. She always feared that one day she would encounter Borath and she knew she would lose, likely to die. To know that Mike and Marina took him down in a blood fest was an honor to have two people like them on her side.

When they arrived in Bay Seven, Marina found the manual release lever and opened the hatch. The men were stunned that, not only was the shuttle cloaked, but it was inside the bay unnoticed. Colby and Margot were loaded onto the shuttle, followed by Borath's corpse in a cryogenic chamber for preservation, thanks to Korick's generosity. The bay cleared and deoxygenated for a quick departure.

Kellen immediately started the engines and ran the diagnostics. When they were ready for departure, he tricked the traffic controller into opening the gates for an 'empty bay' and, once clear of the station, he informed the man that he meant Bay Eight where Borath's ship was docked. He then mentioned that they had a maintenance issue so Bay Eight need not be opened after all. The supervisor laughed it off, assuming Kellen imbibed in a liquid lunch.

As the shuttle sped toward Taurus, Marina inspected the rear control panels of the shuttle. One side housed the power distribution systems. On the opposite side was another panel with the selector switch labeled cloak/transport/off. With her hands on her hips, she was impressed with what Mike accomplished with both the cloaking system and the teleport module but found it odd that only one of the two could be used at a time. She scanned the previous coordinates stored in the module's memory and selected Taurus. A minute after she initiated the 'start' function, Kellen grew frantic and summoned her to the flight deck.

Marina took a seat next to him and was amazed to see the massive space station called Taurus ahead of them. Nervous, Kellen explained that the station just appeared out of nowhere and should have been many days away. Unconcerned by his comment, Marina instructed him to get permission to dock and inform them of their medical emergency.

Sara, the head of the sector security group responsible for Taurus, responded and asked for Colby. Marina informed her that Colby and another crew member needed immediate medical attention. Sara assigned them a berth and arranged for medical personnel to meet them at the hatch.

As soon as Kellen docked the ship and the bay secured, six med-techs entered through the personnel hatch to the bay with their transport vehicle. Marina exited through the hatch and directed the med-techs inside. They promptly moved Mike and Margot onto their vehicle and rushed them to the hospital on the third level. Kellen completed the shutdown of the shuttle and soon joined them.

Sarah arrived with Gemini and Julian, the two senior executives for Universal Shipping on Taurus. No one spoke as they waited anxiously in the corridor for the med techs and the doctors to return with news. Finally, Sara spoke to Marina about her identity and purpose. She was excited to meet the elusive Marina, once again, in person. "I need to be briefed on what happened," she informed Marina. "I'm responsible for all security in this sector."

Marina assured her that they had plenty to discuss and would do so before she leaves the station. Sara then inquired about the details of what happened to Mike and Margot as Gemini and Julian listened intently. Marina revealed that, thanks to Mike and Margot's heroics, Antwan was in the alliance's custody and a very dangerous assassin named Borath was terminated.

Julian was stunned by her words. "You said Borath?"

Marina nodded to him and continued, "The *Blue Eagle* avoided Zim and continued on their course. Had they not, Borath and his men would have surely taken control of the ship."

Sara looked baffled by Julian's concern over Borath. Meanwhile, Gemini stood with her arms folded and a scowl on her face. She was irate over the lack of protection for the *Blue Eagle* and its crew while assisting Marina's rebel alliance. She refrained from saying anything at this time, though.

Julian noticed Sara's concerned expression and explained that Borath was a cyborg assassin with the human portion of him genetically engineered in a lab. "He is very expensive to hire and never failed…until now," he mentioned.

"You seem to know a lot about this, Julian," Sara remarked, curious.

"I do," he replied somberly. "Borath came to Aurora during the regime change to eliminate any obstacles during the takeover. I overheard the Kronos sentries talking about him, and even they were concerned about him if he went rogue. When we saw what he could do, we surrendered. That's how I wound up in prison."

Marina revealed to them the details of how they found their two friends and why she chose to bring them to Taurus. She requested they discuss an urgent upcoming matter once the *Blue Eagle* arrived.

The doctor emerged from the infirmary and informed them that Margot had brain swelling from head trauma and a shunt was inserted to drain the fluid. Her lungs were punctured in three places by broken ribs and were being repaired surgically as they spoke. Colby also had head trauma and a fractured skull. His hands were badly damaged and were also being repaired surgically. The doctor cautioned them that, emotionally, both were likely to suffer severely from their experience - if they survived at all. Marina thanked him and offered any assistance they required.

Sara received a message on her transmitter, informing her that the *Blue Eagle* was now docking. She informed the others that they would meet in the Red Room shortly and departed to meet the arriving crew.

The captain of the *Blue Eagle*, Tisch, ordered the crew to unload the cargo while she inquired about Colby and Margot. When Sara intercepted her at the elevator, Tisch questioned her if they heard from Mike. With a grim expression, Sara answered, "He and Margot are here, as is Marina."

"Oh, shit," blurted Tisch. "What did Mike do now?" The two women and Tisch's engineer Wilmer stepped on the elevator and waited anxiously as the doors closed. Sara explained, "The two of them may have saved us all from a very bad day."

"I don't understand. Why didn't Mike respond to our calls?" Tisch asked, sensing there was more to the story.

"He couldn't," answered Sara. "Nor could Margot." Tisch feared what she meant and trembled. Sara placed her hand on her arm to calm her.

They exited the elevator and approached the Red Room on the seventh floor. The sentries immediately opened the door for them, skipping the security protocol for access at Sara's direction. Inside the secure room, Marina, Kellen, Julian and Gemini sat at the table, looking devastated. Tisch entered with Sara and Wilmer. Marina immediately briefed them on the condition of Mike and Margot. She related how Borath arrived with a crew of mercenaries to capture Mike and the *Blue Eagle* but failed.

"Shit!" blurted Tisch. "We've all heard the myths about Borath. He's the Grim Reaper of the universe."

"Not anymore," remarked Marina somberly. "Mike killed him."

Gemini inquired, "Did you get the parts on Vega?" Tisch affirmed that they did and that they were being offloaded.

Marina pressed Tisch to reveal what they discovered on their expedition to the Scrat world. Tisch related Mike's suspicions about the Kronos' ships and their attack on the Scrat. As if on cue, a Scrat officer named Creeg entered and joined them. When Tisch related that much of the Scrat military was still intact, the Scrat officer pledged to obtain the support of his forces for Marina's alliance.

"I believe there is another valuable piece of information here," mentioned Tisch and she pointed to her crewman Wilmer. Surprised by his unexpected inclusion in the discussion, he retrieved a note from his pocket and handed it to the Scrat officer. At first, Creeg was baffled by its meaning, but then realized what it was. "You found the Kronos base!" he exclaimed.

Marina's eyes widened with joy over the thought of discovering the location of the second of the five bases. "Are you sure about this?" she questioned Wilmer.

"Absolutely," Wilmer replied. He explained how they extracted the information from one of the wrecked Kronos ships' data bases using his pulse pistol to energize the backup system.

Marina then spoke of the cloaking system on Colby's shuttle. She revealed that there were only two such systems and they were designed by the Federation for two specific deep space reconnaissance vessels that were believed to have been destroyed. She expressed her concern over how Kronos got their hands on them.

Marina then revealed that one more attack on Taurus was likely, since Antwan surely would have arranged a last desperate attempt to get control of Taurus. Sara expressed her concerns over the endless number of traitors, thanks to Empire's deep pockets through Kronos, and her depleted resources. She then emphasized that, despite their enemies endless resources, she would not to go down without a fight. Marina assured her that she understood their predicament.

Marina then insisted on speaking with Colby and Margot as soon as possible. The Scrat officer questioned what Marina's plans were for the Kronos base. Marina suggested that the Scrat military should handle it their way. The officer appreciated the gesture and assured her that they would take care of it. With that, the meeting ended and everyone returned to the hospital level except for Sara and Marina. Marina was pleased to see that she had some new, although unusual, allies forming. Still her concerns for Mike and Margot weighed on her.

Sara noticed and reminded Marina that she is the leader whom everyone looks to in the war against Kronos. She mentioned that everyone has a role to play and that they both knew there would be casualties. In an odd act, Marina hugged her and thanked her for her encouraging words.

Marina waited for three days until Mike and Margot's conditions were upgraded to stable, hoping to speak with them. Mike took medication for migraines and was expected to limit his time on his feet to a few hours a day. Margot required a wheel chair due to breathing issues until her lungs were fully healed. In addition, she had soft casts on her ankles and elbows.

Marina met with Sara, Gemini, and Tisch in Gemini's conference room for a final discussion of their plans. Now, Gemini took the opportunity to vent her concerns about the *Blue Eagle's* safety. Marina admitted how some of her allies had failed her, referencing Tarsus' failure to back them up.

Tisch agreed to take the Scrat officer to Archimedes-9 where they would coordinate with Rebecca to meet with the Scrat leadership. They expected to be without Mike and Margot indefinitely and planned to move on without them. Marina requested time with Wilmer to understand the cloaking system on Mike's shuttle as well as what he and Mike planned to do with the teleport module. It had little value to her as she was working with General Lennox of the Federation to install portals in key locations to eliminate the need for the teleport module. They all agreed that the teleport module was too dangerous an item to risk falling into the wrong hands, so it needed to be kept a secret.

After a discussion with Sara over the possibility of a spy on Taurus, Marina announced that it was time for her departure to Zim where she would rendezvous with Faust on her ship. Sara requested that Marina provide any available resources to help defend Taurus from the expected attack by Kronos. Both women were hopeful that this was a parting act by Kronos as they were already retreating from the sector but knew the risk posed by mercenaries within Taurus that could lead to their defeat. Marina had nothing to offer since most of her forces were focused on another region where there was significant Kronos presence. Sara reminded Marina that this looming attack could be a defining moment in the war and losing Taurus could be a significant setback for the rebel alliance.

Sensing her disappointment, Marina assured Sara that she would do her best to free up some resources from other parts of the galaxy but it would be some time before any ships or manpower would arrive. Both were aware that it could be too late by then. Then Marina mentioned something that surprised Sara. "Mike Colby could be your greatest asset," Marina said confidently. "Support him and use him. He's a good man."

The two established an unusual bond during their short time together. Both had responsibilities that demanded sacrifice and commitment, leading to lonely lives. Sara hoped that she would see Marina again soon. She felt invigorated, having someone just like her to bond with.

When Faust docked the *Reaper* at the transportation center on Yord, he was greeted by Marina's good friend Kat and a militia officer named Marcus. Behind them was a personnel carrier (vehicle) with eight militia sentries on top. Faust informed them that he had something for them and led them on board the ship. Faust lifted the lid off the drum and stepped back. When Marcus saw an unconscious Antwan inside the drum, he was eager to get their prisoner into a secure facility. He summoned several men to move their prisoner onto a personnel carrier and they whisked him away.

Kat embraced Faust and mentioned how much she missed him. She then inquired about Marina's state of mind. Faust responded that Marina will always be Marina so, in that respect, she was okay. The two had lunch at an open café, discussing the many events that occurred recently. Kat was surprised to hear about Borath's appearance on Zim and how Marina's new recruits killed him. When they finished their meal, Faust informed her that he had to return to Zim to meet with Marina and she needed to join him.

Kat was disappointed that his visit was short, but was eager to see Marina again. Faust reassured her that all was fine, but then Kat confessed that she was bored and wanted to see some action. Her role as a mentor to the two young Seers was diminished as the girls had their own perception of how things would be handled. Despite Kat's concern that the girls were on the verge of becoming women, the two Seers handled themselves responsibly. Faust questioned Kat on their progress and was amused by her response.

"The girls are ready for their reign of pain with Marina," Kat answered. "They are confident that Marina's grasp on the region as part of her kingdom would be secure under their control."

Faust cringed, wondering how the girls intended to execute their plan. When he and Kat returned to the cruiser, they were met by the two Seers, Kara and Ginna. The girls, now in their middle teens, informed Kat that they needed to go with them. Without further explanation from them, Kat reluctantly agreed. Faust looked uneasy but Kat squeezed his arm affectionately and smiled, thus calming him. They boarded the cruiser and departed for Murgatroyd's Oasis on Zim.

Just as Marina bade farewell to Sara and the Taurus personnel in the Red Room, Mike Colby hobbled in and announced that he would take Marina to Zim on his shuttle. Everyone was shocked that he was on his feet and eager to continue the fight. Then Margot entered, still in a wheel chair, and announced that she was going as well. After some debate, Marina agreed to allow them to take her back. Mike assured them that he would rendezvous with the *Blue Eagle* afterward and all would be fine. Tisch declared that they would travel on the *Blue Eagle* due to their frail condition or not at all. With that, it was settled.

CHAPTER 4

The trip to Zim on the *Blue Eagle* was uneventful at first and Marina used the time to get to know her new allies. Mike appeared to be ready for action should the need arise, but Margot had lingering issues that concerned her. Her worst fears were manifested when Margot attempted suicide by threatening to eject herself out of the emergency airlock. Fortunately, Mike was able to talk her out of it. Margot had the same recurring nightmare over and over: Borath cutting her face off.

Marina went to her quarters and focused on contacting Kat. With Kat's telepathic powers, Marina hoped that she could get help from her. After several attempts, she heard Kat's voice, soft and distant. Kat gave her a name and a location of someone who could help Margot. Marina felt relieved, especially when Kat affirmed that she was on the way with Faust.

Marina joined Tisch in the galley for a friendly conversation. The two spoke of their families' pasts, including Tisch's father, John Mallory. Marina was surprised to meet the daughter of John, who was an important ally of hers until his death. She told Tisch of the missions he performed for the rebel alliance and how much she cared about him as a friend. After a few beers, Marina retired to her cabin to rest.

When the ship was in proximity of Zim, Mike took Marina to Murgatroyd's Oasis in his shuttle. During the short excursion, Marina urged him not to give up hope for Margot. Despite her recurring nightmares and loss of memory, Margot still had feelings for Mike. Then Marina mentioned to Mike that she had information that could help.

"A friend of mine recommended that you take Margot to see Dr. Lowell on a planet called Sargassa in the Nigus star system," Marina suggested. "She might be able to help."

Mike thanked her and assured her that he would do whatever it took to help Margot recover. Then he surprised her with a small package wrapped in brown paper.

"What's this?" she asked, curious.

"A teleport module," he answered. "It's for you." He then related how the first one failed and an Archaenean on the Nims outpost gave him two. The Archaenean mentioned that he'd know what to do with the second one. Marina was pleased that he would provide her with such an asset as this.

After the shuttle was docked, Marina wished Mike well and hugged him. Mike was surprised and offered to be of help to her in any way possible. When Marina departed the shuttle, Mike wondered if he would ever see her again. They both lived dangerous lives and the galaxy was a big place.

Inside the station, Marina hurried down the corridor, eager to see Faust and Kat. Two young women approached her, dressed in robes and sandals. Adorned in make-up and jewelry, they paused in front of her as if waiting for something. Marina thought they looked familiar but dismissed it as coincidence. "Can I help you?" she asked the two women.

Both women embraced her in a group hug until Marina pushed them away, embarrassed. The women were surprised. Finally, one of the women spoke to her. "You don't recognize us, Marina?"

The other woman exclaimed, "It's us, Marina! Kara and Ginna!"

Marina was stunned. "What are you doing here?" she asked, concerned. "And what are you wearing?"

"We're here for you and for our future," Kara explained.

Ginna added, "We're not little girls anymore, Marina. We have a role to play."

Kat and Faust then approached, amused by Marina's expression. Stunned, Marina held her hands out for an explanation from Kat.

"Our girls have grown up, Marina," explained Kat. "They decide their own fate."

Marina turned her attention back to the girls. One a brunette and the other a blonde, their hair was done nicely in a bun with a pony tail protruding out the back. They looked all grown up from the twelve-year-old girls that Marina first took on a while back.

"You both look… stunning!" Marina finally replied. "I didn't recognize you. And I certainly didn't expect to see you here, of all places."

"I can use a drink," Faust mentioned and gestured for Kara and Ginna to follow him.

Kat held Marina in an affectionate embrace that seemed to last forever. Marina savored her touch and realized that her earlier fears of Kat's domination of her had passed. Kat informed her that they had much to discuss. Marina kissed her cheek and assured her that they had plenty of time – for a change.

When they took a seat inside the pub, Marina beamed at her 'family': Faust, Kara and Ginna, and Kat. Elspeth waited on them and was pleased to see Marina back again. Marina and Faust ordered ales, while Kat ordered a red wine. Marina was mortified when Kara and Ginna both ordered white wine.

Kat could see the surprise in Marina's face and placed her hand on Marina's leg. She gestured for Marina to remain calm. Marina reluctantly tolerated the girls' choice and trusted Kat's judgment.

"So, where do we start?" questioned Marina. "There is so much to discuss."

Kat responded that the girls had visions that needed to be addressed. In addition, she had a few of her own. Elspeth returned with their drinks and set them on the table. Marina suggested that she bring a pitcher of ale the next time she passed. Elspeth smiled and left them.

"Come, now, Marina," teased Kat. "It's not that bad."

Marina revealed to her the details from Borath's battle with her friends and why she requested her help earlier. Marina admitted that she believed she was destined for an encounter with Borath that would end her life. Instead, he screwed up two very valuable assets.

"Were they just assets?" inquired Kat, curious.

Marina shook her head and then answered, "Once they were. Then we became friends."

Kat reminded her that war is ugly and casualties will happen. Marina chugged her beer and lowered her head. Elspeth, with perfect timing, arrived with a pitcher of ale for Marina. She filled her mug and then left.

Kat revealed to Marina that she had two visions that concerned her. One involved three Kronos command ships. Another was about the two of them going on one of those command ships together.

"And what of the girls?" Marina asked.

"I need to go to Archimedes-9," announced Kara. "There, I will reside and be an extension of your power."

"And I will reside on Taurus when the time is right," explained Ginna. "There are things that must happen first before we can take residence."

Marina was baffled as to what purpose the girls would have in those locations. Kat suggested that their powers remained strong when they were positioned in certain locations. Then Kat suggested that, with her on Yord, and Marina at someplace to be determined, their powers as a team would remain intact.

Marina considered everything they revealed and then understood what she had to do. She related how Kronos destroyed her little planet and that one of their four ships mysteriously exploded.

"So, you know the location of the remaining three ships?" asked Kat.

"I do," answered Marina, "We're going to pay our Kronos puppets a little visit. In the meantime, the girls need to stay someplace safe." Faust shook his head at her, knowing there was going to be resistance.

Marina also informed Kat that those three command ships have kept Tarsus' group from joining the fight. This was a detriment to the *Blue Eagle's* protection. Kat looked surprised by the mention of the ship. She recalled that a ship named the *Blue Eagle* appeared in a dream but seemed to have no relevance.

Kara and Ginna held hands and their eyes turned white. They were locked in a premonition briefly. When it was over, Kara announced, "The *Blue Eagle* will play a vital role in the war against Kronos."

Ginna added, "There are two individuals on that ship that must be protected at all costs."

Marina was shocked. She knew the girls referred to Mike Colby and his partner Margot. "We have to move fast," she announced. "Kat, you and I are going on board one of those ships for answers. Figure out how." Kat was pleased to be included in Marina's plans.

Marina then sought out Korick, the pub's owner, for a favor. She arrived at his office, where he just finished conducting business with a friend. The man excused himself and left them to speak. Korick greeted Marina and offered her a seat.

Marina requested a ship that would be inconspicuous to transport her on board a Kronos command ship. Korick considered her request and chuckled. "Why in hell would you want to do that?" he asked.

"Just a hunch," she replied. "Besides, I need to find a way to get Tarsus' boys involved in the war."

Korick wrote down a series of numbers on a piece of paper and handed it to Marina. "Be gentle with it," he warned. "It's my personal shuttle." Marina thanked him and hurried back to the pub.

"We have our ship," she informed Kat. "Faust, you take the girls to Archimedes-9 and wait to hear from me."

Faust responded coldly, "Yes, ma'am."

Marina winked at him and then departed the pub. Kat shrugged her shoulders at him and then followed her.

Kat placed the shuttle on autopilot and joined Marina in her quarters. She sat on the bed next to her and hoped for an intimate encounter. Marina nestled against her like a lonely child. Kat caressed her hair and then hugged her affectionately.

"What's wrong, my queen?" Kat asked, sensing her sadness.

"I've become what I feared most – insignificant," she answered. "I'm doing nothing for my people. Kronos is up to something and I have no answers."

"We will find the answers together, if you only let me," Kat suggested. She placed her hand over Marina's eyes and lulled her into a deep sleep. The two lay down together in the narrow cot as Kat attempted to follow Marina's thoughts.

Marina found herself drifting through clouds, wondering where she was going. She saw her parents transform into creatures and dart away. She saw Lilith and Drago in front of a sophisticated control panel. Marina tried to comprehend what they were doing but then she appeared with them. The image faded and soon another appeared. Hundreds of bright lights appeared over Taurus, then Archimedes-9 and soon Yord. Then she appeared on a Kronos command ship with Carl Klingman. She relinquished her title as queen and surrendered all her territories to Kronos. Marina was horrified. How could she do that?

Startled, she awoke and sat up, soaked in sweat. Kat sat up and embraced her. Marina pushed her away and stood, looking panicked. "Did you see what I saw, Kat?" she asked, wide-eyed with fear.

"Yes, I did. Do you understand what any of it meant?"

Marina shook her head, wondering how she could fail so miserably. She paced the floor and suggested that this was her fate if she stayed on this path. Kat commented that the Seers might help clarify the meaning of the premonitions.

Marina stopped pacing and placed her hands on her hips. She turned to Kat and reminded her, "Get soft. Get dead. That was my motto in the old days."

"And?" inquired Kat.

"It's time to unleash some pain on Kronos," Marina announced. "Lilith and Drago play some role in this but we need to know how."

Marina then informed Kat that they needed to board one of the command ships. Ginna and Kara saw the ships land on Yord in a premonition. Those same ships were blocking Tarsus' forces from joining the hunt for the remaining bases but more so, left the *Blue Eagle* defenseless. Still unsure of the *Blue Eagle's* role in this, she was determined to take the battle to Kronos.

Kat requested that Marina leave her alone for a bit to consider their choices. With Marina back on the flight deck, Kat then used her powers to reach out to Kara and Ginna. After hours of what appeared to be meditation, Kat returned to consciousness. She joined Marina on the flight deck, appearing confident. Marina questioned her about her thoughts but Kat suggested that she wait until the details were clearer.

The shuttle darted across the sector toward the three Kronos command ships. Marina was calm and quiet as she piloted Korick's ship, while Kat sat in the copilot's seat, uneasy over her silence.

"So, what is your plan – or lack of – that I should know about?" Kat inquired callously.

Marina smirked at her. She wasn't in the mood for judgment and pondered how she would board one of the command ships without arousing suspicion. Kat turned her seat toward Marina and challenged her to prove her loyalty as a friend.

Irritated, Marina finally responded, "Why do I always have to justify my actions to you, Kat? Can't you just trust me that I know what I'm doing?"

Kat shook her head at her and frowned. She knew Marina was manipulating her into feeling guilty for doubting her. Marina realized that she had to show Kat that she mattered to her and explained, "I'm going to try and reason with them – for now. If that fails, then I will board them and do as much damage as I can."

"Do you want to know what I think?" asked Kat, wondering if Marina cared. "I think your best chance of getting on that ship is by boarding an incoming shuttle. You're going to need backup though."

"And why is that?" Marina inquired, curious.

"Because a shuttle will normally be manned by two to six crewmen. If you wish to commandeer the shuttle without an SOS being transmitted, you need me to watch your back while you take out the pilot and copilot."

Marina considered her suggestion and smiled. She knew Kat was right. "Perhaps I should listen to you more often," she kidded.

Kat began a search with the long-range sensors. The sensors soon picked up the three command ships and after several minutes, two smaller objects, supply shuttles, appeared. Kat pointed to them and announced, "There's our ticket in."

"How long before we catch up to them?" Marina asked. Kat reminded her that they can't cloak in this shuttle like they could on the *Reaper*. Marina grew flustered as she now considered that Kat's plan wouldn't work.

Kat stood and kissed Marina's forehead. She went to the hatch and paused. "We'll send an SOS to them. When they approach us, we'll transport over and commandeer the ship. It all sounds legit to the transport supervisor on the command ship."

Now Marina was elated. She stood and went to Kat. "You earned this," she remarked and embraced her tightly. "And yes, I do care about you. I'm just worried about losing people I care about because of my battle with Kronos."

Kat immediately responded, "This isn't just your battle. This battle is for all of us."

<hr>

Carl Klingman sat in his office on the top floor of Base Five. The office was a long, rectangular room with an elaborate bar near the entrance. The far end had a communication system designed for discrete contact with his facilities. He just learned that three of his bases had been compromised and that the fourth was likely to be breached soon. A tall, blonde woman entered the office and stood before him. Pleased to see her, Carl gestured for her to take a seat in front of his desk. The woman, Tessara, was Carl's first officer and often his most trusted advisor She waited patiently for Carl to address her. He stood and paced the room with his hands behind his back, pondering his next strategy.

"What is it that concerns you, sir?" she finally asked, breaking the uneasy silence.

Carl returned to his desk and sat down. "You heard the latest report on our bases?" he inquired.

"Yes, sir. I have," she replied.

Carl expressed his concerns that someone inside the Kronos organization could be leaking the locations of their resources. He also inquired as to what she thought they should do to handle their current situation. Kronos had lost too many resources recently and failure would not be tolerated by those in the top tier of the organization. At some point, he would have to answer for their failure. Tessara contemplated their options briefly and then suggested, "Let's set some priorities here."

Carl stood and approached the bar. He poured two glasses of scotch and returned to his desk. Sliding one glass to Tessara, he held his glass up for a toast. Tessara obliged and the two tapped glasses. "To our recovery plan, Tessara," Carl announced. "I trust you won't let me down." They each sipped and then set their glasses down.

"Have I ever?" she kidded. Carl smiled at her. "Let's assume they already know where this base is," she commented. "That means you and I should not be here."

Carl nodded, pleased with her first suggestion. Tessara pondered again for a moment and then sipped from her glass. Carl did the same as he anxiously awaited her next response.

"The only mole I can imagine is that bitch Darra," she mentioned. "However, I don't believe it's her – at least not yet."

When she paused to consider her next words, Carl gestured with his hand for her to continue. He was eager to know how she suspected the locations were discovered. She explained, "Your nemesis, Mike Colby, has a knack for being in or around these bases when they are overtaken."

Carl grew somber and asked if Colby could really be that good. He wondered aloud if it could be Marina. Tessara reminded him that both seem to have a vendetta against him but Marina hasn't left her sector to their knowledge, where Colby has been all over the place.

"So, what do we do about it?" Carl inquired.

"Do you really believe that Darra killed Marina?" she countered. "I think she had Marina on the run and used the "chase and kill" tactic by the command ships to convince us that Marina was dead. Meanwhile, Marina is taking advantage of that perception to lay low and plot her next move."

"And what would that move be?" asked Carl, growing more curious.

"Marina is preparing to mount an attack against us, once she has her targets. "Tessara explained. "Colby is acquiring the targets for her."

"Then we should amass our forces for a final stand," he surmised.

Tessara agreed and insisted that they should expect attacks from several vectors. She clarified that Marina doesn't have a lot of support from her home sector and that the Federation is still building up its Fleet in the Nigus star system. In addition, they've neutralized most of her alien allies.

Carl inquired if the laser targeting system they lost to Marina's forces a while back could be pivotal if they could repossess it. Tessara disagreed to its value since they lost the means to control it remotely and it would have to be reconfigured for high-energy discharge, if they expected it to function as a weapon. Therefore, its recovery wasn't a viable option.

"Perhaps we can strike a deal with Marina and Colby," Tessara suggested.

"I think we're way past that. I will give it a try though," Carl responded. "At least a truce will buy us time to regroup our forces."

"I do recommend that we divide our forces into three groups. Let's assume they are monitoring the base and are watching the movement of our ships. Perhaps we can bait them into underestimating our forces and give us a chance to land the first blow of the battle."

"I think I will put my little friend Corbin to work with his new portal project he claims will be ready soon. What better way to ambush Marina's forces."

"Even better," began Tessara. "Let's not defend Base Four at all. They'll likely suspect that our ships are all in dock and rush their attack. Then we ambush them from behind. If they don't appear, then we know Base Four is still safe."

Carl raised his glass as a salute to Tessara. "Once again, you have done yourself proud," he remarked and finished his drink. Tessara smiled and drank the contents of her glass.

Tessara stood and offered her assistance for any additional issues. Carl thanked her and again praised her for her valuable assistance. She smiled and departed the office.

"Damn, I love that woman," Carl remarked to himself. He instructed his secretary to contact Corbin and then used his communication system to send a signal out to Marina.

After ten attempts, he was about to give up, but then Marina responded tersely, "Go ahead."

Carl was ecstatic with the opportunity to speak with her after everything that happened at Orpheus-2. "Well, Marina, I appreciate you responding to my transmission," he mentioned politely.

"You and I have nothing to talk about," she responded. "You killed many of my friends, and for that, you will pay."

Carl frowned as he quickly realized this was hopeless. As a final attempt to win her over though, he asked, "Is there any common ground for us – monetarily or other?"

"Of course, there is," she responded. "Your death will make the universe a better place."

"Then I guess it's game on," Carl replied disappointedly. "See you on the battlefield." He ended the transmission and mumbled to himself,

"Couldn't hurt to try, though." Carl sighed and then reviewed several reports on his computer screen. He returned to the communications set and contacted his fleet commander.

"Commander Zarloff, I need you to send a derelict ship to Archimedes-9 for me," he ordered. "Make sure it has a 10-megaton explosive device on board." Carl grew frustrated as the officer questioned the reason for his order. "Just make it happen ASAP! That's an order." He slammed the receiver down and rubbed his temples, while feeling pained with a migraine.

A few hours passed and Corbin entered the office. He apologized for not arriving sooner and offered to assist Carl in any way possible. Carl gestured for him to sit. Corbin was excited to be in Carl's office and he was eager to know why he was summoned.

"Where do we stand on the portal project?" Carl inquired.

"I heard from my contact earlier," he replied excitedly. "She tells me that the Federation plans to go live with the system next week as part of their preparation for a major attack."

Carl grew interested and questioned Corbin if he knew more. Corbin explained that the contact had access to the system for acceptance testing from their civilian contract engineers and would have the components for him very shortly. Carl approached Corbin and gestured for him to stand. The two embraced in an affectionate hug.

"How long will it take to integrate the components into our model?" Carl asked.

"My contact gave me the details of the linking and connection points. I believe we can be up and running in an hour."

"I can see you have a bright future in my organization, Corbin," Carl commented. Corbin beamed at him, seeing his future blossom before him.

Carl took Corbin by the hand and led him through a doorway in the rear of the office to his quarters. When Corbin saw the elegant bed and fancy bar, he was more than willing to do whatever was necessary to please Carl. The two embraced again and spent the evening bonding.

Faust piloted the *Reaper*, frustrated by Marina's treatment of him. He was capable of so much more, but she only saw him as her love toy. Even then, she rarely was in the mood to make love.

Kara and Ginna entered the flight deck. They sat in the copilot's seat and the jump seat behind Faust. Faust smiled at them and inquired what they were up to. Kara informed him that he needed to take them to Taurus and then to Archimedes-9. Faust laughed at her and reminded her that he takes his orders from Marina.

"You need to take me to Archimedes-9 and then take Ginna to Taurus," instructed Kara. "If you don't, Marina will die."

Faust considered that the girls had unusual powers and were right so far. He also knew that the girls had saved Marina's life already. Reluctantly, he changed course and headed for Archimedes-9.

Ginna, in an attempt to appease him, informed him that Kronos laid a trap for them on Yord and, if they returned there, it would lead to many deaths.

"If I get into trouble with Marina over this, you girls are going to take the heat for it," Faust warned them. Each girl kissed him on the cheek and then they left the flight deck. "Why me?" grumbled Faust.

After a lengthy journey, The *Reaper* arrived on Archimedes-9 first and docked after receiving permission from the transport supervisor. Rebecca was concerned when she heard that the *Reaper* had returned unexpectedly. She hurried down to the transport bay with a contingent of security personnel. The hatch opened on Marina's ship and Faust emerged with Kara and Ginna. Rebecca waited patiently expecting Marina to follow but no one else exited. Faust and the girls approached her.

"Greetings, Rebecca," said Faust politely. "Thank you for receiving us."

"Is Marina okay?" questioned Rebecca, concerned.

"Yes, she is," he replied. "She is on a mission currently."

Rebecca grew more curious. "And who are these young ladies?" she asked.

Faust became uncomfortable, wondering what he should reveal. Frustrated, he gave up and explained, "These are the new Seers that Marina has been caring for."

"And they are here for..." commented Rebecca.

"Kara claims that it is important for her to be here," answered Faust, feeling foolish. "Perhaps she can explain her reasoning to you."

Kara took Rebecca's hand and closed her eyes briefly. When she opened them, she informed Rebecca that there was a ship coming that would endanger the entire station. "She can stay," Rebecca informed Faust. "I will care for her."

Kara and Ginna hugged each other and said their good-byes. Faust thanked Rebecca and returned to the ship with Ginna. The hatch closed and the bay alarm sounded for departure. Rebecca led Kara from the transport bay, escorted by her security detail.

Another alarm annunciated and the personnel hatch latched. The bay became a vacuum and once void of oxygen, the outer gates opened. Faust piloted the shuttle into space and on to their next stop.

On Orpheus-2, General Lennox entered the board room along with four other Federation officers. Six civilian consultants were already present at the oval table. The officers took their seats as General Lennox stood at the head of the table.

"We are one week away from implementing our new portal technology," she announced. "The sixth floor will be off-limits to all nonessential personnel for the time being."

One of the consultants inquired, "Why the one-week delay?"

Lennox revealed that the new portals will be created in conjunction with the itineraries of field assets. This was necessary to prevent Kronos from learning of their existence and destinations. Assets included shuttles that performed monitoring of passing ships in unusual locations, undercover agents in selected public locations and transport bays at various stations to monitor incoming and outgoing ships, along with their cargo manifests. The consultant scribbled on his note pad.

Another consultant asked, "What about testing? We haven't completed the acceptance test yet for the Federation." Lennox assured him that she had the utmost confidence in the technicians that the portal system will work as advertised.

One of her officers inquired about the badges and access to the sixth floor. Lennox pondered briefly and then responded, "I don't see a need to alter anyone's access who is currently working on the project. We will have a sentry posted at all times though to ensure the lab is secure and the system is protected."

General Lennox thanked them for their hard work and invited them to a celebratory dinner in the evening. The meeting ended and everyone but Captain Harville departed. Lennox gestured for him to sit down. She paced the room and then sat across from him.

"General, was it wise to divulge our plans for the new system?" inquired Harville.

Lennox chuckled and informed him that there was a mole and this was an opportunity to flush him or her out. Harville asked what his role was in the plot. "Just monitor the sixth floor to see who attempts to access the beta portal system," she instructed him. Harville nodded and departed the board room.

On the tenth floor of Orpheus-2, Drago and his wife, Lilith, operated the control console for the laser targeting system. Since the battle for Orpheus-2 six months earlier, Lilith and Drago's roles were to interface the targeting system with many of the planets in the quadrant and use its heating capability to hydrate arid atmospheres on various planets for agricultural purposes. They had little interaction with the Federation since their work was strictly for civilian purposes. As such, both were surprised when General Lennox arrived in their lab.

"Good afternoon, General," Lilith greeted her pleasantly. Drago stayed in the background as his role was only to assist and he had little to say on the project. Lilith was the creator and engineer of the targeting system and developed the concept of using lasers to control atmospheres and create rain.

"Good day, Lilith," replied Lennox. "Hello, Drago." Drago nodded to her.

"What can we do for you?" Lilith asked.

General Lennox pulled up a chair and sat down. "The portal system," she remarked. "We have a mole who will have a chance to access the beta system."

"The beta model has sustaining issues," commented Lilith.

"Yes, it does. And that's why we are allowing the mole an opportunity to steal the primary components."

Lilith glanced at Drago, wondering what the General wanted from them. "Is this mole involved with Kronos?" she asked.

Lennox nodded and then replied, "Is there anything we can do to make this more painful for Kronos, if they were to use it?"

Lilith and Drago considered the operation of the portal generator for a few moments and then both their eyes widened with excitement. Lilith revealed that they could change the programming of the primary control module so that the exit location of the portal is the same every time. It wouldn't affect the sustaining issue and the portal would still collapse soon after but they could create a destination that is less than desirable. The destination, however, would be predetermined by Lilith and no matter what coordinates are programmed into it, the destination would always default to Lilith's selection. Lennox was pleased and inquired how long it would take to make the change.

Lilith pondered for a moment and then answered, "We can make the change in just a few minutes. The one question I have is this: where do you want their ships to emerge?"

"What about in the middle of the Aegis Asteroid Field?" answered Lennox. "Right smack in the middle."

Lilith and Drago grinned. "Consider it done," Lilith replied excitedly.

"I'll contact the sentry and make him aware that you are running a test. General Lennox thanked her and left the lab. Lilith smiled at Drago and the two hurried down to the sixth floor.

After another lengthy journey, the *Reaper* arrived on Taurus. This time, Julian and Gemini, the CEO of Universal Shipping Corporation on Taurus, awaited Marina's appearance. The hatch opened and Faust exited with Ginna by his side. Gemini was disappointed as she looked forward to meeting with Marina again. Julian approached and shook hands with Faust.

"This is a most unexpected encounter," quipped Julian. "To what do we owe this visit?"

Faust pointed to Ginna and explained the importance of her role in things to come. Less than enthusiastic about having a teenager to care for, Gemini questioned Faust about the reason for her visit.

"Ginna is a Seer and has the ability to see and do unusual things," Faust explained. "She claims that it is important for her to be here."

Julian, in an attempt to be diplomatic, questioned Ginna. "Why do you feel the need to be here on Taurus?"

Ginna responded, "There is someone among you who is endangering the station and all those here."

"And who might that person be?" he countered.

Ginna closed her eyes for a moment and then opened them. "It is a man in a critical position. He is an unlikely suspect who has access to vital information."

Now, she had Gemini's attention. "Perhaps we should continue this conversation in a more secure location," she suggested.

Julian assured Faust that they would care for Ginna and use her skills where applicable. Faust thanked him and returned to the *Reaper*. They promptly left the transport bay and stepped onto the elevator. The *Reaper* departed the station with only Faust on board.

Gemini questioned Ginna about her ability to see things, but Ginna was evasive and only explained that there are times when she needed to take action, even if Marina wasn't available to approve her choices. Julian questioned the accuracy of her insights, wondering if they really did have a serious security breach on Taurus.

The elevator door slid open before she could respond. Tariq, Sara's replacement as head of GSS and off-site security at Taurus greeted them. "I understand Marina's cruiser just docked here," he commented.

Ginna eyed him and cast a concerned glance at Julian. Julian realized that he fit the description she gave earlier. "Just a social call," he replied, unwilling to share information until he knew more.

"That's strange," Tariq inquired. "Marina doesn't go anywhere unless it is part of an action plan." Tariq then followed them down the corridor to Gemini's office.

Gemini noticed his interest in the *Reaper's* appearance on Taurus and was curious. She paused at the entrance to her office and asked innocently, "Is there something we can help you with, Tariq?"

Tariq hesitated and then inquired, "And who might this young lady be?"

Julian quickly interceded and replied, "This is a servant girl from Yord who worked for Marina. She's very intelligent and Marina hoped that we could find her employment here." Tariq eyed her suspiciously but had no rebuttal.

Gemini performed the retina scan and the door slid open, allowing them access to the office. Julian and Ginna entered first. Gemini commented to Tariq, "I will let you know if we need you for anything. Thank you, Tariq." Tariq nodded and departed.

Julian looked concerned and sat at the conference table. He motioned for Ginna to sit as well. Gemini poured herself a drink and paced the room. She contemplated aloud, "If he is, in fact, a mole for Kronos, then that would explain the assaults on the *Blue Eagle* at each stop on their itinerary."

"He also has access to critical information on the station, especially incoming and outgoing flights," added Julian.

"So, how do we handle this?" Gemini asked, concerned about consequences from Kronos if they apprehended him.

Julian turned his attention to Ginna. "If Tariq is the spy, what can you tell us about a Kronos response?"

Ginna responded, "You must do what you must."

"But, how do we know that he is the spy?" asked Gemini, growing impatient.

"I can only tell you what is shown to me," Ginna replied. "You must determine what needs to be done on your own."

Realizing that there was no further point in questioning Ginna, he offered to show her to her quarters. Gemini gestured with her hand for him to proceed. When they left the office, she guzzled her drink and swore. If there was a mole, she wanted him to suffer.

As Julian and Ginna approached the elevator, Tariq met them from the other direction. "I'm sorry to bother you again," he said in a somber tone. "I have to know if Marina mentioned anything about her intentions."

Julian pressed the button for the elevator and stared at him, wondering if he could trap him into revealing his true intentions. "She did say that she was here in the sector for a crucial meeting."

"Did she say where?" Tariq pressed. "I really should be there and I do need to speak with her."

Julian felt confident he could now prove that Tariq was the mole. "She said it was a private meeting with a man named Korick at a pirate haven on Zim." Tariq thanked him and hurried off.

Once Tariq was alone, he used his wrist transmitter and instructed one of his officers to take a team and discretely follow Faust's ship. It was a long shot, but he hoped that Faust would lead them to Marina.

The elevator door opened and Julian led Ginna inside. The doors closed and Gina inquired, "Why would you give him that information if he is a suspect?"

Julian smiled at her and pointed out that he had no idea where Marina was but, if Kronos showed up, then they would know for sure that he was the mole. The elevator stopped and the doors slid open. Julian gestured politely for Ginna to exit first. He then led her down the corridor to her quarters.

Ginna questioned him about what she should do in the meantime. Julian promised to introduce her to some friends at dinner. Pleased, she entered her quarters, while Julian returned to Gemini's office.

Gemini was surprised to see Julian so soon and refilled her drink while taking an expensive brand of beer from her refrigerator. She sat at the table and handed the beer to him.

"What do you think?" she asked.

Julian revealed what transpired between him and Tariq. He recommended that they inform Korick of their plan and let him handle it. Gemini agreed.

CHAPTER 5

Still far out, a derelict freighter glided toward Archimedes-9. The station's transport supervisor attempted to contact the pilot of the ship but received no response. Immediately, he contacted Rebecca and informed her that something was wrong.

Rebecca summoned Kara and briefed her on the situation. Kara, just as Ginna responded, explained that she can only reveal what she sees. She suggested cryptically that they do what needs to be done. Concerned, Rebecca summoned her security team and discussed the situation with them. The team expressed their concerns about destroying the ship without knowing what its cargo was, fearing that it could unleash a dangerous shockwave toward the station, even at such a distance.

Rebecca took it upon herself to take a shuttle out to the derelict ship and investigate. Her team was shocked at the idea but she refused to risk lives to save her station. It was a race against time, despite the distance.

On Yord, Darra's shuttle landed at the transport center. Keeping a low profile in plain clothes and a cap on her head, she took a long walk around the town before reaching the palace. She needed to confirm if Marina was still alive and, if so, she needed to terminate her before Klingman turned on her for failing her mission.

Once she reached the palace, she noticed that there were no guards at the gate. That was unusual and likely a sign that Marina wasn't there. As she ascended the steps to the entrance, Marcus and a sentry stepped into the doorway, blocking her path.

"Can I help you?" he asked politely.

"I hope so," Darra replied. "I need to speak with the Queen. Is she available?"

"I'm afraid not," he replied. "We haven't heard from her in quite some time. Unfortunately, that's normal for Marina."

Darra looked down at the floor, disappointed. Suddenly, she had an idea. "Can you tell me anything about the three orphans that were brought here? I was hired by their mother to locate them."

"I'm afraid I don't know anything about their whereabouts," Marcus responded.

The sentry became wide-eyed, feeling the opportunity to be helpful, and announced, "The orphans were taken to Archimedes-9! They were transported there about two months ago."

Marcus was stunned that one of his men would disclose information to a stranger like that. He maintained his calm and suggested that she pursue the sentry's comment, remembering that it was old information that may or may not be accurate. Darra thanked the men and departed. As soon as she was out of sight, Marcus shoved the sentry inside the lobby and threw him against the wall.

"You stupid fool!" he shouted at the man. "Do you know who that was?"

The sentry shook his head, knowing he was in serious trouble. Marcus punched him in the face several times before summoning other sentries to the lobby. When six men arrived, Marcus instructed them to imprison the man and that he was to be tried for treason for giving classified information to a potential enemy of the kingdom. The sentries were surprised that their peer would be so foolish, but they obeyed Marcus' order. Marcus promptly went to the communication office. He instructed the officer to contact Rebecca on Archimedes-9 and warn her of the likelihood of an unvetted stranger arriving in search of the orphans. Marcus returned to the lobby and banged his head against the wall in frustration. He could see his dream as a high-ranking militia officer ending abruptly.

Marina studied the monitor for the long-range sensors, while Kat piloted the ship. The sensors detected three large ships; likely the command ships Marina was searching for. Marina saw them and blurted, "Son of a bitch! Those command ships are headed to Calamaar!"

Kat was startled by Marina's outburst and asked, "Why would they go there?"

"They're going to destroy another one of my allies! That's their strategy!" Marina exclaimed. "Follow them at full speed!" Kat promptly accelerated the ship to maximum speed. Marina maintained a somber mood as she contemplated how she would retaliate against Kronos.

When the Kronos command ships appeared on the short-range monitor, Marina was horrified by the size of the attack. The command ships selected random targets on the planet while ground forces had been launched to the planet's surface. The Calamaarian forces fought valiantly against the Kronos forces but they were significantly outnumbered.

"There's our opportunity!" exclaimed Marina. "Dock on the nearest command ship."

"Are you out of your mind?" blurted Kat. "That's suicide!"

"Just do it," ordered Marina. "Let me worry about suicide." Kat groaned at her but obeyed.

The officers in the control rooms of each of the ships were focused on the battle and failed to notice Marina's shuttle approach one of the ships from behind. Once the shuttle was docked inside the end bay, the gates for that bay closed automatically.

Kat glared at Marina and asked sarcastically, "Now what, your Wise-assness?"

Marina grabbed her head with both hands and kissed her forehead. "Don't leave without me," she instructed her. Kat was surprised by Marina's reaction and covered her eyes, fearing what her plan was. Marina left the flight deck and hurried to the hatch. She checked her pulse pistols to ensure both were charged and her daggers to make sure she had all four. Taking a deep breath, she uttered to herself, "Let's kick some ass, just like the old days."

Marina stepped off the shuttle and hurried across the dock to the personnel hatch. With all the troops engaged in the ground war, she encountered no resistance. "What a bunch of fools," she uttered to herself. After wandering down several corridors, she reached a stairwell that led to the control room. "Looks like show time," she quipped. Then she recalled what Kat said about this being suicide. "Or that," she added and ascended the stairs.

The door to the control room required a retinal scan for access. Marina sighed and leaned against the wall next to the door. Suddenly, the door slid open and one of the officers stepped out. He was caught off-guard by Marina when she gave him a chop to the throat. Now wedging him in the doorway to keep it from sliding closed, she took his pistol from him and shot him twice in the chest.

Nine officers in the control room were startled by the pulse fire and turned immediately toward Marina. Three drew their pistols and fired at her, but she ducked back into the stairwell and dodged the pulses. She leaned inside the doorway, still using the dead officer to prevent the door from closing, and fired several shots. The three officers fell to the floor, dead or dying. Marina entered the control room again and marched forward with two pulse pistols pointed forward. She ordered the officers to step away from the consoles with their hands behind their heads. Two hesitated and she promptly shot them both in the chest. They fell to the floor with lethal wounds.

"Alright boys," announced Marina. "Backs against the wall." The officers reluctantly complied. Then Marina inquired, "Where is the commander?"

A voice startled her from behind as an oriental officer entered the control room. "I'm right here, Marina." Marina quickly turned and pointed one of her pistols at him. He held his hands up innocently. "There's no reason for any more bloodshed," he added.

Marina gestured for him to join the others by the wall. He walked slowly, keeping his eyes on her. "You got a name?" Marina inquired.

"I am Commander Zhi of the *Celestial Queen*," he responded, somber over the turn of events. "What brings you to such an extreme act as boarding a Kronos command ship? Surely it must be something of significant importance to you."

Two of the officers glanced at each other and quickly reach for the pistols, holstered on their belts. Marina fired two shots into each of them without looking at them. Zhi instructed the remaining two officers to stand down. Both turned and reached for their pistols, but again Marina was ready, and fired twice into each one. The officers were dead before they hit the floor.

"Looks like it's just me and you, Commander," Marina commented.

The commander pointed to a chair and asked, "May I?" Marina nodded and leaned on one of the consoles, while facing him. The commander sat down and eyed Marina for a moment.

"That was quite a number you did on the *Imperius*," he commented.

"Funny you should bring that up," Marina remarked. "I was going to ask you about that. As much as I'd like to take credit for it, I cannot. I did speak to Commander Horan earlier and he mentioned someone named Darra that I should be concerned with."

Commander Zhi revealed that there were suspicions among the other commanders that Darra may have used a rogue crew to destroy the *Imperius* when the nearby planet was destroyed as well. "It was all too easy to justify your death," he remarked. Marina tied him up and informed him that she would spare him and his ship. Zhi was relieved until he realized what Marina's intentions were.

Marina programmed the weapons on the ship for 'auto' and then selected the other two command ships as the targets. She initiated the program and watched on the monitor as the *Celestial Queen* unloaded an arsenal of cannon fire on the other two unsuspecting command ships.

Zhi lowered his head in shame. Marina pulled up a chair in front of him and questioned him about Klingman's location. Zhi responded that Klingman doesn't stay in one place too long but isn't necessarily at one of their bases either.

"I want you to give your boss a message for me," Marina instructed him.

"Perhaps you should give it to him yourself," he replied. Zhi then gave Marina instructions to contact Klingman from the communications console. Marina eagerly attempted to make contact with Klingman.

Tessara, Carl's first officer, prepared Klingman's shuttle for departure. A beep from the transmitter caught her attention. "Go ahead," she replied, careful not to give away her identification without vetting the caller.

"I need to speak with Klingman," Marina announced into the console's microphone.

"Who is this?" Tessara inquired. "And what is your identification?"

Marina was amused and responded, "Tell him a friend is calling."

Tessara suspected it was Marina and summoned Carl to the flight deck. She whispered to him that it was likely Marina. Curious, Carl sat next to her and spoke up. "What can I do for you, Marina?" he asked in a friendly tone.

"Well, Carl, since we're becoming such good friends, I thought I'd share some of my good fortune with you."

"Ah, you are always the optimist," commented Carl. "Please continue."

"I'm sitting in the control room of the *Celestial Queen*. I'm about to take out your ground forces on Calamaar. You now have two less command ships as I have disposed of them."

Carl's face went taut and he felt rage build up inside him. Tessara gestured for him to remain calm. "What is it that you want?" he asked tersely.

Marina chuckled as she considered her next words. "You see, Carl, this is personal. You attacked my kingdom, my allies, and my friends. I feel it's only fair that I return the favor. Therefore, I'm giving you fair warning: I am coming for you. I will go through your entire organization and your fleet until I get to you."

Carl whispered to Tessara to validate where she was transmitting from. Tessara promptly operated the controls on another console. "You do know that Kronos is a big operation. Huh, Marina?" he reminded her.

"Let's see," Marina began. "I know that you've lost three bases already and several command ships. I know where two of your main forces are located. It is just a matter of time before you lose everything and it will be me who takes it all from you."

Tessara nodded to Carl, affirming that Marina was indeed on the *Celestial Queen*. Carl rubbed his temples with a pained expression. "How did you get aboard that ship?" he demanded to know, his anger showing.

"The same way I plan on getting to you," she replied. "I'll see you soon, my friend." Marina ended the transmission and focused the cannon fire from the *Celestial Queen* on the ground forces. Within a short time, she gave the Calamaarian forces a fighting chance to defend themselves.

For some reason, Marina took a liking to Commander Zhi and untied him. "I'm letting you go free as a professional courtesy, Commander," she remarked. "Perhaps, when the war is over, we can share a drink or two and become better acquainted."

Commander Zhi was grateful for her generosity and assured her that he would like to learn more about her strategies over a drink. She wished Commander Zhi well and departed the control room. A tear streamed down Zhi's cheek as he evaluated the destruction of the other command ships by his own ship.

Kat watched the monitor in front of her and was stunned as two command ships were pummeled with cannon fire. Marina returned to the shuttle and surprised Kat when she boarded. Kat stared at her and then chided, "What the hell did you do? This ship just destroyed the other two!"

Marina sat next to her and replied, "Yes, it did."

Kat was beside herself. She had no idea Marina would pull something like this off. When Marina piloted away from the dock, the bay doors opened, allowing them to exit the transport bay into space.

"How's that for a wise-ass?" Marina joked.

Kat shook her head in disbelief. "Where to next?" she asked, still wondering what just happened.

Marina thought for a moment and then answered, "The Strontarian Galaxy, Ramses-3."

"What the hell is there?" Kat asked, stunned by Marina's response.

"We're going to see what forces we have available for the big battle. I'm not pleased with what I've seen of Tarsus and his forces thus far."

Kat sighed and went to the hatch. "I need a drink," she commented and then exited the flight deck.

Marina contacted Golgar, eager to inform him that he owed her for saving his scaly hide. Golgar was stunned that Marina would help him after his reluctance to ally with her. She commented that she needed to leave but his troops should be able to finish off the remainder of the invaders. Golgar thanked her and assured her that he would be there for her in the future. Pleased, Marina ended the transmission.

Marina then contacted Faust and inquired about the girls (Kara and Ginna). Faust informed her that, while at Taurus, Sara's replacement Tariq was identified as a spy for Kronos. He explained that Julian was handling it and had a plan. Marina then realized that all the attacks on her allies on the *Blue Eagle* were a direct result of Tariq's betrayal. She felt relieved that the source of the leaks had been discovered and handled. Marina then requested that Faust meet her at an abandoned outpost called Situ-Minnus at the edge of the sector.

After the transmission ended, she thought for a moment and then contacted Korick at the pirate haven called Murgatroyd's Oasis on Zim. Korick was pleased to hear from her and caught her up on all things related to her alliance. When he informed her of the conquest of Empire Shipping and his inheritance of its domain as his new base of operation, thanks to Mike Colby, Marina was ecstatic. Kellen would now be the owner of Murgatroyd's Oasis. Then he revealed that the third base had been discovered and was now a shipping hub in the Nigus star system under Federation protection. Now her alliance had complete control of the sector as well as another stranglehold on Kronos' forces. Kronos was now on the run, a sign of Colby's success.

Marina requested that he forward a message to Tarsus. Korick became anxious, sensing that the message meant good news. She related how she commandeered a Kronos command ship and stopped their invasion of Calamaar. Now he had no excuses to avoid the war.

"Oh, and there's a Kronos command ship, the *Celestial Queen*, in the vicinity of Calamaar. It's not a threat."

"What?" blurted Korick. "How did you pull that off?"

"Small targets are harder to hit," she responded. "I'll be in touch with you or Kellen when the time is right." Korick thanked her for the good news and the transmission ended.

When Kat returned to the flight deck, she was somewhat inebriated from the wine. She sat in the copilot's seat and giggled at Marina. Marina groaned and complained that she would need to restock the wine cabinet after this trip. Kat slid off the seat and knelt next to her, gazing at her with puppy-dog eyes. Marina placed her arm around Kat's shoulders and thanked her for being there for her.

"What about some play time?" Kat asked coyly.

Marina smiled and requested a few moments to change their course. Kat was surprised and asked what their new destination was. Marina revealed that it was an abandoned outpost named Situ-Minnus. There they would rendezvous with Faust. Once the new coordinates were programmed, Marina followed Kat to her quarters.

On Orpheus-2, a woman named Dr. Zelda Fielding stepped off the elevator onto the sixth floor. With a small suitcase, she approached the lab which housed the beta-type portal generator and was stopped by two sentries. They requested that she show identification and state her purpose for entry into the lab. Dr. Fielding explained that she was part of the acceptance team and needed to remove some of the test equipment prior to the system going live. One sentry made a call to General Lennox and received permission to allow her access.

Dr. Fielding entered the lab and waited patiently for the doors to close and latch. Once secured, she activated a security protocol to prevent access during testing. A second set of latches secured the door and a red light flashed outside the lab, indicating that testing was in progress.

On the seventh floor, General Lennox sat with her security team and watched Dr. Fielding on a monitor. "Looks like our rat took the bait," she remarked. The other four officers grinned with satisfaction.

Dr. Fielding unlatched one of the panels on the side of a console and swung it open on its hinges. She glanced warily about the lab once more before removing three components from the inside assembly. One of the components was a cylinder-shaped tube with a glowing green substance inside it, used to power the generator. The second was a small PC card with four square components in the center, used for control and positioning of the portal it creates. This is the component that Lilith and Drago preprogrammed to deliver the Kronos fleet into the asteroid field. The third component was an interface between the generator itself and the logic control section of the panel. Without those, the portal generator was useless.

Dr. Fielding slipped all three components into her suitcase and hurried to the door. She deactivated the security protocol and pressed the 'open' button for the door. The flashing light in the corridor extinguished and the sentries stepped aside. Dr. Fielding thanked them for their support and hurried down the corridor to the elevator. When she entered the elevator, one sentry notified General Lennox that she just exited the floor. General

Lennox was pleased and monitored the elevator's status on a security panel. When the elevator stopped, the screen indicated it was on the second floor.

Dr. Fielding was confident that no one would suspect her and hurried off the elevator to a stairwell at the end of the corridor. She descended the stairs to the main floor and quickly walked to the transport bay. When she reached bay seven, she looked back once more and then entered the bay through the personnel hatch.

Inside the transport bay, Corbin was excited to see her and the two embraced. She gave him the suitcase and he handed her a satchel with several gold bars in it. Corbin kissed her cheek and thanked her. He boarded his shuttle and Dr. Fielding left the bay. As soon as the bay was void of oxygen and sealed, the outer doors opened and Corbin departed Orpheus-2. Eagerly, he transmitted a message to Carl Klingman that he was successful and on his way back to Base Five with the components.

Meanwhile, ten sentries filled the corridor at opposite ends and trapped Dr. Fielding. She pretended to be ignorant of the accusations but the sentries confiscated her satchel and escorted her to a holding cell in the prison section of the station. There she would remain until her trial where she would be charged with espionage and treason.

Darra piloted her shuttle away from Yord and was confident she could recover the three orphans for her pet lover Tia. When the transmitter beeped, she cringed. It had to be Klingman. When she acknowledged the transmission, Carl's face appeared on the monitor with a frightening scowl. "We have a problem, Darra," he remarked. "It seems that you lied to me about Marina."

"I didn't lie, Carl. She's dead," Darra responded, sounding emphatic. "We destroyed everything! There's no way she survived."

Carl shook his head and continued, "I just spoke with Marina. She was on the bridge of one of my command ships, the *Celestial Queen*."

"What is she doing there?" Darra asked, baffled.

Carl informed her of the damage Marina did to his forces and that he just put a bounty on her head for her failure to terminate Marina. Darra was panicked, knowing there was more punishment to come. Then he announced that she no longer had an apartment to live in and all her assets were confiscated.

"I'm on my way to Archimedes-9. I have contacts who will help me find Marina. I'll make sure I kill her with my own two hands," she promised.

"I'll help you out once more for all the good work you've done in the past," Carl said coldly. "A derelict ship with a plasma bomb is on its way to Archimedes-9 as a message to Marina. I suggest you stay away from there."

"What about Tia?" she asked, hoping she could salvage something of her life.

"You know the rules," Carl replied. The transmission ended.

Darra went into a rage. She raced her ship at maximum speed toward Archimedes-9. "That son of a bitch!" she shouted. "He can't do this to me!"

Pacing back and forth with the ship on autopilot, Darra fretted how she would explain to Tia that her children died in an explosion caused by their own people. She cherished the relationship she had with Tia, something she never had the opportunity to have with anyone else. In her line of work, friends and lovers were a liability. Since Tia was already a liability, being Antwan's wife, there was nothing to hide. Darra's success was supposed to ensure Tia's safety.

When Archimedes-9 appeared on the long-range sensor monitor, Darra grew hopeful that she could disarm the derelict ship. Knowing it would anger Klingman even further, he would likely increase the bounty on her head. Her mind raced as she sought a way to fix all this. She couldn't bring back the lost command ships but she had to think of something. Perhaps, she would consider taking Tia with her to a distant planet where they could avoid Kronos' detection.

Soon, the derelict ship appeared on her long-range monitor. She programmed her transport control system to place her on board when her ship was close enough. "This has to work," she uttered repeatedly to herself. "Screw Klingman! That son of a bitch!"

On Archimedes-9, Samson Gorsham the security officer informed Rebecca that another ship was closing on the derelict ship at a rapid rate of speed. Rebecca wondered if it could be Colby in his shuttle. Who else would approach a ship rigged with plasma explosives. "Let me know if anything changes," instructed Rebecca. "I'll prepare a team to board with me just in case."

"But you can't go out there!" Samson responded frantically. "What if you get killed?"

Rebecca stared at him coldly. "What if everyone gets killed?" Samson looked away, embarrassed, but he knew she was right. Rebecca departed the Red Room and met with a boarding team in a conference room on the same floor.

Rebecca informed them that they had two objectives in boarding the derelict ship. One was to disarm the weapon, if possible. The second was to change the ship's destination to its point of origin, also if possible. If not, the shockwave from the blast could severely damage Archimedes-9 to the point where it was uninhabitable.

The six men and women looked doubtful about their mission. Rebecca then informed the group that another ship was approaching the derelict ship at a high rate of speed. They would not attempt to board until they determined whether the ship was an ally or an enemy. Everyone seemed relieved, hoping that someone had a better idea what was on board and how to deal with it. Rebecca ordered them to stand by for transport if she needed them to go. She also mentioned that she would be joining them. Her team realized the severity of the situation if Rebecca was going, too.

Darra's ship approached the derelict ship and hovered over it. She assembled a tool bag from a locker as well as a pulse pistol. "What the hell am I doing?" she uttered to herself. "This is friggin' insane."

Darra pressed the 'sequence initiate' button on her remote and a flash filled the main quarters. She transported onto the derelict ship in the cargo hold. The ship had an eerie atmosphere with the only lighting provided by the necessary panels powered by a backup source. The hull creaked, an indication that it had significantly eroded and could fail at any moment. "I am so screwed," she mumbled.

Darra searched the bay but saw nothing resembling a bomb. Curious, she checked the flight deck but then her worst fears materialized. The plasma bomb was rigged to the controls with a detonator programmed for close proximity to Archimedes-9. She inspected the connections to the panels and then the controls for the ship. She attempted to alter the ship's destination but could not access the program. As she attempted to change it, she realized that there was nothing to change. It was a simple program designed for only one thing – detonate its cargo on its approach to Archimedes-9.

When her time before detonation reached ten minutes, she began to panic. In desperation, she managed to take the ship out of autopilot and attempted to alter its destination. Three times she entered new coordinates but the system would not accept them. Then, as a last resort, she entered the coordinates of its origin. This time the system accepted them and the ship turned around. The hull creaked from the strain and buckled. Darra fumbled her remote and dropped it on the floor. The squealing sound from the hull told her that her time was up. She dove for the remote and pressed the 'return' key. She transported just as the hull ruptured and the cold vacuum of space tinged her skin. The derelict ship would now drift as debris back toward its origin.

When Darra appeared on her ship, she lay on the floor, exhausted. "This had better be worth it," she complained to herself. The transmitter beeped for an incoming message. Darra was surprised and feared it was Klingman with another threat. She sat in her pilot's seat and acknowledged the incoming signal.

"To whom do we owe our thanks?" inquired Rebecca.

Darra hesitated, unsure of what to say. Finally, she responded, "I'm a friend of Marina's."

"Well, we are extremely grateful for what you did," Rebecca commented. "You saved a lot of people."

"Yes, well it had to be done," answered Darra diplomatically. "I do need a favor, though."

"Of course," replied Rebecca. "What is it?"

Darra mentioned the three orphaned children who were transported to her station a few months prior. She explained that their mother was a friend and was heartbroken to have lost them. Rebecca recalled the warning from Marcus on Yord about a stranger looking for Tia's children.

"Is there any chance you can help me find them?" asked Darra. "It would mean a lot to my friend."

"The children never made it here," Rebecca informed her. "Marina arranged for them to be taken elsewhere for security reasons."

Darra was quiet as she considered that she was played by the militia officer on Yord. Finally, she thanked Rebecca and was about to end the transmission when Rebecca added, "If I know Marina, the children will be somewhere that no one would expect to look. Perhaps among unlikely people like pirates or in a poverty zone on a distant planet. Just a hunch."

Darra thanked her again and ended the transmission. She wondered if she could be played again and maybe the children were on Archimedes-9 after all. "Screw it!" she shouted and piloted the ship away from Archimedes-9. "Tia's just gonna have to be satisfied with me. I've done enough for her."

With no idea where to go next, Darra scouted the sector for days, hoping to find a clue as to where Marina could be hiding. She finally took a chance and contacted a mercenary friend named Varick. She inquired if he had any news on Marina's whereabouts. Varick informed her that they were shadowing a known accomplice of Marina's, hoping that he would meet with her. When he revealed that they were headed to Situ-Minnus, Darra became excited and announced she would meet them there. Varick warned her that the bounty was theirs and theirs only.

Darra didn't care about the bounty. She had her own idea though about how to handle the situation. Then Varick mentioned the bounty on her head. Darra assured him that he stood to make more by working with her than by turning her in. Varick agreed to give her time to prove it and then ended the brief transmission. Long transmissions increased the chance of being located and identified, which was bad for pirates and bounty hunters.

Rebecca ordered her crew to stand down and informed them that the threat was handled by someone else, an ally or enemy undetermined. Grateful to be excluded from the mission, her team dispersed and returned to their quarters.

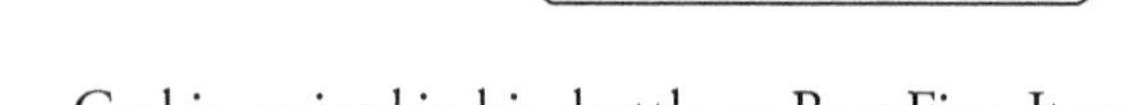

Corbin arrived in his shuttle on Base Five. It was a long journey and he was irritable. When he exited the shuttle with the suitcase, Carl and Tessara were there to greet him. Carl was eager to hear how Corbin arranged to get the critical components. Before they could speak, Dr. Sianni Kepler and Dr. Kimo Stylus barged into the bay. Carl calmly turned to them, waiting patiently for the reason for their interruption.

Kimo exclaimed, "We can't use those components!"

Sianni added, "They are from a failed beta system. Our contact just confirmed that."

"Get lost! You two have been milking this project way too long," chided Corbin. "It's time for me to show my leadership skills." Carl gestured for calm among his scientists.

"But, Mr. Klingman," pleaded Kimo. "He could be putting us all at risk. They allowed his contact to take those components so that Corbin would sabotage the project himself."

"The Federation is counting on his arrogance to do their work," added Sianni.

"My plan was perfect," Corbin responded confidently. "There is no way they knew what me and my contact were doing."

"Your arrogance will be our downfall," chided Sianni.

Carl pondered the warning from the two women and then advised Corbin to proceed but with caution. Then he added that Drs. Kepler and Stylus would oversee his progress and report directly to him. The two women weren't happy about it but with no other options, they agreed to follow orders.

Klingman then instructed Tessara that they needed to depart the base immediately. He was eager to reap the benefits of Taurus' demise while also safe from any retaliation by the Federation or Marina's rebels.

Corbin went to his lab and, anxious to please Klingman, he immediately went to work, installing the stolen components into his system. Sianni and Kimo stood by and eyed him keenly, knowing they would have no results until Corbin attempted to operate the portal generation system. Corbin sneered at them and mocked them for their lack of vision. Sianni was about to reply but Kimo touched her hand and shook her head at her. They would have their time soon enough.

Once the components were installed and the system energized, Corbin ran several tests. Everything seemed correct and a small portal was generated in the center of the room. Kimo questioned how Corbin would prove that it works if he sends something elsewhere. There would be no way of knowing if it made it to the location if he couldn't bring it back. Corbin laughed at her and modified the program through a programmable logic controller. He opened his desk drawer and took out a ball. Holding it up for the two women to see, he then threw it into the portal. The ball disappeared briefly and then shot out to him. Corbin caught it and beamed proudly at them. "And now we are ready for the real deal," he boasted. "I told you it would work."

Kimo whispered to her partner, "That wasn't a valid test. The ball might have been rejected from the portal."

"He's a fool," responded Sianni. "And he's going to take us all down with him."

Corbin rushed to the communication set and attempted to contact Klingman. Appearing on his monitor, Tessara responded to him and was wary of his eagerness in implementing the components. After several questions about the system's reliability, Tessara sent him coordinates for the portal they required to send their fleet to destroy Orpheus-2.

Tessara requested to speak with Dr. Stylus while Corbin programmed the system to create the new portal. Kimo sat in front of the monitor, wondering why Tessara requested her. Corbin was caught up in his big moment and paid no attention to the conversation between Kimo and Tessara.

"Dr. Stylus, if the portal system should fail in any way, you and Dr. Kepler are to take action against that fool," Tessara instructed her.

"With what restrictions?" Kimo inquired, curious.

"Do whatever you and Dr. Kepler feel he deserves. I have concerns about these components as well but Carl seems to think the kid is a genius."

"Understood," replied Kimo. "We'll handle it, if necessary."

Corbin observed a large screen on the system's console and watched a green shape form in the center. He scrolled through several screens and then jumped up in the air with a fist pump. "Yes! It worked!" he shouted and then rushed to the monitor on the communication console, arrogantly pushing Kimo out of the way. "Tell Mr. Klingman that the portal is ready."

Tessara nodded and suggested that he standby for clarification of the results. She ended the transmission.

In Carl's office, Tessara relayed Corbin's response to him. She advised him that he should consider that Kepler and Stylus may have credible information. Carl was impatient and pressing for a victory. He ordered Tessara to initiate the transport of his main fleet through the portal to Orpheus-2. Tessara reluctantly sent his orders to the fleet commander.

Assembled near Base Five was Kronos' prized fleet, led by Commander Jean Willits. The fleet consisted of twenty-seven cruisers and five command ships waiting eagerly for word to attack. Commander Willits received her orders from Klingman through Tessara and promptly passed them on to the command ships. From there, the orders were given to the cruisers. Commander Willits' ship, the *Artemis*, led the way and was the first to pass through the portal.

Corbin danced around the lab and offered to buy drinks for Drs. Kepler and Stylus to celebrate his success. When they declined, he expressed pity that such beautiful women were bereft of the intelligence that he was gifted with. Both women hoped that the new portal would fail, just so they could take out their thirst for vengeance against this pompous ass.

Corbin reached into his desk drawer and took out an expensive bottle of champagne. It was obvious he had planned this for some time. The women waited anxiously to hear if the fleet's crossing was successful. Corbin popped the cork and guzzled greedily from the bottle. "It's a shame the two of you can't appreciate my genius. I might have kept you on as my assistants."

Kimo had enough of his disrespect. She clenched her fist and took a step toward him, but Sianni grabbed her arm. "Let's wait for the results," she urged her peer.

Carl waited anxiously for the view of Orpheus-2 to come up on his screen. After several minutes, he became uncomfortable and ordered Tessara to verify that the portal was operational. Before she could contact Corbin, she received a message directly from Commander Willits.

When she acknowledged it, Commander Willits' frantic face appeared on her monitor. Smoke billowed from several consoles behind her.

"We're in the middle of an asteroid field!" Willits exclaimed, "Casualties are high and we have critical damage!" A loud bang followed by Willits piercing scream was heard and then the transmission ended.

Carl leaped up and shouted, "What the hell just happened? Get her back!"

Tessara tried repeatedly to contact Commander Willits as well as any other ship in the fleet but there was no response. She looked somberly at Klingman for her next instructions.

"Have them kill that little shit!" he ordered, his face red and his fists clenched.

Tessara promptly contacted the lab. When Corbin acknowledged her transmission, she requested that Kimo speak with her. Corbin suspected that something went wrong and retreated away from Kimo. Sianni was quick to block his exit and waited for Tessara's instructions. Tessara informed Kimo that they lost the entire fleet. She then ordered her and Sianni to handle it as previously discussed. "Oh, and Carl wants him to suffer more than anyone could imagine," Tessara added.

Kimo glanced back at Sianni with an evil smile and replied, "We will do more than that." Tessara then ended the transmission and their monitor went blank.

Kimo stood and approached Corbin with a sinister leer. Sianni grabbed him from behind and bull-dogged him to the ground. Kimo operated the system and programmed a man-sized portal with a destination inside the thick outer wall of the base. Corbin pleaded for mercy and swore he could bring the fleet back. Neither woman cared to hear his excuses. When the portal was completed, the two women shoved Corbin through it.

Before he could return, Kimo removed the power from the control console and shut down the portal. Smoke quickly filled the room and then cleared. An impression of Corbin in the wall was visible. If he returned, he would have been a horrible mess on the floor. At low power, the portal system actually worked with objects up to the size of a man, unfortunately for Corbin. By powering the system down, he remained permanently in the wall for eternity, a staunch reminder of how failure and hubris are dealt with in the Kronos organization.

Kimo approached the impression and placed her hand on it. "He did achieve his place in history. We now have the wall of shame as a reminder of his brilliance." Sianni gave Kimo a high-five and suggested they go out for drinks. The two women shut down the lab and paused at the doorway. "Good night, Corbin, you genius son of a bitch!" mocked Kimo.

"It sucks to be you," added Sianni. The two women laughed hysterically and left the lab. The door slid closed and secured. The impression of Corbin's corpse in the wall was a lasting one.

⸻ ⸻

Tariq arrived on Zim and went promptly to Murgatroyd's Oasis. He planned to keep his visit short and sought out his closest allies. At the bar, near the entrance, three men and two women drank ale and laughed giddily. Recognizing Tariq from images sent from Taurus, Elspeth approached him and offered to seat him.

"I'm meeting some friends," Tariq answered. "I believe they are at the bar."

Elspeth stepped back and allowed him to proceed. She went behind the bar and informed Stosh that Tariq had arrived from Taurus. Stosh reached under the bar for a small bag of gold coins. He filled a mug with ale and walked down to the end of the bar.

Tarsus, Marina's bearded field general, gnawed on a leg of lamb and paused when Stosh reached him. Stosh set the mug in front of him along with the bag of coins and mentioned, "The ale is on the house." He patted the bag of coins and added, "This is for the man standing in front of that noisy bunch. You know what to do." Tarsus smiled and continued gnawing on the leg of lamb.

Stosh left the bar and went to Kellen's office. Kellen had just finished a discussion with two men. They departed and left Stosh to speak in private with Kellen. Stosh informed him that Tariq was there and Tarsus was handling it. Kellen thanked him for dealing with the problem and immediately contacted Julian on Taurus to update him on the situation. Stosh returned to the pub.

Tariq informed one of the men that Marina was on the premises, while the others continued their banter to cover their words. He asked specifically about Marina but was told that no one had seen her in some time. "Even the rebel leader's lady friends haven't been seen here in some time," the man commented. "We got your message and brought in extra help. If she's here, she's doing a damned good job hiding from us."

Tariq grunted and departed the pub. When he returned to the open hatch at his ship, he was overpowered from behind by Tarsus. Tariq tried to fight back but was knocked down and barely conscious. Tarsus chastised him for jeopardizing his plans. At first Tariq was baffled, unsure of what he meant. Then Tarsus explained that everyone on Taurus knew he was spying for Kronos and they no doubt followed him there. Tariq pleaded for mercy and promised to disappear but Tarsus had to finish him to protect his own credibility.

Tarsus sat on him and, with a curled dagger, cut Tariq's face off. Tariq squealed and cried frantically. When his face was completely removed, Tarsus placed it in a green plastic bag. Next, he cut out his tongue and dropped that in the bag. Tariq was in shock at this point, but Tarsus wasn't finished with him yet. He proceeded to cut Tariq's genitalia off and placed it in the bag as well. Tariq could only stare with a distant gaze as he bled out. He couldn't fathom how everything could go so wrong, so fast. Tarsus laid him across the entrance to the ship and pulled the external lever to close the hatch. Tariq's head was severed by the hatch.

Inside the pub, Stosh was surprised to see Tarsus return so quickly. Tarsus handed him the plastic bag and returned to his seat. He chugged the mug of ale and resumed gnawing on the leg of lamb. Stosh looked inside the bag and was pleased. He took it to the kitchen and disposed of it.

Korick met him and related his conversation with Marina. Stosh was excited and returned to the bar where he relayed Marina's message to Tarsus. Tarsus was less than thrilled that Marina would think he was ineffective, offering 'excuses' for their failure to protect the *Blue Eagle*. Before Stosh could leave, Tarsus inquired, "What's so special about this *Blue Eagle?*"

Stosh leaned on the bar, close to Tarsus, and answered, "The *Blue Eagle* has been Marina's most effective ally. The third base has just fallen into Federation hands thanks to them."

Tarsus pondered Stosh's words and then commented, "That means Kronos is no longer in control of the region."

"Yes, it does," replied Stosh.

"And there are only two bases left,"

Stosh nodded to him and suggested that the time for war was drawing near. Tarsus smiled and promptly left the pub. Stosh glanced at the plate and empty mug. "I'm sure he won't be returning for a while," he mumbled and removed the plate and mug from the bar.

CHAPTER 6

Situ-Minnus was a small outpost used by early space miners. When the miners failed to find critical ores in the region, they abandoned it, leaving some equipment and tools on site in case they ever returned. Faust guided the *Reaper* into one of three small bays on Situ-Minnus. He was not thrilled about arriving on an abandoned outpost by himself. There was something spooky about the small station that haunted him. Delaying his exit from the ship, Faust spent time with the teleport module that Colby gave to Marina. It took several hours to install and run a diagnostic test but he finally finished. Marina still hadn't shown so he reluctantly departed the shuttle. There was only one way out of the bay so he passed through the personnel hatch and ascended the stairs to the control room.

A shuttle with six mercenaries approached the outpost and docked in the third bay, hoping to avoid detection, should Marina arrive for their rendezvous. They left the bay and crept up the stairs to the control room. Unaware of their approach, Faust studied the consoles, looking for a means to turn on the lighting. Two of the men ambushed him from behind and tied him up in a chair. The others were amused at the ease with which he was captured. If only Marina was as easy a prey.

Varick, the leader of the mercenaries, stood in front of Faust. "Well, it looks like you are in quite a pickle, my friend," he commented.

"What do you want with me?" Faust inquired, knowing he would likely die.

"Where is Marina?" he asked. "She's been quite elusive lately."

Faust hesitated as he considered how to avoid endangering Marina. "I haven't seen her in a long time. When we last met, she instructed me to be here at this time. She didn't say why or where she was going. That is why she is so hard to catch. Her own people don't even know where she is or what she is doing?"

One of the men mentioned that there was a rumor circulating around the sector that Marina was dead. Faust shrugged his shoulders at him and suggested that they wait and find out. Varick grew impatient and turned irritable. "If you don't know, then she may not even appear," he grumbled and punched Faust repeatedly, hoping to change his response. Faust laughed at him hysterically until Varick lost it and gutted him with his dagger.

Varick's partner questioned him that he should have kept Faust alive in case they needed to negotiate with Marina. Varick scoffed at the idea and reminded the man that he could handle Marina and she would come whether Faust lived or died.

Marina's shuttle approached the outpost and docked in the second bay. She thought it strange that the bay doors to the first and third bays were closed. When people abandon a station or outpost, they tend to leave the doors open in case they return. Ironically, the middle bay door was open. Marina's face was taut as she feared for Faust's safety.

Kat noticed and inquired, "Something you want to share?"

"Someone else is here, too," Marina answered. "Stay here."

Kat flailed her arms in the air in frustration. "How long are we going to play this game of yours?" Kat complained.

"Alright, then," relented Marina. "Give me ten minutes and then come in."

Marina exited the ship and encountered four of the men at the base of the stairwell. The first two men who rushed at her were quickly disposed of with a kick to the throat of one and a knife slit to the throat of the other. Both fell to the ground and died quickly. Marina drew a second dagger and poised to fight the remaining two coming down the stairwell.

Welcoming a knife fight with Marina, the two mercenaries drew their daggers and stalked her. She chuckled at their stupidity and then threw a dagger at each one's head. Both daggers were buried deep in the mercenaries' heads through the eye sockets. Marina retrieved her daggers and wiped them off on the corpses' clothes. "Fools," she uttered as she looked down at them in disdain.

Marina continued up the stairwell to the control room. Varick and another mercenary were surprised to see her. "After all this time, we finally meet. Eh, Marina?" he remarked.

Marina saw the pool of blood at Faust's feet and knew he was dead. She contained her rage for now and inquired, "Who might you be?"

"I'm one of the fiercest bounty hunters in the galaxy and there's quite a bounty on your head," he replied. "Oh, and a friend of yours is on the way. I believe you know Darra."

Now, it was time for Marina to vent her rage. "Since neither of you is Borath nor a fierce bounty hunter, I'll give you an option: which one of you pussies wants to die first?"

Varick's partner was eager to take up the challenge. He and Marina traded punches with Marina repeatedly striking at his throat and left ear, inflicting significant pain to the man. When he became reckless in his desire to cripple her, he left himself vulnerable. Marina used a leg sweep and floored him. His head bounced off the concrete floor with a thud. He lay motionless and ceased breathing.

Marina stood up, blood trickling from her mouth and dripping off her chin. "You know," she began, "I might have spared you had you not killed my friend."

Varick laughed at her and explained, "I needed to make sure I had your attention in case you had thoughts of not showing."

Kat stepped into the control room, much to Marina's annoyance. "How about you save one for me?" complained Kat.

Varick drew two daggers, confident that Kat was no threat. Marina pointed to Faust and replied, "He took something from us. Take something from him."

"Black magic?" Kat requested.

"Of course," replied Marina. "I think he deserves it."

Kat raised her hands in the air and uttered an incantation. Red smoke formed in a circle around Varick. He panicked when he realized Kat was a witch. "Let me go! Please, I'll do anything!" he pleaded.

"Can you bring our friend back to life?" she inquired cynically.

Varick knew he was screwed. The smoke rose around him to his waist. Kat uttered another incantation. Marina was horrified as she watched Varick's soul separate from his body and hover in front of Kat. Kat held her hand out, revealing a large ruby on her forefinger ring. Varick's soul was sucked into the ruby and his body was just a mindless corpse.

Stunned, Marina asked, "What did you do?"

"His soul will be my prisoner to be used for my own personal pleasures," she explained. "Would you like to know how?"

Marina held her hand up and replied, "No, I think I'll pass. Now we wait for Darra."

Kat informed her that she received an image from the Seers and that they needed to leave now for Ramses-3. She also mentioned that Darra's destiny with Marina was already decided and would come in due time. Reluctantly, Marina followed Kat's suggestion and they left the outpost in her cruiser, the *Reaper*.

Marina was pleased to have her cruiser back but was devastated by the loss of Faust. Kat sensed her pain and commented that Faust served them both well and died an honorable death. Marina snapped at her, "He was killed by a bounty hunter! How is that honorable?"

Kat explained that Faust knew the possibility of an ambush if he was followed. He also knew that Marina needed her cruiser back because of its unrivaled speed. As always, he followed orders without question, but now he paid the ultimate price for his loyalty – death. With the cruiser on autopilot, Marina paced the flight deck.

Kat complained, "Will you please sit down? You are annoying me!"

Marina sat in the pilot's seat and mourned. Kat inquired about her prolonged sadness over Faust's death. Marina responded coldly, "Because he gave me great sex when I needed it."

"And that's it?" Kat countered.

"No. He helped me control myself," she answered as a tear streamed down her cheek.

"And I can't!" challenged Kat.

"It's different with us," Marina answered. "Faust never took anything from me. You took my innocence that day on Magnus. You used your black magic and took advantage of me."

"It had to be done," Kat responded defensively.

"So that's what you call our encounter – it?" Frustrated and hurt, Marina left the flight deck and locked herself in her quarters.

"Damn it!" blurted Kat. "She's always so damned difficult!"

The journey to the Strontarian Galaxy was a long one and Marina rarely came out of her quarters. Her interaction with Kat was always brief and only when necessary. Finally, Kat had enough. She barged into Marina's quarters and demanded to know what she could do to fix their relationship. Marina responded that only time will tell.

Darra's shuttle arrived at Situ-Minnus and docked in bay two. When she exited her ship, she checked each of the other bays. Bay one had Korick's shuttle, which she didn't recognize but assumed it had something to do with Marina. She verified that bay three was Varick's ship before approaching the darkened stairs to the dimly lit control room. Unfortunately, her easy feeling was short-lived when she encountered the corpses of two of the mercenaries on the steps. At the top of the stairwell, she saw two more mercenaries lying in pools of blood.

"Varick?" Darra called out, but there was no response. She reached the top of the stairwell and entered the control room. She was horrified to see Varick's twisted, contorted body lying next to the chair with Faust's corpse next to it. "Oh, Varick, you poor fool," muttered Darra. "What did she do to you?"

Darra departed the control room and returned to her ship. The hunt for Marina would have to continue. Fortunately, Marina was without one of her accomplices now, leaving Darra with one less fighter to deal with. Frustrated, she searched the area with her long-range sensors, hoping to pick up a heat trail or some other clue to Marina's next destination. After hours of pondering where to look, she decided to do something that would draw Marina to her. Like the others in Kronos, she finally realized that you do not find Marina. She finds you.

"That's it!" Darra exclaimed. "I'll take someone close to her and I'll make sure there isn't much left when Marina finds them."

Darra sent messages to several of her contacts offering a sizable bounty from her Kronos reward for anyone who would abduct any close friend of Marina's that would draw her out. Two of her contacts responded quickly, asking for more details. She explained that she needed a hostage for a negotiation. None of her other contacts were eager for a challenge like that and feared the consequences that came with it. Darra suggested one or two hostages that Marina would give her life for. Both contacts agreed to accept the job after discussing the amount of payment for completing the task.

Marina finally let loose about the way Kat used her when they first met and, whether it was physical or spiritual, she felt violated by Kat. Feeling the need for redemption, she grabbed Kat and kissed her hungrily. Then she threw her on the bed and tore her clothes off. Kat was stunned as Marina undressed quickly and pounced on her. She realized that Marina would do everything she could to humiliate her for what she did to her.

Kat never wanted Marina this way but she knew Marina was right. She deserved this. Marina did things to her that she always dreamed of with her but this was different. This wasn't love. This was, for all practical purposes, rape. She wanted to stop Marina but she knew this was the only way to fix their relationship; it was her penance.

When Marina finished using Kat, she dressed and left the quarters. Kat cried, feeling humiliated. She never imagined Marina could be this way. When she summoned the courage to return to the flight deck, Marina grabbed her once more and shoved her against the rear wall of the flight deck. She again used Kat in every way possible, finally pushing Kat to her knees and ordering her to pleasure her. Kat wanted to retaliate with magic but refrained. This would be the last time though.

Marina finished with her once more and then returned to her quarters. Kat lay on the floor of the flight deck in tears. She now knew what it was to be a defenseless victim. What she did to Marina was meant to help her heal, but in retrospect, she did use her. Kat curled up in the corner and sobbed.

Marina finally returned and stood over her. "How does it feel to be used like that?" she asked, anger still in her voice.

Kat tried to speak but burst into tears again. Marina remained still, determined to get a response from her. Kat struggled to stand, exhausted and hurt. Marina realized that she made her point and helped Kat to her feet. Kat stared into her eyes and then apologized for what she did.

"That's all I wanted to hear," Marina responded.

"I thought I was helping," Kat explained. "Now I understand how you felt. I'm so sorry."

Marina embraced her and hugged her. "You are a valuable friend but that was always the rift that kept us apart."

"Has this healed the rift?" asked Kat. "Will you forgive me?"

Marina kissed Kat's forehead and sat in the pilot's seat. She pondered her feelings and then responded, "I think so. I'm glad you now understand how I felt about our first encounters all this time. They haunted me and created doubt in my mind about why you stayed by my side."

Kat sat in the copilot's seat and was silent for quite a while. She was concerned about what would come next for them and how this altered their feelings toward each other. Marina sensed her remorse and concern. She stood and went to the hatch. Kat's eyes followed her, wondering what she was up to.

Marina paused and looked back at her. "We have a few hours before we reach Ramses-3. Why don't you join me in my quarters?"

Kat hesitated, fearing another fit of rage against her. Marina took her hand and led her to her quarters. This time, she treated Kat as a lover and showed her what could have been all this time.

Afterward, Marina confessed that she never expected to engage in this behavior with Kat but their experience together would further their friendship. Kat inquired if there would be more or if this was a one-time thing with Marina. Marina's response didn't surprise her. Marina explained that Kat's purpose was to rule Yord on her behalf and Marcus would be there with her in whatever capacity the two needed. Marina also mentioned that, when the war with Kronos was over, she likely would not be returning to Yord, Taurus, or any other location they were involved with.

Kat's sad eyes laid a feeling of guilt on Marina. She requested that Kat keep the memories of the good times that the two shared and never forget her. Kat asked about the Seers and how they fit into their future. Marina chuckled at her.

"Weren't you the one that told me they don't need us?" she teased. "Besides, we will still be able to communicate with them no matter where we go."

Kat lowered her head and turned away, disappointed by how things turned around between them so quickly on this one trip. Marina looked around and noticed the teleport module was gone from the top of the control console. She wondered if Faust would have taken it but then considered he might have figured out how to install it. She left her quarters and went to the power distribution panel in the rear of the cruiser, where a new trio of wires trailed into an adjacent panel. The second panel held control circuitry for the shuttle as well as two servers for the ship's computer. Then she found it! Faust had installed the module in her absence, but unfortunately she would have to wait to test it. After closing both panels, she returned to the flight deck alone.

Carl Klingman sat in his quarters, stunned that he could let a snot-nosed, arrogant punk like Corbin ruin his grand moment. Tessara knocked and entered through the open hatch. "Permission to speak, sir?" she requested. Carl gestured for her to enter.

"Tessara, this is one of those moments that I really need your advice," he confessed.

Tessara sat in a chair, facing Carl. She placed her hand on his leg and inquired, "When is a predator most dangerous?"

Carl looked up and responded, "When it is cornered."

"Exactly. We have played this game of chess far too long." After a brief pause, she suggested, "Perhaps it is time to come out swinging and go for the knockout punch."

"I'm surprised that someone of your tactical ability would recommend something so reckless and daring," he commented.

"When the situation changes, so must we," she responded. "I have given this much thought since we lost the heart of our fleet and I have several ideas."

Carl stood and leaned against the hatchway. "You have my interest," he replied, growing hopeful of a recovery from their losses. "Enlighten me, Tessara."

Tessara recommended that they lighten their defensive forces at the fourth and fifth bases to form two new armadas for the offensive. Then she recommended that they target Yord, Marina's home planet, and then Ramses-3, since they know Marina's rebels are hiding out there.

"But those aren't significant targets," Carl remarked. "Why not go after Taurus and Archimedes-9?"

"First," she began, "Marina is your main obstacle. If she falls, the rest of her alliance falls. This is a psychological move. Yord is her home and Ramses-3 is likely any source of backup she has in reserve for a major encounter."

Carl understood and realized this could be done with minimal losses. Then he considered that they could just take over the planet Yord instead of destroying it. Perhaps that would force Marina to reveal herself to them. He related his thoughts to Tessara, who agreed that this move would have merit as well.

"But what of bases four and five? Won't they be vulnerable?" he inquired with concern.

"We already suspect that Base Four has been compromised," she explained. "Base Five is safe for now."

Carl grinned and instructed her, "Give the orders! It's time to take the battle to Marina." Pleased by the return of Carl's confident nature, Tessara stood and left the quarters.

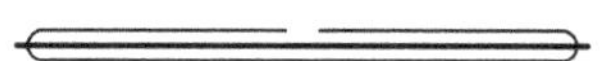

Ten Kronos cruisers and one command ship raced toward Ramses-3 in the Strontarian Galaxy. Ramses-3 was once the location of a massive shipbuilding facility, controlled by a dominant alien race. All that was known of its demise was that a mysterious nuclear explosion wiped out the facility and the military installation adjacent to it. The contamination left behind in the aftermath made Ramses-3 the ideal location for rebels to rebuild their forces. So long as they were underground or distant from the blast location, they would not be harmed by the radiation.

Commander March of the *Intrepid* command ship provided the target locations on the planet's surface for the cruisers to attack. Aware of the planet's history with the nuclear explosion, he emphasized to the captains of the cruisers that they were to destroy anything on the surface that was recent. Three cruisers landed in a ground assault against the suspected headquarters while the other seven destroyed any infrastructure or housing from the sky.

Within a few hours, what little surface infrastructure existed was decimated. The ground assault killed over fifty rebels while destroying several weapons caches. The few prisoners taken had no information of value to them and were executed immediately. With the operation deemed a success, the ground forces returned to their ships and departed the region.

The second armada consisted of one command ship and five cruisers, led by Commander Sanchez, a young but experienced officer. He understood that they were only there to draw Marina out and their presence was temporary. Knowing the fate of their fleet in the portal disaster, his goal was to accomplish this while incurring as few losses as possible. When his armada approached Yord, they were met by eight militia vessels, prepared to defend the kingdom.

Commander Sanchez contacted the leader of the militia fleet. He advised them that a battle would be catastrophic for both and recommended that they stand down for the short duration that the planet would be under their jurisdiction.

Captain Frost of the militia battle cruiser *Stark* contacted Marcus at the palace to discuss the terms. Marcus recognized what their goal was and knew Marina would not be baited into a scheme like this. He agreed that the consequences of a battle would be horrendous to both sides and ordered Frost to agree to their terms, so long as no civilians were harassed or harmed. He insisted that any act of aggression would lead to the battle they both hoped to avoid. Captain Frost agreed with the decision and relayed the message to Commander Sanchez.

Commander Sanchez assured Captain Frost that his ships would land in various locations but no one would disembark from any ship. This would assure the militia that an air attack would not occur and no hostages would be taken. In a surprise request, he asked that Frost ensure no communications were made off-planet, warning of their presence. Reluctantly, Frost agreed. When he informed Marcus of the additional request, Marcus wasn't surprised. He trusted that Marina and Kat would handle it, as they always did. At least in this manner, the planet and its people were not ravaged by war.

Klingman was ecstatic when he heard that Sanchez executed his plan to perfection and knew it was only a matter of time before Marina responded to their presence on Yord. When she did, he would give her his terms for her surrender.

Commander March sent word that their attack was a success as well. Tessara recommended to Klingman that they immediately return to the fourth base in support of a potential attack. She was confident that, due to the speed and success of Commander March's attack, they could still defend the fourth base, while plotting their next attack.

Klingman had other ideas and instructed Tessara to send March's force to Archimedes-9 and launch a full-scale attack. Tessara advised Klingman against it, but he smelled blood and wanted more. Reluctantly, she instructed March to proceed to Archimedes-9 and attack.

While focusing on the monitor for the long-range sensors, Marina received an incoming signal in code. It was someone from the rebel base on Ramses-3, requesting identification from her. After responding, she was given clearance to approach. Kat joined her on the flight deck and warned her of images sent by both Seers. Mike Colby, Marina's most valuable ally, was in danger. In addition, she received images of Yord and the Kronos armada.

Marina was baffled why the images did not show an attack on her kingdom. Perhaps it was yet to come. Kat used the short-range sensors to scan the surface of Ramses-3. She was shocked to see the damage to the battle craft and warehouses.

"Marina, did you see this?" Kat asked, concerned that something terrible happened.

"We're cleared for landing," she replied. "What's wrong?"

"The damage! They've been attacked."

Marina approached the transport area and was horrified when she saw the burning ships and camouflaged warehouses. "Those sons of bitches!" she shouted. "How did they know?" Kat informed her that she was getting no response from Marcus on Yord. She returned and continued her attempts to make contact.

As soon as the *Reaper* was docked and shut down, Marina hurried off the ship, fearing that her main force was destroyed. Two young boys emerged from the trees and instructed her to follow them. Marina followed the boys along a rough path for almost a mile. They reached a cave in the side of the mountain that was camouflaged by the foliage. Along the way, Marina attempted to question the boys but they said nothing.

A militia officer named Cheska, tall and blonde with sharp features, stepped out of the cave and blocked Marina's entrance. With folded arms, she stared down Marina, patiently waiting for a response. At a loss for words over what happened, Marina asked, "How bad was it?"

"What do you think?" Cheska countered. "How the hell did they know we were here?"

"We had a mole on Taurus but he would not have had this information. Has there been any traffic to or from the planet?"

"Only one," answered Cheska. "A Kronos freighter with some former Special Forces people in search of their old unit."

Then Marina recalled bringing a confiscated class four Kronos freighter here several months ago with a male officer and a female sergeant. "Where is the Kronos freighter?" she questioned Cheska.

Cheska pointed to a valley between two mountains. "We parked it away from headquarters in case someone came looking for it."

Marina paced about with her hands on her hips. How could she have been so careless? "What do we have left here?" she inquired.

Cheska frowned and responded, "About twenty personnel, no weapons, no fighting craft. We're basically out of the war."

Marina instructed them to gather everyone and whatever resources they had left and load up the Kronos freighter. Cheska looked baffled by her decision. Marina then explained, "This was a desperation move on Kronos' part. They must have known about this place since I brought that freighter here. Think about it: why didn't they attack before?"

"Fair enough," Cheska answered. "Where are we going?"

"Yord – my home planet," she responded. "I have a plan."

Marina returned to the *Reaper* and entered the flight deck. Kat just ended a transmission and turned in her copilot's seat toward Marina.

"Yord has been occupied by Kronos. There have been no demands and no response to any communications by Rebecca's people or by me."

"What about Lennox? Have we heard from her?"

"They allowed defective components for their new portal generation system to be stolen by Kronos spies. Kronos attempted to transport the main part of their fleet to Orpheus-2, but the malfunction placed all their ships in the middle of an asteroid field that destroyed them."

"Then we still have a chance to defeat them," Marina surmised. "Get us to Archimedes-9, now." Kat immediately programmed the coordinates and placed the ship on autopilot.

During the journey, Marina slept in her quarters with the hatch open. Kat monitored the controls with the flight deck hatch open as well. She was lonely but knew better than to bother Marina when she was in one of her moods. She attempted to contact the Seers (Kara and Ginna) but with no luck. Her mind drifted to thoughts of better days, recalling her palace inside Magnus, her personal space station. She thought about all the black-market vendors she knew and her influence over them as their guardian.

Suddenly, Kat heard Marina scream. She rushed to her quarters and found Marina sitting up in bed, wide-eyed and terrified. Kat sat with her and embraced her. "A nightmare?" she asked Marina.

Marina nodded to her and returned an affectionate hug. "I saw Britt and Faust," she uttered. "They scolded me for losing control of the war."

"It was just a dream," Kat assured her.

"No. They're right," Marina admitted. "I'm not fighting the war. I am trying to manage it."

"Then let's fight it," urged Kat. "What do you want to do?"

"I need to find out what Colby was doing on the *Blue Eagle*," Marina replied. "He seems to be the key to winning this war."

"I hope you're right," fretted Kat. "There's a lot happening right now and we have no control over anything."

"Just get me to Archimedes-9," ordered Marina.

Rebecca sent her security team to find Kara. She expected her to remain in her quarters but, as most teens do, Kara disobeyed her orders. Samson Gorsham, Rebecca's long-haired and bearded security officer, entered and informed Rebecca that Kara was in the pub with a young man. Rebecca's first question was, "Is she okay?"

"No worries, Rebecca," he answered. "The boy has a good reputation and his father is one of us. They were only talking."

"Are they still there?" she inquired.

"Yes, ma'am," he responded, hoping to display a calm demeanor. "I thought it best to speak with you before we took any action." Rebecca thanked Samson and hurried down to the pub.

When she arrived, the pub was only about half full of patrons and Kara sat in the middle area at a table with her new friend. Rebecca approached them, but Kara didn't seem concerned. "Kara, I was worried about you," said Rebecca, feigning coolness. "The station is a big place and it's easy to get lost."

Kara gestured for Rebecca to sit with them. "I needed to clear my head in case I have images to reveal," she mentioned. "My friend Nathaniel was keeping me entertained."

Nathaniel offered to leave and assured Rebecca that they only talked. She insisted that he stay, if Kara wished. Kara thanked Rebecca and reminded her that she is a young woman now and was responsible. Rebecca sensed that she became defensive and took Kara's hand in hers.

"I am here as your friend, not a task master. I do need to know where I can find you in case of an emergency, though."

Kara apologized for worrying Rebecca and promised that she would keep her informed of her location. Suddenly, Kara's eyes fluttered and turned white. Nathaniel panicked and asked if he should get help. Rebecca assured him that Kara was okay and suggested that he come back later. Nathaniel stared at Kara with a concerned expression and then departed.

Rebecca again took Kara's hand in hers. She only knew enough about seers to know that she should not interrupt Kara while her premonitions occurred. Nathaniel returned with a glass of water for Kara and then left again. Rebecca acknowledged his thoughtfulness and felt that he would be a good influence on Kara. As such, she knew she had to tread carefully with Kara.

When Kara's eyes returned to normal, she warned Rebecca that Marina was in danger and would not finish her journey. Rebecca pressed her for more details, especially about her location, but Kara reminded her that visions are not often clear. Rebecca asked Kara how they could warn Marina but Kara gave the usual cryptic response that Marina will do what must be done.

Rebecca stood and paced the floor, contemplating how to get word to Marina, especially when she had no idea where she was. The bartender approached them and asked if the two women needed anything.

Kara answered, "I'll have a scotch on the rocks and a double for my friend. She's a bit stressed right now." The bartender smiled and left them.

Rebecca was embarrassed and stunned that Kara would have an alcoholic beverage at her age. But then she realized, Kara was a young woman. *How odd?* she thought, recalling the stories from Marina a few years back about two young girls being in her custody and now reminded herself that her daughter Aries would one day be a grown woman as well.

Nathaniel hung out by the entrance to the pub, eager to see that Kara was okay. Rebecca gestured for him to return to the table to Kara's surprise. He returned and sat nervously across from Rebecca but near Kara.

"Look, Kara, I have a little girl and I don't want her picking up any bad habits," cautioned Rebecca. "Heck, I don't want to pick up any bad habits."

Kara reached for her hand and guided her back into her seat. "I am here to help," she commented to Rebecca. "Not to give bad habits."

Nathaniel pretended not to hear the conversation and focused on anything else in the pub to occupy his attention. Kara held his hand for reassurance.

"Well, I certainly don't think Marina will see it that way," Rebecca responded. "What is your role that brought you here on my station?"

Kara explained that she and Ginna are part of Marina's reign of power, as was Kat. They would help Marina to succeed over the enemies of the kingdom and once victorious, they would help maintain peace in the kingdom. Ever more curious, Rebecca asked, "How would the four of you ensure victory and then peace? There are plenty of mad men out there in the universe."

Kara's expression turned somber and she replied, "We are the reign of pain. Those who seek to destroy what Marina has built will feel our wrath."

Rebecca became uneasy, sensing that Kara was either psychotic or possessed powers other than the ability to see. Kara assured her that she and her station would fall under their protection. Breathing a sigh of relief, Rebecca asked no more. She excused herself from the table and left the bar.

"Is everything alright?" Nathaniel asked.

"Yes and no," Kara replied. "I am fine but a friend is not. Rebecca is looking for a way to help." Nathaniel nodded as if he understood.

Rebecca entered the security office and requested Samson contact Marina, if possible. After what seemed like hours, Marina finally responded. When Rebecca informed her of Kara's premonition, Marina requested that Rebecca summon General Lennox to meet with them on Archimedes-9. Rebecca sensed the urgency and assured her that Lennox would be present. When Rebecca left the office, Kara waited in the corridor for her.

"Is something wrong?" Rebecca asked Kara.

"Yes. I saw another premonition," she replied.

"Come with me," instructed Rebecca. "Marina is on the way and I need to contact General Lennox."

The two women took the elevator up to Rebecca's floor and proceeded to her office. Rebecca closed the door to keep their discussion private. Kara immediately revealed that someone of importance to Marina will be taken by a dangerous person and harmed. Once again, Rebecca pressed Kara for more detail but was frustrated by her lack of clarity of the images.

Rebecca arranged for General Lennox to come to Archimedes-9 to meet with Marina for an urgent issue. Until then, she spent much time with Kara, hoping to understand her role as a Seer more clearly. Kara opened up to her about how Marina insisted on treating her and Ginna like children, even though they were now older teenagers. Embarrassed, Rebecca found herself learning about the problems of teen girls.

Rebecca realized that this was a conversation she would one day have with her daughter. She was still adapting to having a career and dealing with motherhood as a single mom but she always thought she would have time to deal with it later. Now, Kara was looking to her for guidance and she was speechless.

Finally, Rebecca related the story of how she and Marina met and the hardships they both faced. Rebecca told her about how Marina saved her life but couldn't save her sister. Then she confessed that Marina made her the person she is today. At one time, she was a cold-blooded killer as a rebel leader fighting against the tyrant Victor and his thugs. Now, she ran a shipping facility on the outer edges of civilization and was raising a daughter.

Kara inquired as to what happened to the father of Rebecca's child. Rebecca became teary-eyed as she related how an evil woman murdered Cristos. Kara realized that Rebecca, like Marina, harbored much anger inside of her for her past. She apologized for not understanding that before but promised to be open with Rebecca and more accepting. Feeling a bond develop between them, Rebecca asked if Kara would be staying on Archimedes-9 or if she would be moving on.

"Would you mind if I stayed here with you?" Kara asked politely. "That was the plan but I will only stay if you want me to."

Rebecca reached for her and embraced her. "Of course, you can stay here," she replied.

Then Rebecca was startled by Kara when she asked, "Will you be my mother? My mother was killed by bad people on Yord."

Rebecca was stunned. She never expected this but was honored. "You do know that I have to discuss this with Marina," she mentioned. "I have no problem with it, but she might be hurt."

"I'll speak to her as soon as possible," Kara promised, now smiling.

Kara returned to the pub where Nathaniel sat with four of his friends. Nathaniel eagerly introduced her to his friends and slid out a chair for her to sit. One of Nathaniel's friends, Nall, inquired immediately about Kara's premonitions and her importance to Rebecca, the station executive. Kara grew defensive and questioned Nathaniel about why he would reveal something so personal. He didn't think it was a big deal, which angered Kara even more. She glared at him and then left the pub. Nathaniel's friends laughed over her reaction but Nathaniel realized what he had done. He hurried after her.

Two men at the bar, Seth and Hester, noticed the commotion and overheard Nathaniel's friend mention premonitions. They approached the table and sat down. The four boys were surprised by the men and asked what they wanted. Seth questioned them about Kara and claimed that she was his niece. He demanded to know what was said to upset her so. Not knowing better, Nall revealed what Nathaniel told them about Kara. The men thanked Nall and left the pub. The bartender, Dolores, took note of Kara's anger with Nathaniel leading to her departure and the men's interest in her afterward. Korick's employees were trained to look for anything suspicious that might be a threat to the rebels.

Nathaniel found Kara sitting alone in the transport bay. She watched several of the crews, transferring cargo on and off the ships. Nathaniel sat next to her and apologized for his ignorance. Kara didn't respond to his presence, feeling betrayed. Before anything else could be said, the two men from the pub approached Kara and Nathaniel from behind. Seth grabbed Kara and covered her mouth. Hester punched Nathaniel and knocked him out. The two men hustled Kara into one of the smaller ships and closed the hatch.

Seth immediately contacted Darra and inquired how much she would pay for a girl who had premonitions. Doubting the credibility of his hostage, Darra asked where they were. When Seth mentioned Archimedes-9, Darra grew more interested. She arranged to meet the two men and interview their hostage. Seth, unsure if he could trust her, warned her that she needed to pay them once she validated Kara's relationship to Marina. Seth insisted that Darra come to Archimedes-9 as they were not leaving the station with Kara. If Darra failed to show, then they would release Kara and depart before they were identified. Darra knew she was taking a risk by appearing in the station but this might be her only chance to bait Marina into a trap.

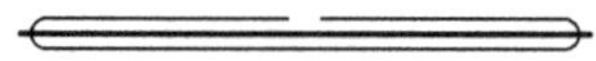

The *Reaper* approached Archimedes-9 in short time due to the teleport module that Colby provided to Marina. Kat was impressed with the advantage that the module provided and commented, "Perhaps you don't need a big military force after all. This Colby seems to be as effective as you are against Kronos, using only wit and tact. We could use this teleport module to our advantage."

"Perhaps you are right," Marina replied, realizing that Kat's perception of Colby's success made sense.

Instead of requesting permission to dock, Marina decided it was best to keep her presence on Archimedes-9 a secret. When a freighter departed from the station, Marina programmed the *Reaper* to teleport into the open bay, while in cloaked mode.

Marina contacted the transport supervisor and informed him that her 'freighter' experienced some mechanical problems and returned to the bay for repairs. The supervisor closed the outer gates and released oxygen into the bay, allowing Marina and Kat to exit.

"So, what's your plan now?" inquired Kat.

"Low profile, all the way."

Kat nodded and provided a spell through an incantation, masking them as Federation soldiers. Marina was still in awe of Kat's magical powers as she watched her perform her spell. Kat gave her a smug grin and commented, "And you didn't like my black magic."

"Ah, shut up," grumbled Marina. "Let's go."

The two women departed from the cruiser, appearing as members of General Lennox's security team.

CHAPTER 7

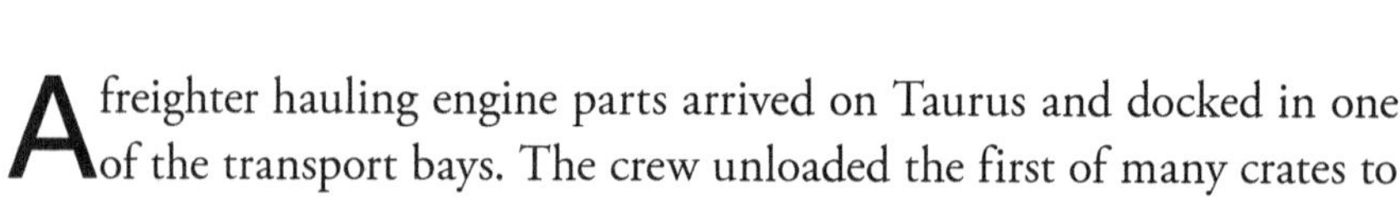

A freighter hauling engine parts arrived on Taurus and docked in one of the transport bays. The crew unloaded the first of many crates to be transferred to other locations. Two men split off from the crew and entered the facility.

Julian met with Gemini's CFO and engineer Dax in one of the conference rooms. The two discussed several projects that were in the works. Dax had been away, working for General Lennox and the Federation for some time on the portal project and was glad to return to Taurus.

Gemini worked from her office and just finished a conference call when one of her security officers entered. "Excuse me, Gemini, but you have a guest – a young lady from Yord." he announced.

"Send her in," she replied as she inserted a stack of papers into a folder.

Ginna entered and stood across the table from Gemini. "Can I speak with you?" she asked.

Gemini was annoyed at first but then considered that she might learn something of value since Ginna had spent time with Marina and may have overheard details of her operation. "Yes, you may. Have a seat," Gemini replied, trying to avoid her business voice, which was terse and bitchy, even on a good day. "What can I do for you?"

"What is it like being in charge of everyone?" Ginna inquired.

Gemini thought that was a strange question, but she took the time to relate how she learned the business from a good man and how he was murdered by bad people. She explained how it cost her a marriage and led to many enemies. "Why do you ask?"

Ginna lowered her head and answered, "Good people always lose loved ones to evil people. My friend Kara and I lost our mothers to bad people and we are learning that everyone we meet, who is good, has lost a loved one needlessly to bad people."

Gemini recalled John Mallory, who helped her with her drug addiction and taught her how to run the shipping business. Together they built the corporation into the biggest shipping organization in the universe, but then he was murdered on their own station. "It is quite tragic how things happen to all of us," Gemini responded.

"Do you have any children?" asked Ginna.

Gemini chuckled at the thought. "Heavens no. When I worked for Special Forces, I had to forego my ability to have children. It seems the SF didn't want their women getting pregnant after all the training they received."

"Do you ever wish that you did?" asked Ginna.

Gemini didn't know how to answer that. There were times when she was lonely and wondered if having a child or two would have saved her marriage to Mike Colby. Finally, she responded, "If things were different, I would have liked to have a family."

"I could be your daughter if you want to have a family. I am old enough that you don't need to take care of me, but I could be your family."

Gemini was shocked. Why would anyone want her for a mother? She was cruel and cold-hearted, but most of all, she never cared for anyone in years. Being a female CEO in a man's world hardened her.

"Why would you come to a new place, meet a strange woman and ask her to be your mother, Ginna?" questioned Gemini. "That's a very unusual way to find companionship."

Ginna explained that fate has a mysterious way of bringing people together and her destiny was with Gemini. "Sometimes things were meant to be," she added.

"And what does Marina have to do with this?" questioned Gemini, wondering if this was a ploy for Marina to keep tabs on her corporation.

"I am a part of her destiny, but she does not control mine. My future is here on Taurus as a protector."

Gemini considered the idea and the fact that Ginna was a teenager, she was right that she didn't need to be cared for like a child. "Are you interested in learning the shipping business?" she inquired.

"I'd love to!" replied Ginna excitedly. "When I came here, the plan was for me to stay and protect all of you. Now, I would have a real purpose."

"Then we will begin tomorrow," Gemini informed her. "I do hope that you can handle Marina when she learns of this. I doubt she'll be thrilled."

Ginna rushed around the table and hugged Gemini. "I will make you proud of your new daughter." She hurried out of the office, leaving Gemini uneasy.

Julian and Dax entered the office and were amused to see Ginna leaving with a smile. Dax walked around the table and kissed Gemini. "I missed you," he whispered and then hugged her.

"I missed you, too," she responded. She and Dax had become involved but then his early research and development of portal technology made him valuable to the Federation. When he was assigned to their secret lab for six months, Gemini feared that this is what ruined her marriage before. Colby was away for lengthy periods of time and she struggled with loneliness, leading to her drug addiction.

"Are we interrupting anything?" Julian asked.

"Ginna wants to be my daughter," she replied without hesitation. Both men waited for a punchline to what they perceived as a joke, but none came.

"I assume you declined her offer," Julian remarked. Gemini looked away and was silent.

Dax quipped, "I never imagined you for the motherly type Gem. What brought this on?"

"Screw you assholes! I am taking her on as an apprentice. Besides, why couldn't I be the motherly type?"

Dax rubbed her arms affectionately to calm her down. "I didn't realize you were serious. It's just something I never expected to hear from you."

"Look, you can leave if you like and I won't hold it against you," she informed Dax.

Julian pondered what might have brought this on. He commented, "Perhaps having someone to mentor would be good for you. With the knowledge you have of the business, she could become an asset down the road."

"It just seemed like something that I needed in my life." Gemini confessed. "I can't explain it and neither can she."

Gemini maintained a fixed stare on Dax, waiting for his next response. He fidgeted, knowing he had to commit to something here. "If you want to start a family, regardless of whether you choose a young woman or through a pregnancy, I am there for you. I'm just surprised."

Gemini embraced him and reached out to Julian for his hand. Julian offered to assist in any way with Ginna's training while Dax suggested that he could help handle Gemini's workload while she mentored Ginna.

Ginna returned to her quarters, excited to be part of something other than Marina's war. She sat down on the bed and suddenly felt Kara's fear. Kara projected images of her abduction and instructed Ginna to notify Kat. She also projected her emotions to Ginna as calm and safe.

Ginna knelt on the floor and focused on a wall-mounted picture of Gemini with the crew of the *Blue Eagle*. She knew that Marina was going to Archimedes-9 where Kara was. In a few minutes, she established a link to Kat and informed her of Kara's situation. With no other options available to her, she left her quarters and went to the station's pub for lunch. She was only at the bar for a short while before several young men approached her, offering to buy her a drink and strike up conversation. She declined the offer from each of them until one young man caught her eye. He sat down a few stools from her and glanced over.

"Good afternoon, ma'am," he greeted her. She responded kindly and then looked away. He turned his attention to the bartender and ordered a sandwich and a cup of tea. Ginna was curious why he didn't make a move on her like the others so she asked, "Are you here alone?"

"I am," he replied. "Just got off of shift. I work the docks here."

"My name is Ginna. And yours?" she inquired.

"I'm Dante," he answered politely. "It's nice to meet you."

Ginna invited him to join her for lunch and patted the stool next to hers. Dante moved down to the stool and turned his attention to her. The two engaged in a lengthy conversation about the station and the events that are hosted for entertainment. After three fruit-flavored beverages with rum in them, Ginna became tipsy. Dante paid the bartender and escorted Ginna to her room.

Longing to be held by a man, Ginna invited him in. To her disappointment, he declined and suggested another time. She wondered what she did to blow her opportunity with a nice boy as she closed her door. No sooner had she turned away, there was a knock. She anxiously opened the door and found Dante standing there, grinning. "You change your mind?" she asked.

Dante embraced her and kissed her. "I wanted to make sure I could see you again. How about dinner tomorrow night?" he requested.

"Another kiss like that and I'd have to say yes," she replied, excited to have her first date. Dante embraced her again and kissed her passionately. When he finished, Ginna sighed with a smile.

"See you tomorrow evening at dinner," he repeated and then left. Ginna stared at him from the doorway as he walked down the corridor. She admired his ass as he turned the corner.

"Oh, yes. He'll do," she whispered to herself and closed the door.

General Lennox arrived in a Federation cruiser and was escorted by six sentries. She was an imposing figure with her short blonde hair cropped up under her beret and a stone-cold expression. She was met by Samson Gorsham, Rebecca's security officer, and led from the transport area to the lobby elevator. Four armed mercenaries stood guard at the elevator and were at attention when Lennox and her sentries arrived. She instructed her sentries to remain there with the mercenaries while she tended to business. Gorsham stepped aside and allowed Lennox to enter first. Once he was on, the doors closed and the elevator ascended to Rebecca's floor.

When the elevator stopped and the doors opened, Rebecca was there to greet General Lennox. The security officer remained at the elevator while Rebecca and General Lennox proceeded to her office. Lennox sat across from Rebecca's desk and removed her beret.

"I assume Marina isn't here yet," she remarked.

"I haven't heard anything recently, but then that's Marina's style," Rebecca explained.

The door slid open and Marina stepped in. With Kat's spell now removed, she knew they could see her. "Miss me?" she asked with a hint of humor in her voice. Kat entered behind her and in her usual mysterious manner said nothing, but nodded as a greeting.

"Welcome," said Rebecca, pleased to see her. "I didn't know you were on site." Marina smiled, knowing that she proved her elusiveness was still effective. Then Kat slid out of the room without a word.

"You look good, Marina," Lennox complimented her. "I see you've been working out."

"Of course. I am on the Kronos Limited plan. I've worked my way up to command ships."

"Yes, I've heard," Lennox responded, amused. "So, what is it you wish to discuss that requires my presence?"

Marina congratulated General Lennox on the destruction of the second Kronos base and then related the success that her alliance was having against Kronos, primarily because of Mike Colby and his ship *The Blue Eagle*. She then inquired as to the progress that Lennox's engineers were having with the new portal generation system. When Lennox revealed that it was operational and how they trapped a portion of the Kronos fleet in an asteroid field, Marina was pleased. She requested the placement of three portals in strategic locations.

One was to be placed in the Nigus star system to reduce long distance travel to and from the former third Kronos base, now known as Genesis, from Archimedes-9. The second was to be placed near Marina's home planet of Yord, connecting it to Archimedes-9. The third portal was to connect Taurus with Archimedes-9. Each of these portals was vital to her battle plan.

General Lennox reminded her that there would be a fee for the use of the portals to cover the Federation's cost for R&D and for the manpower to maintain those portals. Marina urged her to be patient as the long-distance shipping business would need time to mature. Then Marina reminded her of the services that her rebels and Colby's shipping friends have been providing to the Federation free of charge. Rebecca, sensing this was a point of contention, suggested that they save that topic for another day. Both Marina and General Lennox agreed to give it time before addressing the issue.

General Lennox was eager to hear if Marina had any information on the fourth and fifth Kronos bases, but Marina admitted that they had nothing. She mentioned that her asset Colby was onto something in the Nigus star system. When Lennox grimaced, growing impatient, Marina explained that Colby was high on Kronos priority list next to her and that he was risking a lot to help find the two remaining bases.

"When will I know where we stand on the fourth and fifth bases?" pressed Lennox.

Marina informed them that she was going to the Nigus star system next and that was the reason she requested a portal to get there. When they caught each other up on their encounters with Kronos, Marina asked Rebecca where Kara was.

"She's probably in the pub with her boyfriend," Rebecca confessed, knowing a scolding was coming. "She isn't a child anymore."

"I'll speak to her about it," Marina replied, drawing a chuckle from General Lennox.

"I understand that you took out two Kronos command ships and commandeered the third," mentioned Lennox. "Pray tell, how you pulled that one off."

"It was easy," she said, proud to take credit for it. "They were so obsessed with destroying the Calamaarians that I walked right into their control room and took over."

"You are a treat," teased Lennox.

Marina stood and kissed her on the forehead. "As are you, Sandra," she kidded, knowing that Lennox wasn't very receptive to displays of affection.

Rebecca received a message over her wrist transmitter from her security team. She became uneasy and announced, "Twelve Kronos vessels are approaching at a high rate of speed."

General Lennox sent a message from her wrist transmitter and waited. When she received a reply, she informed Rebecca that she just dispatched fifteen Federation vessels to intercept them. When she stood to leave, Rebecca remarked, "You've done a hell of a job rebuilding the fleet and restoring its integrity. We'll do our best to get you the locations of the last two bases."

"Thank you, Rebecca," Lennox responded. "You've done a great job working in the shadows for Marina as well as running this facility. Keep it up."

Marina commented, "Whoever the commander is of the approaching Kronos fleet, remind them what happened to Commander Zhi's fleet. Tell them Marina sends her thoughts and prayers for them. They'll need it."

General Lennox was amused and assured her that she would. She then left the office, eager to participate in the battle. Marina hugged Rebecca and promised to spend some time with her before she departed.

Marina entered the pub and searched for Kara. As much as she resented Kara growing up and hanging out in adult places, she was disappointed not to see her. When she approached the bar, the bartender Dolores greeted her and immediately mentioned the two men who might be a threat to Kara. Marina thanked her and requested a glass of whiskey. It had been a while since Marina had a drink but her frustration was like a crack in her armor. It was eating at her.

Kat entered the pub and sat next to Marina. She gestured to Dolores for whatever Marina was drinking. Dolores served them each a glass of whiskey and then suggested that Marina start her search for Kara in the transport bay.

"When young girls need time to think, they tend to go to places where they can escape from their troubles," she mentioned, "even if they don't plan on leaving."

"How would you know that?" inquired Marina, wondering why Dolores would say that.

"Because I was once like that," she replied. "I was upset about a boy and I sat in the transport bay for hours, watching the freighters unload their cargoes. They always had to escort me out when the freighters were ready to depart so they could secure the bay for access to space."

Realizing that the woman was speaking from experience, Marina thanked her. Kat turned her seat toward Marina and asked if she was worried about Kara. Marina knew she was poking her about her maternal instincts, which she believed she had none. Marina pondered and sipped from her glass. "No," she finally answered. "I just don't want her to grow up too fast. I miss the young girl who was always excited to see me."

Kat sipped from her glass and was about to speak when her eyes turned white. Marina noticed and set her glass down. "What is it, Kat?" she asked anxiously.

Kat didn't answer until her eyes became normal. "It's Kara," she finally responded. "I think she's in trouble."

Marina stood, ready for action. "Where is she?" she asked, concerned. "Is she alright?"

Kat tried to focus but had difficulty. "She's nearby and unhurt," she explained. "That's all I received."

"Then what are we supposed to do?" Marina fretted.

"I sense that she and Ginna are handling it," Kat answered. Marina stormed out of the pub with Kat close behind. "Where are we going, Marina?"

Marina stopped and waited for the elevator. "The transport bay. Dolores thinks it's a good place for young women to hang out to think."

On board the freighter, Kara was tied up in a chair with tape across her mouth. Seth sat calmly across from her while his partner stood watch outside the ship. Seth taunted Kara, telling her she was worth a lot of money to them. Kara didn't seem concerned and stared at him, not at all intimidated. She made no effort to escape from the cords that bound her nor did she try to speak with the rag in her mouth. That bothered Seth.

"What's with you?" he shouted. "Are you some kind of S&M freak?" Kara's eyes told him that she had no idea what he was talking about. Irritated, he removed the rag from her mouth. "Well?" he asked angrily. "Say something." She just smiled at him, angering him even more. Now he suspected that Darra set him up, unsure why she would since she contacted him.

On Taurus, Ginna sat on a bed in her quarters. She could see through Kara's eyes what was happening and directed her power to her. She projected an image of the freighter to Marina and Kat.

Marina and Kat paced the dock area, searching for any sign of Kara. Then, from a distance, they saw the freighter with Hester in front. "That's it!" shouted Marina. She and Kat hurried past several other freighters toward the last berth.

Kara smiled at Seth and suggested that he and his friend have a very short life expectancy. Seth raised his hand to strike her but Kara shouted. "Stop!" His arm froze in the raised position. Then his arm bent backwards until it was in an unnatural position and snapped. Seth howled in pain and cursed Kara for being a witch. Tired of his tirade of profanity, Kara focused on his jaw until it cracked and hung loosely from his skull. His eyes were wide with fear as he could only moan guttural sounds.

Kara easily slid the cords off her wrists and ankles. She opened the hatch, surprising Hester. "I think your friend needs some help," Kara suggested to him.

Hester panicked, seeing her free on their ship. He grabbed Kara by the arm and ushered her back inside, leaving the hatch open. When he saw Seth on the floor with his arm and jaw disfigured, he drew his pistol and aimed at Kara's head. Kara smiled at him and then gazed at the gun. Hester suddenly had no control of his arm and turned the gun toward his knees. He fired a pulse of energy into each knee and, after falling to the floor, turned the gun on Seth. He fired a pulse into each of Seth's knees, leaving him in tears. His eyes showed his desire for mercy but Kara would have none of that. She forced Hester to fire another pulse into Seth's shoulder, rendering his good arm useless. Once more, she had Hester fire a pulse into his own shoulder.

Marina and Kat barged in. Both were surprised to see Kara sitting calmly in the chair, now holding one of their pulse pistols, with her two captors lying on the floor in a smoldering mess. "Kara!" Marina cried out. She rushed to her and embraced her, kissing her cheek repeatedly. "I was so worried about you."

Kara smiled at Kat while in Marina's embrace. Kat returned a smile, nodding to her that she understood her ability to protect herself. Marina glanced at the wounded men and then chastised Kara for 'playing' with their lives. Kara apologized and then fired a pulse into each of them, ending their misery.

Marina was appalled. "Why did you do that?"

"You said don't play with their lives," she answered. "Now they are gone. No more playing."

Marina feared she was becoming like her and hugged her. "Please don't do this," Marina pleaded. "You are better than this."

Kara touched Marina's cheek affectionately and replied, "You do what you do to make things right. Ginna and I do what our fate requires us to do to make things right, as well."

Marina, grew more frustrated and chided her, "Fate and destiny are bull shit. How many times do I have to tell you that?"

Kara kissed her cheek and replied, "We can't change what you are and you can't change what we are. That's how it is and always will be."

"Since you are here and not on Yord, I suppose Ginna is also not on Yord," Marina commented cynically.

"Nope," replied Kara innocently. "She's on Taurus."

Marina looked to Kat for support but Kat could only shrug her shoulders. She had nothing to offer Marina when it came to acting motherly. "Shit!" blurted Marina as she paced the floor. "What am I gonna do with you, Kara?"

Kara stood and walked to the hatch. "Nothing right now," she replied. "I have to meet someone." With that, she left them.

Nathaniel paced the docks, searching frantically for her. His eye was swollen from the punch he received earlier. He asked several crewmen and dockworkers if they had seen Kara but none had. Then he saw her walking toward him and was elated. He rushed to her and threw his arms around her.

"I'm so sorry, Kara," he blurted. "I never meant to hurt you."

Kara warned him to never reveal any of her business or anything about her premonitions again. He promised and begged her for another chance. Kara found it hard to stay mad at him. She agreed and took his hand in hers. "Let's get out of here," she suggested and the two of them left the transport bay.

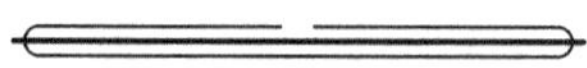

Marina shook her head in disbelief at Kat. She complained to her, "And you were no help whatsoever." She sat in the chair, wondering what she should do about Kara.

Kat rubbed Marina's shoulders and urged her to relax. Marina rubbed her temples, a sign of an impending migraine. Kat offered to see if General Lennox provided the portal yet for their trip to the Nigus.

"What will you do?" Kat inquired, concerned about Marina.

Marina looked up from the chair at her and replied, "I'm going back to the pub to finish my drink and perhaps, have another. See you there." Kat smiled approvingly.

Marina returned to the pub and sat at the bar. Dolores approached and inquired if Kara was safe. Marina thanked her for her insight and assured her that all was okay with Kara.

"You met the young man?" questioned Dolores.

Marina was surprised and realized that Kara might have a man in her life. Panic swept over her for a moment. "No," she responded and chugged her drink. "I imagine that will come soon enough." She held her glass up to Dolores for another.

Dolores poured her another glass of whiskey and set it on the bar. She glanced over at the pub entrance just as Kara and Nathaniel entered.

"Well, here's your moment to shine in front of your girl's new flame," Dolores teased.

Marina jerked her head around in a panic and saw the two of them. Her heart broke as she realized she was no longer the center of Kara's life anymore. *What a shitty mother I am*, she thought to herself. A tear formed in her eye and streamed down her cheek.

Kara and Nathaniel sat at a table in the corner and ordered lunch with drinks. Marina glanced at them repeatedly, wanting to join them, but she knew it was better to stay away.

Rebecca entered the pub and took a seat next to her. "Got room for one more?" she inquired. Marina gestured with a nod to her. "I see Kara has a friend," she remarked. Then she noticed the tear on Marina's cheek. Rebecca pointed to a table in the opposite corner.

A young girl and boy sat there with his mother, eating their lunch. Rebecca continued, "That's Aries, my little girl. I know what you are feeling and I know I will feel that way one day, too."

"Life is so friggin' confusing," complained Marina. "And painful as well."

"Watching your daughter become an adult can be more painful than the wounds we suffered in battle," commented Rebecca. "Those didn't strike the heart."

Marina held her glass up for a toast. "Touché," she responded. The two women tapped glasses.

Marina thanked her for looking after Kara and admitted that she knew it was a tough task, given Kara's age. "You're better at this than I am," she confessed.

Rebecca took her hand in hers and assured her that she is every bit a good mother as anyone, especially under the circumstances. Marina considered that she was right but she felt that Kara and Ginna deserved better.

Kat entered the pub and joined them. "I see we're having a party," she kidded and gestured with her hand to Dolores for a drink. "I think we are long overdue for one."

Rebecca responded enthusiastically, "Amen, sister."

"And I'm the one with issues," Marina teased. She held up two fingers to Dolores for more drinks.

While waiting, Marina emphasized her concerns for Colby and Margot. They have been so good together but she feared that their success would be their demise. Rebecca commented that Marina survived all these years with wit and tact. She pointed out that, between Colby and Margot, they seemed to have a lot of both.

Kara noticed Marina and her friends at the bar. She took Nathaniel by the hand and brought him over to meet them. Marina was surprised and tried her best to act like a normal person. Rebecca sensed her tension and placed her hand on Marina's hand for support.

After introductions, Marina thanked Kara for introducing them. She mentioned to Nathaniel that friendship was difficult for her because of her line of work. Then Marina added that her defensive reactions to people might affect Kara but perhaps he could help with that.

Nathaniel admitted that he learned a valuable lesson with Kara recently and would do his best to keep her safe and happy. Marina thanked him and, for some odd reason, gave him a hug. Kara kissed her cheek and the two of them returned to their table.

"Well done, Marina," praised Kat.

"I'm impressed," added Rebecca. Marina chugged her drink and requested another.

"So, what did Sandra tell you?" asked Marina.

"Sandra, huh?" teased Rebecca.

Embarrassed, Marina explained that Lennox was not really the hard-ass she pretended to be and that there was a human being underneath that armor she calls a body.

"Lennox assured me that we'll have our portal by morning," Kat announced. "She has to deal with Commander March from Kronos right now."

"Just another Kronos prick that needs to be humbled," commented Marina sarcastically.

Kat added, "Lennox gave him your message. He says he's not Zhi and she informed him that she's not Marina so charity is off the board."

Marina held her glass up and toasted with the women. "Lennox is okay in my book," she remarked. "I hope she kills every one of those bastards."

Rebecca chuckled and responded, "She probably will."

After conversing more about the girls, Rebecca inquired about Marina's plan for Yord. Marina was baffled at first, unaware of the siege of her home planet. Then Rebecca realized that Lennox purposely withheld that from Marina so the Federation could handle it.

"Why didn't Lennox tell me about this?" Marina demanded to know.

Rebecca admitted her thoughts that the Federation was handling it so Marina could focus on finding the fourth and fifth Kronos bases. Marina requested the details of the siege and was confused as to why the siege was peaceful. Then Kat suggested that Kronos' forces were at a critical stage and they couldn't afford more significant losses. She also surmised that a peaceful standoff was a way of drawing Marina out of hiding.

"I need to know the results of General Lennox's encounter with the Kronos armada," Marina instructed Rebecca. "This could be an indicator that both their remaining bases have minimal protection right now. It could be an optimum time to strike if we can find them."

Marina finished her second drink and stood up. "We need to leave now. Things just got real," she announced. "Please tell Kara that I'm sorry we didn't have more time together."

Rebecca stood and hugged her. "Of course, I will. Be safe out there," she said, saddened by their urgent departure. She hugged Kat and asked her to keep Marina out of trouble. Kat chuckled at the idea. Marina and Kat left the pub for the transport bay.

Rebecca remained at the pub, sipping from her glass. She always feared that each time Marina left, it might be the last time she ever saw her. Her thoughts were interrupted when the little boy's mother brought Aries over to her. Aries called to her and reached out. Rebecca lifted her in her arms and held her. She became teary-eyed when Aries rested her head on her shoulder.

"Aries had enough playtime and missed you," the mother remarked. Rebecca spoke with the woman for a few minutes and then they both departed the pub.

When Darra's ship approached Archimedes-9, she reported to the transport supervisor that she was a private courier delivering business documents to one of the freighters. The supervisor was reluctant to grant her permission to dock until she informed him that she would only be there for an hour and she was the only member on the ship. After a scan of her ship to confirm her statement, the supervisor allowed her to dock. She was given access to the dock area but no other area of the station.

Darra left her ship and sought out her associates. She walked along the docks until she found Seth's freighter. When she saw the open hatch, she knew that something was wrong. She placed her hand on the pulse pistol under her belt and behind her back, before approaching the hatch warily. When she entered, she saw the corpses of the men and became enraged.

Three dockworkers noticed Darra when she entered the ship and got a good look at her face. When she exited, one called out to her and asked if she was performing services for a price as if she were a prostitute. She grew more irate but kept her composure as she approached them. Again, she placed her hand on her pulse pistol.

"And what services are you interested in," she asked.

The first man, young and anxious, replied, "A little action would be nice. I could use some comforting."

Darra sidled up to him and replied, "That's not asking too much." She drew her pistol and fired a pulse through his chin and into his head. His eyes rolled back in his head as blood and brain matter streamed out from under his chin.

The other two men were horrified and ran for help. Darra cussed as she would now be wanted on the station for murder. She hurried to her ship and requested an immediate departure from the transport supervisor. He informed her that there was a security issue and he couldn't allow her to leave. Darra warned him that if he didn't open the outer gates, she would blast them open and everyone in there would die. The transport supervisor reluctantly complied but notified security that she was departing. Four assault craft were manned and departed from the security section of the station in pursuit of Darra.

Knowing that the station security had a limited range of jurisdiction, Darra continued at full speed away from the station. The assault crafts fired at her but only caused minor damage. Just as she reached the limit of their range, a pulse of energy from one of the craft struck the side of her ship and damaged the hull. Reluctantly, they ceased their chase and returned to the station.

With damage to the environmental compartment, Darra had to perform a series of valve manipulations and system alterations to maintain survivability on the ship. Once the oxygen level was stabilized and the compartment leakage through the fractured hull isolated, she continued her journey to a small outpost, inhabited by other mercenaries, looking to avoid detection.

When she arrived, she met with Regis, the owner of the outpost. Regis was a rough-looking, scar-faced man, armed with a machete and a pulse pistol. His first question to her was, "Why shouldn't I turn you in for the bounty?" Darra was quick to explain that she would pay more than the bounty for his help and informed him that, due to their recent string of losses, Kronos was short on funds, meaning he might not see payment. She inquired if he had any shuttles available for purchase. Regis was more than happy to show her an expensive model that was recently stolen. Of course, he wanted payment in full for the shuttle.

Agreeable, she also offered him a sizeable reward for any information on Marina or her friends. When they agreed on a price, Regis mentioned that a man named Colby was on his way to Taurus. Colby was Marina's pit bull in the war. Darra wasn't anxious to go on another wild goose chase and questioned the validity of his information. He assured her that it was good as it came from an ally at the pirate haven on Zim – one of

Marina's field generals named Tarsus. He removed a photo from his pocket and handed it to her. "This is Mr. Colby, if you haven't met him already. Another five-percent for the photo."

Darra offered another ten-percent if he could arrange for two mercenaries to meet her on Taurus. Regis pushed for fifteen-percent but Darra countered that the men had to be near Colby when she arrived for the abduction. Regis reluctantly agreed to arrange it. When Darra was finished doing business with him, she departed the station. She was determined to capture Colby and force Marina to face her, even if it killed her.

Carl Klingman pondered from his office on Polaris. There, buried inside a mountain, was the emergency Kronos base. It was built in case of a devastating loss in the war. A place of refuge, Carl and his most trusted peers would join him in rebuilding the Kronos empire once more if it ever fell. Carl knew that if he ever needed to use the base on Polaris, then things were going really bad in the war.

Tessara reminded him that remaining on Polaris was just a precaution and, since they didn't have the latest information and many of their contacts had been captured or killed, they should stay put for now. Carl swore that one day he would get his revenge on Marina and her friends.

Tessara made several attempts to contact any of their spies and finally reached one of them – a man named Tarsus. She promised a reward much larger than the last two for a favor. Tarsus reminded her that he hadn't been paid for the information about Ramses-3. When she offered to double his fee and was willing to transmit the credits immediately, Tarsus was eager to listen to her offer. "What is it you need me to do?" he inquired.

"I need you to guarantee me that your forces will not engage us when the big battle comes," Tessara informed him. "I trust you still have your credibility with the rebels."

"Of course, I do," he assured her. "That's why I had to kill your spy Tariq. They were onto him."

Tessara thanked him for his loyalty and began the transfer of a large sum of money. Then she surprised him with another offer. "You are familiar with one of our agents, Darra."

"Yes, I know Darra," he replied.

Tessara informed him of the bounty on her head and offered twenty-percent over that if he took her head and displayed it to them. She mentioned that Darra stole the reward money offered for Marina's death and was using it to pay off anyone who might be a threat. Tarsus considered that he might collect a reward from the Federation for Darra's execution as well.

"I'll handle it," he responded. "Make sure you are good for it."

Tessara agreed to give him an advance for his expenses to ensure he was properly motivated for the job. Tarsus gave a sinister laugh and ended the transmission.

CHAPTER 8

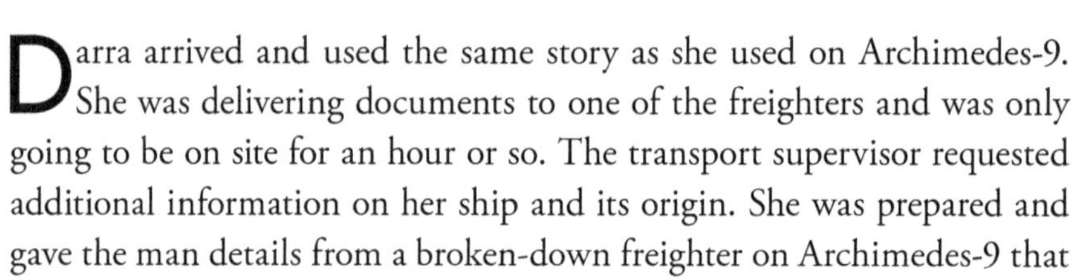

Darra arrived and used the same story as she used on Archimedes-9. She was delivering documents to one of the freighters and was only going to be on site for an hour or so. The transport supervisor requested additional information on her ship and its origin. She was prepared and gave the man details from a broken-down freighter on Archimedes-9 that she remembered seeing. It was transferring a cargo of fertilizer onto another ship while repairs were underway. The supervisor warned her that she had an hour and a security officer would be down to inspect her credentials.

Darra thanked the man and ended the transmission. She hurried off the ship and waited near the elevator for the security officer to arrive. When he stepped off the elevator, Darra stopped him and questioned him about where she might find Mike Colby. The man mentioned the executive level but informed her that she needed to get clearance first. Darra surprised the officer with a chop to the throat. Then she grabbed him from behind and snapped his neck. After removing his badge, she blocked the door open with one of his boots and dragged his corpse behind a large wooden crate.

When she stepped back onto the elevator, she inserted his badge into the card reader and selected the executive level. She was anxious as the elevator rose several floors and then stopped. As the doors opened, Darra was ready to fight if she encountered any resistance, but the hall was clear. She stepped off the elevator and walked down the corridor.

Mike Colby exited the conference room and entered the men's lavatory. Darra noticed him but kept her distance. In his haste, he didn't notice the two men dressed as custodians, standing across from the lavatory entrance. Now, Darra seized the opportunity and motioned for her two accomplices to stand by.

Mike was relieving himself when Darra startled him. "Well, Mr. Colby. It's about time we had some face time."

"Excuse me," he replied, unsure of who she was. He finished and turned around. "Who are you?"

Darra stood, leaning against the wall, fingering a dagger. "You don't know me but everyone at Kronos, including myself, know all about you."

Mike wasn't concerned and suggested that they carry on the discussion someplace other than the Men's Room. Darra approached him and placed her dagger against his neck. She inquired, "Where is Marina?"

Unintimidated, Mike shrugged his shoulders and replied, "Marina doesn't tell anyone where she was, is or going to be. That's why she is so hard to catch."

"Where is the *Blue Eagle*?"

Mike chuckled and answered, "You really are having a bad day. I don't work for the *Blue Eagle* or its captain."

Darra turned away with her head down. Mike knew better than to let his guard down. Suddenly, she turned and attempted to cut his throat. Mike blocked it and slammed her against the wall. "There's a hefty bounty on your head, Colby," she mentioned. "Someone wants you alive. Otherwise, you'd be dead."

"I doubt that," he responded, confident. Then she caught him by surprise. She dropped to the floor and elbowed him in the groin, doubling him over. Before he could react, she rolled on her back and kicked upward, striking him at the bridge of his nose with both heels in her boots.

Mike staggered backwards and fell to the ground, out cold. She summoned the two men from the corridor to drop him in the trashcan and carry him back to her ship. They lifted him into the can and placed a trash bag over his head. The accomplices promptly exited the lavatory, pushing the trashcan with Mike inside it. She trailed the men in case someone asked questions and she needed to create a diversion.

Julian emerged from the conference room, suspicious of Mike's prolonged absence and hurried to the Men's Room. He entered the men's lavatory and found it empty. Seeing blood on the floor, his worst fears were realized. The elevator display indicated that the kidnappers exited on the ground floor. Urgently, he inserted his card and called for the elevator. He scanned the corridor in both directions, hoping for a clue but there was nothing of use to him. The elevator came and he stepped inside. As the elevator descended, Julian punched the wall, wondering how this could happen on the executive level of Taurus with all the security they had in place. He notified Sara of the abduction through his wrist transmitter and instructed them to stay put.

When Julian stepped off the elevator, he met Major Tieg on the ground floor. Tieg informed him that a small schooner just left the station on an unscheduled departure. He ordered Tieg not to contact them but only track them. He then returned to the elevator.

In the conference room, Sara briefed Margot and Julian's wife Deidra of the abduction. Margot fretted as to who would kidnap Mike, especially there on Taurus when no one knew they were there. Sara suggested that it was a random opportunity by pirates. After all, there was a bounty on Mike's head.

"But Korick's men are the pirates and they are loyal to him," Margot countered.

"Then Kronos must be involved somehow," she responded. "Their pockets are deep and someone could have been bribed."

Julian burst into the room and ordered Margot to get to her shuttle and follow the tracking coordinates coming from Major Tieg. Sara was eager to help and followed Margot out of the conference room. Julian took a deep breath and prayed that he was right about this.

Mike awoke in the main quarters of Darra's shuttle, surprisingly with no restraints. The cobwebs in his head began to clear and he recalled his initial encounter with Darra in the Men's Room on Taurus. The hatch to the flight deck opened and Darra emerged. "Well, it's nice of you to join me, Colby."

Mike still couldn't believe she knocked him out and how she did it. Everything happened so fast. "So, how much is Kronos paying you to deliver me?" he inquired sarcastically.

Darra laughed at him and then replied, "I'm not doing this for Kronos. I'm doing this for revenge against Marina for killing two of my sisters."

"And that has what to do with me?" he asked, curious.

"All in time," she answered confidently. "All in time."

Mike stepped toward her but she held her hand out for him to stop. "Try anything stupid and you may not get up next time," she warned. "Sit down and enjoy the trip."

"Where are we going?" he asked. "Not that it matters."

Darra informed him that he was leverage to get the bounty on her head lifted since there were some very important people who wished to speak with him. She mentioned that these people weren't very happy about his interference in their operation. Then she strolled over to him and suggested, "If you tell me where Marina is, I won't deliver you to your enemies."

Mike suggested that she start with Marina's home on Yord. He was pleasantly surprised when Darra slipped and responded, "I'm tired of Yord. I have an apartment with a view of the palace and I know she hasn't been there for quite some time."

Mike then suggested that she hang out at the pirate haven on Zim and wait for her to show. She laughed and replied, "Those people are all her allies. I know what they did to my friend Borath, so why would I go there?"

"Therapy," he kidded. "Seems like you need to feel loved."

"Last chance," Darra offered, irritated with Mike's comments. "I'm going to request authorization to land and I have to tell them why."

Mike countered that it was her last chance to work something out with him. Once she turned him over to Kronos, she might never find out where Marina is. Darra grimaced, knowing he was right, and returned to the flight deck. Mike searched the cabin for anything useful but found nothing. He hoped that his friends were smart enough to track or follow them.

Margot and Sara monitored the schooner with Mike on board on the long-range monitor as it approached the Kronos base. The women were ecstatic that they would learn the location of the fourth base. Sara positioned the cloaked shuttle close to the schooner until they were nearly beneath it. The transport bay gates of the base opened and the schooner glided in with the shuttle beneath it. Darra had no idea as the shuttle never showed on her short-range sensors due to the cloaking mode. Once inside, the shuttle veered into the next empty dock.

On board the schooner, Darra argued with the transport supervisor on the transmitter. He refused her admission to the facility and requested she leave immediately. He accused her of using an active tracking device that could jeopardize the base. Unsure of why she was suspected of emitting the tracking signal, she checked all the systems on her schooner and found nothing.

Again, the transport supervisor warned her to depart immediately. The bay gates opened and Darra had no choice but to leave.

Mike sensed her fear and inquired what her problem was. Then she considered that there was a device on Mike's body. "Stand up!" she screamed at him. "Are you wearing a tracking device?"

Mike chuckled, knowing that his friends must be nearby. "Nope. I don't wear trackers in the Men's Room," he responded sarcastically. "It's a distraction."

Darra retrieved a scanner from a locker and checked Mike from head to toe. Frustrated, she threw the scanner at the wall and shattered it. Mike inquired why she was so upset about being denied access to the Kronos base. She grabbed Mike by his chin and replied angrily, "Because, if there is a tracker on my ship, then Marina and the Federation know where I am. Even worse, they know where this base is and it's my fault. Do you think that will go without consequences?"

"But I thought you wanted to find Marina?" taunted Mike. "Don't worry about Kronos. They'll get over it." Pissed off, Darra spun and karate kicked him in the head, knocking him out.

Once Marina received the coordinates, she and Kat boarded her cruiser and departed the station. They identified Margot's tracking signal and darted toward it. "We have one chance to catch them," Marina announced.

"Where are you going?" questioned Kat as Marina left the flight deck. Once again, Marina left her clueless as to what her plans were.

Marina opened the panel in the rear of the ship and studied the teleport module. There were three small buttons and five slide switches.

After manipulating each of them and observing the display, she figured out how to enter the coordinates and set the timer sequence.

Kat came back to see what she was up to and inquired, "Do I want to know what you are about to do?"

"Just be prepared for anything when the module is activated," Marina advised her. Kat shook her head and returned to the flight deck. She realized that she would never understand Marina and perhaps it was better that way.

Marina programmed the last coordinates from Margot's ship, not accounting for their movement, to avoid hitting them when they arrive at their destination. She set the timer for one minute and synchronized the timer on her wrist transmitter. Content that she could do nothing more, she returned to the flight deck. She glanced at Kat as she took her seat.

"Do I get a countdown or anything?" asked Kat.

"Yeah," replied Marina smugly as she glanced at her wrist transmitter. "Now." Suddenly, two small ships appeared on their long-range sensor monitor. Marina chuckled as Kat frowned at her.

"Looks like the path of the signal transmissions changes direction after a brief stop," Kat commented.

"Find out where that ship stopped," Marina instructed her. "Then we'll resume following the trail."

Kat repositioned the long-range sensors to the coordinates where the signal changed direction. A large image appeared on the monitor. She activated the cameras for the sensors and was stunned. "Marina, we found it! The fourth Kronos base!"

Marina leaned over, staring at Kat's monitor and instructed her, "Notify Lennox with the coordinates and tell her that it's their baby now. We're going after Mike." Kat happily relayed the message via transmitter.

Mike entered the flight deck, looking pissed. Darra charged at him and the two exchanged a series of punches. When Mike slammed her to the floor on her back, Darra attempted to scissor-kick him but with no luck. He rammed her head into the bulkhead and choke-slammed her to the floor. Darra was dazed and lay still. She tried to move but her ribs were badly injured.

Mike attempted to contact the *Blue Eagle* but with no luck. He then tried to contact his shuttle. To his surprise, Margot responded. When she revealed that they were still in the transport bay of the Kronos base, Mike instructed her to turn off the beacon and wait until he returned before doing anything else.

As Mike piloted Darra's schooner back to the Kronos base, he considered that he should have Darra contact them instead of himself. When he requested her help in docking, she was more cooperative than before.

"Why do you want to go inside that base so bad?" she inquired, curious. Mike explained that he had some things to settle with Klingman. "Jack or Carl?" she questioned him. Surprised that there were two of them, he figured that they both had to be dealt with.

Then Darra revealed Jack's condition as a result of a machine malfunctioning on Sargassa. Jack was more like a seal than a person. Carl was the quiet psycho who was the more dangerous of the two.

"Will you help me?" Mike asked.

Darra snickered and replied, "I'm more than happy to help you get yourself killed. You'll never get near him and he's very good at traps. He'll snare you." Mike shrugged it off as inconsequential.

Darra contacted the transport supervisor and informed him that the issue with the beacon was resolved and she needed to pick up some parts for her ship. She assured him that it was a short visit and she'd be leaving immediately after her procurement. The transport supervisor gave her the okay but warned her that she'd be arrested if the beacon became an issue again.

The schooner was allowed to dock without further incident. Just as Mike was about to exit the hatch, Darra called out to him, "You're wasting your time. The Klingmans aren't here."

"I expected as much," he replied. "As a courtesy, I suggest you leave immediately before the Federation blows this place to pieces."

"We will meet again," she warned. Mike nodded to her and left the schooner. Darra punched the console and immediately prepared to leave the station.

With the shuttle still cloaked, all Mike saw was Margot's head sticking out of the hatch. He rushed to her and, after an affectionate hug, closed the hatch behind him. "We have to get out of here, fast," he warned. Then he saw Sara on the flight deck and gave her a hug as well. When he turned around, Marina and Kat stood before him. Sara and Margot were awestruck to see the two women appear out of nowhere.

"How did you get here?" he asked, amazed to see them.

"We followed the tracking signal," replied Kat. "The Federation will be here shortly to blast this place, so I suggest we get going."

"There's someone in the schooner next to us that wants to meet you. I believe she's a friend of yours named Darra."

Marina checked the outside monitor and saw that the bay just depressurized and the gates opened for the schooner to depart. She kidded, "I came all this way to find out what ails that bitch. I guess she'll have to wait for another day."

Margot and Sara anxiously started the shuttle and departed the bay behind the schooner. Mike mentioned to Marina that Darra's beef with her was about two of her sisters that Marina killed. Marina smiled and recalled Fiona and Willow had a third sister that must be Darra. Now she could look forward to defeating the last of the psychotic litter of bitches.

"What can you tell me about the remaining plans for Kronos?" Mike inquired.

Marina touched the bruises on his face from his brawl with Darra and commented, "You should really consider retirement." Mike groaned in frustration as, once again, he didn't get the answers he wanted from her.

Marina explained that they were reserving the rebel forces for the attack on the fifth base. This allowed them to keep their existence a secret, while reducing the possibility of a spy alerting Kronos. In addition, they wanted to capture the Klingmans before the Federation did for other reasons. Marina hoped to learn their entire organizational structure and discover who funded them during the last war, allowing them to become the monsters they were. Everyone involved needed to pay.

Margot returned from the flight deck and hugged Marina. "It's been a while," she commented. "I thought you forgot about me."

"Never. By the way, congratulations, Margot," Marina commented sourly. "Thanks for inviting me to the wedding."

Margot was embarrassed and responded, "It was a spur of the moment thing. I'm sorry."

"Relax. I'm glad for you," Marina replied. "Not sure why you did it, but I'm glad." Mike frowned at her but she replied, "Only kidding Colby.

You and your team did well." Kat stood by her, ready to transport back to the *Reaper*.

"Will we see you again?" asked Mike.

"Of course," she replied with a rare smile. "We'll be right behind you. I think me and Ms. Kat need a break." In a flash, she and Kat were gone, transporting back to their own ship.

Sara pointed out that the gates were closing and they should leave while they had the chance. "Get us out of here," Margot ordered her. "Take us to Terran."

On the planet Terran, the local inhabitants were in a festive mood over the new long distance trade routes that Colby's team established. Mike's friends from the *Blue Eagle* were already there. Marina and Kat sat at one of the tables and drank ale. The ship's captain, Tisch, joined them, hoping for an update on the war and how it would affect her business. Marina introduced Kat as her second in command and her replacement on Yord. Pleased by Marina's perception of her, Kat shook hands with everyone.

When she held Mike's hand, she hesitated and grew concerned. Mike noticed and questioned what was wrong. "You play a dangerous game, Mr. Colby. Beware," she warned.

Marina glanced at Margot and Tisch, fearing what Kat saw. The women suspected Kat had special powers, particularly since she was allied with Marina and was unique in her appearance. It seemed wise not to question her warning.

To break the tension, Margot teased, "Here that, Mike? Don't piss me off."

Mike was unaffected by their words and pressed Marina about the last Kronos base. He was eager to know if they had any idea where it might be. Marina suggested he focus on his new life with Margot and let them handle it. When he changed the topic to the portals, Marina gave him the message from General Lennox. "You owe her the location of the fifth base before she'll commit to any negotiations with you."

"How can I find it if I don't know if I'm in or out of the game?" he asked, fearing he would be forgotten.

"You have a way of figuring things out," Marina complimented him. "I'm sure that, between you, Margot and your friends, you'll solve the mystery, if we don't."

Tisch emphasized that their focus would remain on the trade routes and continuing their development. Marina reminded her that their progress was vital for a lot of reasons. She saw it as a way to unite the distant sectors and bring peace to the region.

When Zenith joined them, Tisch introduced her to everyone as her new partner. Mike was surprised and impressed. Zenith immediately inquired about the locations of the first two bases and requested their coordinates. Marina agreed to send them to the *Blue Eagle* and wondered why she wanted them. Zenith only mentioned that it was a hunch.

Mike suggested that Marina seek out Antwan's wife on Yord and see if she knew anything that would help. He revealed what Darra told him about the apartment overlooking the palace. Marina responded with the story of how Carl Klingman punished Antwan and sent the kids to be sold off as slaves. "We took advantage of that and procured the children," she announced proudly.

Kat mentioned that there were few buildings that had an upper view of the palace to search for Antwan's wife. With the return of her children, they had no doubt that Tia would be cooperative.

Marina then inquired as to what their immediate plans were. Tisch revealed that they would stop at Sargassa to deliver some items and then proceed to Archimedes-9. After that, she wanted to make a return trip to Taurus to discuss their progress with Gemini. She indicated that Mike would likely want to coerce Gemini into providing additional staples for the ship – like rum and beer. Again, everyone had a good laugh while Mike shook his head in disbelief. "The disrespect I get for all my accomplishments," he complained. "It's just not right."

Margot kissed his cheek and reminded him of the rewards he got as well. He sighed and relented that things would never be the same. After some hesitation and several stares, he added that he was happy and grateful for the adventures he had with all of them.

"You'd better keep your wife happy, Colby," warned Marina. "Don't make me come back and kick your ass."

Margot responded, "I'm sure he'll be a good boy. Little boys want their candy. Right, Mike?"

Mike smiled at her and replied innocently, "I love candy."

Marina received a message over her transmitter and informed them that Antwan was sold to a sex slave operation and, without his genitals, he was of no use to women. "So, you know what's left for him?" she kidded.

Mike chuckled and remarked, "He always had a thing for men, especially me."

"We were able to withdraw the sex video from the galactic servers for his wife Tia. She was very appreciative and willing to cooperate with General Lennox's people."

"What did you learn?" questioned Mike, eager to know.

"Don't worry about it," replied Marina. "Just take care of my girl and let me handle the rest." She thanked them again for their help.

As she and Kat returned to the *Reaper*, Marina had a strange feeling that she'd be seeing them soon. Marina questioned Kat, "What did you see that warranted warning Colby?"

Kat glanced at her, wondering if she should reveal her premonition. When Marina stepped in front of her and blocked her path, she relented. "Something isn't right about all this," Kat mentioned. "Klingman isn't on the fifth base and he has contrived a trap for you and Colby."

"That's nothing new," Marina retorted.

"This is different," warned Kat. "I don't have details but nothing about this trap is familiar."

The two women boarded the *Reaper* and set off from Terran to Yord. Three days into their return, Marina instructed Kat to slow down while she programmed the teleport module in the rear of the ship. She returned to the flight deck and asked Kat, "Where is the *Blue Eagle* now?"

Kat sent out a signal and waited. Soon, she received word back that they were on the way to Taurus. Marina announced excitedly, "We're going to Taurus!" She returned to the module and reprogrammed it for Taurus.

"Contact Tarsus for me," requested Marina. Kat sensed that Marina recalled something significant and promptly obeyed. It had been a while since Marina was cheerful about anything.

Surprised, Kat received a quick response back. "Tarsus is on, Marina," she announced.

Marina stepped in front of the monitor and, without even a greeting, ordered Tarsus to gather his forces at Orpheus-2. She told him that the time was nearing for the final battle. Tarsus acknowledged her command and ended the transmission. Marina thought it strange that he had no questions and ended the transmission before she could say anything more.

Kat commented that Tarsus might have been part of the premonition that she had. There was something about him that worried her. Marina wasn't concerned and assured her that time will sort everything out.

"You know he won't be there when you need him," commented Kat.

"Of course. I'm counting on it."

The sequence timer activated and the *Reaper* was transported to Taurus. Marina was assigned a bay to dock in and, as soon as she exited the ship, she was met by Julian and his wife Deidra. They greeted her with a hug and welcomed her inside the station. Kat remained on board the *Reaper* to monitor any communications. Kat wasn't very good at interacting with people she didn't know and often left Marina to handle any interaction with others.

"I'm surprised to see you here, Marina," admitted Julian. "Not that I'm disappointed."

Smiling, Marina thanked him for his decision to have Colby's kidnapper tracked to the fourth Kronos base. Julian kidded that he only considered what Mike would have done. "What can we help with?" he asked.

"I need to meet with the crew of the *Blue Eagle*; Zenith in particular," she replied.

"I'll let them know to join us in the conference room when they finish their cargo transfer," he responded, eager to know what she was up to.

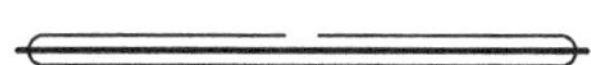

In the control room on Polaris, Carl and Tessara sat in front of a large console with several monitors on it. Behind them were four panels containing servers for a complex computer system. Tessara operated the communication portion of the system in a desperate attempt to find their missing fleet in the asteroid field.

Carl read several messages that had been received during their travel. One caught his interest. He commented to Tessara, "It seems that our girl Darra is still out there and in one piece. We may have to up the ante on her bounty."

Tessara chuckled but then replied, "Perhaps we should forget about her for now. I think we need to make some moves before it's too late."

"What do you suggest, my dear?" he inquired.

Tessara surmised that Marina had limited resources. She was unaware that the Scrat (aliens) had any remaining ships to fight with. She believed that her forces destroyed all of them when they attacked the Scrat worlds previously. The two of them both assumed that it was the Federation and not the Scrat that defeated their forces and destroyed the second base. With Tarsus' assurance not to interfere, and Marina's forces on Ramses-3 in shambles, Tessara considered that the Federation and a few ragtag rebel units were all that Marina had left.

"That ragtag group includes our nemesis Colby as well as Marina," Carl reminded her.

"They are human and they can bleed," she remarked cynically.

Carl grew concerned with Tessara's new arrogance. He understood that she was tired of their losses and wanted a big play to regain control of the quadrant. Tessara noticed his prolonged silence and stated that the Federation, while rebuilding since their catastrophic losses in the battle for Orpheus-2, is only a shell of what it once was. She suggested that they recall their forces from Yord and prepare to defend Base Five. Before Carl could respond, Tessara contacted Kimo in the lab.

"Kimo, what's the status of the projects you and Kepler are working on?" Tessara asked.

Kimo responded over the speaker, "The portal generator isn't complete yet. There are still issues and after Corbin's disaster, we'd like to be thorough about our testing."

"And the other project?"

"The cyborg soldier project is ready," Kimo responded. "We've just completed testing and have forty soldiers ready for deployment. The other cyborg shells are awaiting volunteers and critical components that haven't arrived."

Tessara glanced at Carl with a smile and then continued, "Stand by for further instructions. We'll be in touch."

Tessara ended the conversation and then contemplated how to use the cyborg soldiers. Carl considered how best to implement them as well. Then Carl suggested, "Why not use our drones to deliver our new soldiers to Archimedes-9? Then we can use Sanchez and March's fleets to take out Orpheus-2 and the Federation with it, leaving Archimedes-9 with no other option but to surrender."

"That's dangerous, Carl," replied Tessara. "We're risking a lot if it fails."

Carl explained that his expectations would be for the cyborgs to inflict significant casualties to personnel on Archimedes-9, while their fleet engages the remnants of the Federation's fleet. Archimedes-9 could become their new home if the cyborgs live up to their promise.

Tessara pointed out that Marina is known for surprises and might still have resources that they were unaware of. Carl's ego got the better of him and he ordered her to amass all remaining ships behind the asteroid field. Then she was to direct Dr. Stylus to use her drones to transport the cyborg soldiers. Tessera was concerned about abandoning Base Five knowing that an attack there was possible.

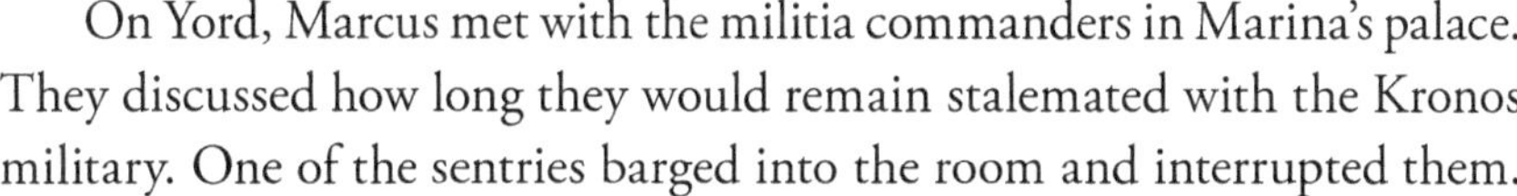

On Yord, Marcus met with the militia commanders in Marina's palace. They discussed how long they would remain stalemated with the Kronos military. One of the sentries barged into the room and interrupted them. He announced excitedly that the Kronos ships were departing.

"Report to your ships," ordered Marcus. "Be prepared in case they turn on us."

"Shall we attack first?" asked one of the commanders.

"No," he replied. "Just be ready. I think something must have happened to force this."

The commanders exited the conference room, eager to enter the war once more. Marcus sat in silence, considering what to do. Eventually, he went to the communication room and spoke with the officer. "As soon as those ships are out of range, I need you to contact Marina," he ordered.

Marcus paced the small office as he pondered what Commander Sanchez might be up to. The security officer suggested that he contact him and see what his intentions were. At first, Marcus was reluctant but then he considered that he could ask if this was an attack or if the siege was over.

While waiting for Marina's response, Commander Sanchez responded to their signal request.

Marcus inquired if their truce still held or if the departure was a prelude to an attack. Commander Sanchez expressed his appreciation for their cooperation in avoiding unnecessary casualties and losses. He informed Marcus that they had been reassigned and would be departing the sector. Marcus thanked him for handling the situation like a professional and for avoiding losses as well. He ended the transmission and breathed a sigh of relief.

"What do you think?" asked the officer.

"Something big is going on," answered Marcus. "First of all, they were eager to avoid any losses, which tells me that their forces are thin. Marina must be winning the war." He continued to pace the floor and then continued, "To leave on short notice like this, they were summoned for something significant. Perhaps Marina knows what it is."

Marina finally responded and was eager to know if everyone was okay. Marcus related the strange arrangement with Commander Sanchez to avoid losses. Marina was interested in the size of the armada and where they might be going.

"There was a command ship and five battle cruisers," Marcus answered. "They left in a hurry but I have no idea where to."

"Send your forces to Orpheus-2 to join up with General Lennox's fleet," ordered Marina. "Tarsus forces should already be there."

"Who will defend Yord?" he inquired.

"Cheska's group will remain along with the class four freighter she has," Marina replied. "Let me speak with her."

Baffled by her request, he responded, "There's no Kronos freighter here and no one named Cheska."

Marina instructed Marcus to attempt to make contact with her and see if they were nearby. She wanted the class four freighter with its superior weaponry to defend Yord. It would also be available to support the Federation if needed.

"Let either me or Kat know when you reach Cheska," ordered Marina. "I need to go now."

The transmission ended and Marcus instructed the officer, "Try to reach Cheska on a Kronos freighter if it's in the area. Keep the signal short-range so Sanchez's people don't intercept it. Marcus sat down finally and covered his face to hide his frustration.

After the fourth try, a female voice responded to the communication officer's signal requests. "This is Cheska. Go ahead," she responded.

Marcus rushed over to the transmitter on the console. "Cheska, this is Marcus. I'm coordinating all military operations here on Yord. Where are you?" he asked, anxious.

Outside the palace, the class four just landed. Three militia officers rushed into the room in a panic, thinking that Kronos had returned. Marcus gestured for silence as Cheska spoke with him.

"If you look out your window, Marcus, you will see exactly where we are," she answered. "I'll be reporting shortly." The transmission ended.

Marcus shook his head and complained, "I have no idea what the hell is happening anymore. These Kronos ships keep coming and going and… Oh, never mind." He then directed the officer to inform Marina of Cheska's arrival.

As he exited the office and entered the palace lobby, he encountered Cheska. "Marina was worried about you," he remarked.

"Sorry, pal. We had to wait until your date with those Kronos jackasses was over before we could show ourselves."

"Fair enough," Marcus replied. "Let's talk."

Marcus led her into the conference room and the two traded stories about their Kronos encounters.

CHAPTER 9

Marina sat in the executive floor conference room, discussing the latest events with Julian and his wife Deidra. Julian informed her of how they identified Tariq as the Kronos spy and how he was responsible for the *Blue Eagle's* misfortunes. Marina's main concern was that there were no more information leaks coming out of Taurus. Julian assured her that they've been very discrete about critical information since Tariq burned them.

Tisch and Zenith, the *Blue Eagle's* co-captains, entered the conference room. Both were excited to see Marina again, viewing her as their role model for women. Marina immediately asked for Margot and her partner Mike.

Tisch and Zenith chuckled. "They'll be along shortly," answered Tisch. "They are, let's say, busy at the moment."

Marina realized that her most prized assets were having a romantic interlude. "Well, I don't need them right now," she remarked. "More important, I was hoping that Ms. Zenith made some headway with the Kronos database, using the coordinates I gave her."

Zenith was suddenly the center of attention and grew nervous. "I, um… I mapped out the locations of the four bases and then overlaid the origins and destinations of their numerous communications over the map."

Marina waited anxiously for her to reveal what she found. Zenith looked down, disappointed by her failure to locate Base number five. "So, what did you find out?" questioned Marina.

"The point that I isolated is an empty area of space," she uttered sadly. "I remapped the locations with the origins and sources of each base's communications several times but it always came out the same."

"I'd like to see the map if you have it," Marina requested.

Zenith reached into her back pocket and removed a container with a data disk in it. She handed it to Marina and accepted that she failed to find the last base. Marina passed the disk to Julian and asked him to display the map on the wall monitor.

While Julian installed the disk into his computer and set up the monitor to display the contents of the disk, Marina pressed Tisch for information on the Nigus star system. She had been there once or twice to visit Sima Lowell, her alien friend on Sargassa, and to visit Terran, after Colby's rescue along with the destruction of the fourth Kronos base.

Margot and Colby entered the conference room, all smiles and holding hands. Marina was amused and commented, "Nice of you two to make time for something as insignificant as a galactic war."

Mike's eyes widened with excitement. "You found the fifth base?" he asked Marina, excited by the thought.

"Calm down," she responded. "I thought you were handling him, Margot." Margot shook her head and admitted that it was hopeless. Marina embraced Margot and asked if Colby was treating her well. Margot assured her that she kept him in line – most of the time. Marina then gave Colby a friendly punch in the arm. "I'm proud of you both," she complimented them.

Julian displayed Zenith's map of the four Kronos bases on the wall monitor. Zenith explained how she used this map with the sources and destinations of the communications for each base on the database to predict where the fifth base might be.

Julian then accessed the second file which was a copy of the system logs off the Kronos database. Zenith pointed out the signal strength of the communications which was determined by distance and the fact that the signal strength was strongest for two of the bases but showed up as weak for the other two and therefore, must have come from the fifth base which was equidistant to bases two and four but further away than the distances between bases one and three as well as one and four.

Marina studied the logs for each of the bases for a moment. She was impressed how Zenith used simple math to draw her attention to the empty area. "Perhaps, you didn't fail," Marina commented to her. "I think we may need to look into the area you highlighted and see for ourselves if it's really a void in space."

"If it's possible, I'd like to visit the Kronos freighter on Yord," requested Zenith. "There's something else I have a hunch about."

"I'll let them know you're coming, assuming Tisch can take you there without impacting her schedule."

"I'm sure we can make a short visit," Tisch replied.

Marina apologized for not taking her on board the *Reaper* but feared putting Zenith at risk in the event of an attack on her ship. Zenith understood and wasn't anxious to leave her partner Tisch to run the *Blue Eagle* alone.

Zenith offered the disk to Marina so she could study it further. Marina was grateful and accepted it once Julian shut down the system. She then related the strange siege of Yord by Kronos and the armada's mysterious departure.

Eager to know more about the battle plan, Mike pressed Marina for details on her plan. She related her defensive strategy for Yord using the hijacked class four freighter that she turned over to Cheska. "The ship will be a little insurance, in case we need it," Marina mentioned.

Marina revealed that she believed Kronos' leadership would likely target Orpheus-2 to take on the Federation's forces while they are still rebuilding in addition to defending the fifth base. She felt that Kronos would likely do all they could to maintain their last base for a resurgence in power, if they were victorious at Orpheus-2.

Mike inquired, "Where would they amass their forces if they were planning an attack on the station?"

"I'm going to assign my field general the responsibility of finding and destroying that fleet, wherever it may be," she answered.

"And what about the fifth base?" Mike asked, growing more interested. "What happens when we find it?"

"What do you want me to do with it?" Marina countered.

"Klingman. Your friend Darra. The Kronos leadership. What about them?"

Marina enjoyed Colby's intensity and continued to frustrate him with vague answers and questions. "I have my own plans for them, Mike. Don't worry."

Margot finally spoke up and asked, "What if Klingman isn't there?"

Marina looked over at the bar and requested a glass of something strong from Julian. She hated answering questions that she didn't have answers to and her request for a drink was a distraction from the question. When Julian served her a scotch on the rocks, Marina sipped it and savored the taste while everyone waited for her response.

With her drama moment building, she finally responded, "When Kronos is defeated, I'm retiring. I'm tired of fighting and losing people I care about."

Everyone in the room was stunned. "Besides," she continued, "I'm sure Mike won't sleep until he finds them and beats them to death."

Everyone laughed except for Mike. As usual, they mocked him for his success in the field. He stared at Margot, disappointed by her lack of support for him. She kissed his cheek and promised to make it up to him. Marina groaned at their affectionate demeanors and finished her drink.

Julian served drinks to the others in the room as a celebratory gesture. He hoped that one topic wouldn't come up, though. And then it did. Marina asked Julian, "Can I see my girl Ginna?"

Julian grew uneasy and hesitated. Everyone noticed and wondered what was wrong. Marina gave him a terse stare. He took her glass and went to the bar. He returned with two full glasses and gave her one. "Alright, Julian. Cut the theatrics," warned Marina. "What aren't you telling me?"

"Ginna… She, uh…" he started reluctantly and then paused. Marina chugged her drink and handed it to him for a refill. Julian refilled it and handed it to her. Marina gestured for him to continue. "She is in a serious relationship with a boy," he muttered.

Marina sensed that it wasn't the worst of it. "So?" she inquired.

The *Blue Eagle's* crew including Mike and Margot took the opportunity to take a drink during his pause. Julian chugged his drink. Deidra placed her hand on his to ease his nerves. She answered for him and explained, "Ginna is in training to be Gemini's new executive in the corporation."

Mike coughed and spit out his drink all over himself. "Oh, Julian. What have you done?" Mike chided.

Julian held his hands out innocently. "It was her idea and Gemini agreed to it before any of us knew about it."

Mike explained to Margot that his ex-wife Gemini was not the person you want spending time with a young girl if you care about her. "Sometimes people change," Margot responded. "Look at you, for instance."

Mike returned a stare, baffled by her remark. She clarified that he wasn't the lone wolf that he used to be and that he listens to her when she gives him an order. Everyone chuckled at him. Mike shook his head, knowing he was ambushed again.

The laughter ceased when Ginna entered the room with her boyfriend Dante. She was dressed in black slacks and a white blouse. Her hair was set in a bun with a long curl down each side. She had diamond earrings and a gold cross for a pendant around her neck.

"Marina!" Ginna exclaimed. She rushed to her and embraced her.

Marina's eyes were wide with surprise. She stood and ogled Ginna. Her heart broke as she now saw Ginna as a woman and not a girl. "You look… stunning," she blurted.

Ginna then introduced Dante and revealed that they were in a committed relationship. Now Julian's eyes were wide with surprise. Marina approached him, unsure of what she should do. She studied him for a moment and then embraced him. "Take care of my girl or I'll take care of you," she warned in classic Marina style. Dante smiled and assured her that she was safe with him.

Gemini burst into the room, unusually cheerful. "Hello, everyone. Sorry, I'm late," she said apologetically. Without a second thought, she shook hands with Marina. "Welcome to Taurus. We're always glad to have you as our guest," she remarked.

Mike was even more shocked. "Julian, what the hell are you giving her?" he asked, concerned. "That's not the Gemini I know."

Julian shook his head at Mike and replied, "Things have changed a lot since the early days."

The group conversed for a lengthy period of time. Gemini was quite generous with the drinks until Mike asked about procuring several cases of rum. Gemini stared him down and replied, "My kindness only goes so far, Colby."

Again, everyone laughed at him. "It didn't hurt to try," he answered humbly.

"We'll talk about that later," she commented.

Marina excused herself and asked Margot to join her. The two of them walked along the corridor that followed the circular perimeter of the station. "I sense that something is bothering you, Marina," Margot began the discussion.

Marina stopped and took her hands in hers. "Are you happy with Mr. Colby?"

"Of course," she replied. "Why do you ask?"

Marina released her hands and the two walked again. "You and I are alike in many ways," Marina explained. "When I assigned you to work with Colby, I never imagined the two of you would become inseparable."

"Neither did I but sometimes you feel a chemistry develop that tells you it's the right person." Then Margot stopped and gazed at Marina with a surprised expression. "Oh, my, Marina! You've fallen for someone!"

Marina smiled at her and denied it. "I'm tired of fighting and I'm tired of being alone. I'm serious about retiring after Kronos is defeated."

Margot's curiosity got the better of her and she inquired, "Does that someone know how you feel?"

Again, Marina smiled at her and responded, "It's hard to tell. I have Kat nipping at my heels but I don't feel the same way about her. When I first encountered Mike, I wondered if he might be the one. Unfortunately, I realized I'd kill him before we got too close."

Margot chuckled at the thought. "So, you saved him for me. Thanks, Marina," she teased.

"I guess time will tell. I don't know what I want other than peace," she confessed. "I've lost Britt and Faust. Those were big losses in my life. Maybe I just want a friendship or someone to be a sister to me."

Margot placed her arm around Marina's shoulders and assured her that she would always be there for her if she needed a sister. The women embraced and reached the end of their walk. They entered the conference room and joined their friends.

"What's next for you?" Mike asked Marina.

Marina thought for a moment and then replied, "I'm returning Kat to Yord to handle things there. Then I think I need to return to Archimedes-9 and spend some time with Kara before she does something crazy."

Ginna commented playfully, "It's too late, Marina. Kara has chosen her path as well."

Marina sighed and responded, "I guess no one needs an old, beat up rebel leader anymore."

"I'm available for the position!" Mike answered, anxious.

Marina and Margot glared at him. Marina pointed a finger at him. "Don't even think about it. You just worry about taking care of your wife. It's time for other people to take responsibility for the safety of the galaxy."

Mike looked disappointed and Margot elbowed him in his side. "We talked about this 'hero stuff' already," chided Margot. "Or did you forget?"

Mike groaned, while Marina winked at her in approval. Mike's captain, Tisch, beamed with pleasure, proud of how Margot changed Mike for the better.

Marina stood and looked at each of her friends as if it would be the last time. "It's been a pleasure spending time with all of you. I feel like you are my family." Each of the group hugged her and wished her well. When they finished their goodbyes, Major Tieg entered and offered to escort Marina to her ship. Marina glanced at them once more and left the room.

Before entering the transport bay, Marina encountered Zenith. "I hoped I'd see you before I left," Zenith said giddily.

"Yes, I wanted to thank you again for your help with the database," replied Marina. "No one else would have thought to uncover the programming behind it."

"I have to tell you; I think we can control the firing system of any Kronos craft around a ship using the program in the database to override each ship's existing one."

Marina knew the importance of an advantage like that and was elated. She embraced Zenith and praised her for being a special individual. She gave Zenith her signature code so she could contact her at any time. Zenith was ecstatic and promised to keep working on the database. The two hugged once more and Marina entered the transport bay. Zenith was sad to see Marina leave. She had hoped to learn so much from her about the technology used by Kronos in the war.

Marina boarded the *Reaper* and sat down in the main quarters. Kat entered from the flight deck and sat with her. "What's wrong?" she asked Marina.

Marina looked at her with sad eyes. "I fear that when the war is over, we will all go separate ways and never see each other again," she confessed. "I don't want to rule anywhere. I just want peace and happiness. Unfortunately, happiness doesn't seem to be in my destiny."

Kat reminded her that she has a connection with her and Ginna and Kara. She also reaffirmed that they have a unique power that binds them and protects them. Then Marina revealed that Ginna was involved with a nice young man. Kat was pleased by the news.

"Let's get to Yord before I change my mind," Marina instructed her. Kat patted her arm and then returned to the flight deck.

"I've been in touch with Marcus," Kat informed Marina. "Cheska arrived right after the Kronos armada departed the sector. She and Marcus are awaiting your orders."

Marina left the flight deck. Again, Kat was left wondering what was bothering her now. Marina sat in the main quarters and listed the possible targets that Kronos would likely attack by priority. Next, she considered the apparent losses that Kronos incurred, including their bases. Then, she listed the last locations of any Kronos forces and the time that elapsed since they were last spotted.

Kat joined her and inquired sarcastically, "You want to talk about it or should I leave you to your mood swing?"

"You can stay if you promise not to nag," Marina responded coldly.

Kat sat beside her and studied Marina's list for a moment. "See anything obvious?" she asked.

"I'm not sure," Marina answered, baffled. She explained to Kat that the Kronos armadas appeared to head in one general direction and then vanish. There wasn't anything out that way in terms of planets, stations, or outposts except for an asteroid field.

Kat agreed with her but then questioned her about why Kronos would focus all their forces in that region. She commented that it would leave their fifth base unprotected unless it was in that vicinity.

Marina brought up a star chart of the area and used the projector to display it on the wall. "If you were going to launch an attack from this region," she began, while pointing to the vacant region in front of the asteroid field, "what would you target?"

Kat studied the chart and inquired the location of Orpheus-2, Archimedes-9, and the former Kronos Base Three called Genesis in the Nigus star system on the map. When Marina pointed the location of each one, Kat stood and approached the image.

"Genesis is too far away to be a target," Kat mentioned. "Their armada would be detected long before they got there." She studied the other two locations and continued, "You'd have to know where their forces are gathering in relation to the asteroid field. That's a really big field. While Archimedes-9 and Orpheus-2 are both likely targets, there is no way of knowing which one would draw them into battle."

Frustrated, Marina decided that they would need to go out to the asteroid field and track down the amassing Kronos armadas. She was sure that Tarsus' forces combined with the Federation's would be able to handle an all-out attack by Kronos. Her concern was that Archimedes-9 could be attacked before she learned the location of the fifth base and organized a quick assault on it to put Kronos on the defensive.

The *Reaper* landed on Yord at the transport center. Marina and Kat took the short walk to the palace and were greeted by Marcus on the steps. After a friendly embrace with Kat, he led the two women into the palace. When they entered the conference room, Cheska and seven of the militia captains sat at the table, anxiously waiting for them.

Marina stood at the head of the table, while Kat and Marcus were together at the back of the room. Marina noticed Kat's giddiness with Marcus. She couldn't keep her hands off him. Marina wondered if she was that bad to be around that Kat would be so eager to be away from her.

Marina started the meeting by thanking all of them for their loyalty and support. Then she discussed Cheska's primary role in defending Yord. She informed Cheska that Zenith will be visiting in the near future and she should give her whatever support she requires. Cheska questioned the significance of Zenith's visit and why on Yord.

Marina was aware of the interest on the faces of the other militia commanders and was glad to see their concerns about winning this war. She revealed how the entire database was obtained by her assets on the freighter *Blue Eagle*. Then she revealed how one of the crew, Zenith, may have found out how to use the programming for Cheska's class four to disrupt the operation of other Kronos ships during an attack.

"When will this woman arrive," questioned one of the commanders. "It will be soon. Don't worry," she assured them.

Marina instructed Cheska that, when the battle starts, she will be summoned at some point, assuming Yord is not part of the Kronos attack. She emphasized that, should Yord be attacked, it was vital to protect it until help arrives.

"And what of us?" questioned Marcus from the back of the room.

Marina ordered them to take their forces to Archimedes-9 and stand by for further instructions. Again, one of the commanders questioned the logic of this. She informed them that there was a chance that they might learn the location of the fifth Kronos base and that all the Kronos forces could be amassed there in defense of their last base. If that occurs, then the militia forces could be deployed to that location. Everyone in the room was pleased with the progress Marina made and were eager to meet Zenith when she arrived. Marina cautioned them not to pressure Zenith as this was still a long shot.

Marcus questioned where Tarsus and his forces would be positioned. Marina replied, "Tarsus and his fleet should be at Orpheus-2 by now or at least on the way." She explained that between the forces of Tarsus, the Federation, and the militia, they could mount a significant stand against Kronos. "Orpheus-2 is the most likely target since that is the home of the Federation," she added.

Marina then reminded everyone that the closer they get to defeating Kronos, the more desperate they were likely to become. Marcus walked to the front of the room and asked the question that was on everyone's mind. "Are we close to defeating them?" he asked, eager to know if an end was in sight.

Marina explained that Kronos suffered significant losses but there was no way of knowing what their reserves are. Kronos was a well-funded organization with roots all over the universe and could have other assets that Marina and her people were not aware of. "This is the reason we are approaching the battle cautiously. I don't want our forces going into a trap and getting wiped out. The commanders nodded in appreciation of her concern for their welfare. Marina announced that Kat would be acting on her behalf and she would work with Marcus to handle things on Yord in her absence. There were no additional questions so Marina ended the briefing and departed the room.

Marcus and Kat followed her out of the palace to the transport center. Both wanted to know what Marina's immediate plans were in case she needed their help. Marina paused as she considered her next move. "I'm going out to the asteroid field to look around," she announced. "Something's not right about that region and I need to know what."

Kat and Marcus wished her safe travels and embraced her. Kat reminded her that she had a team; Kat herself, Ginna and Kara. She urged Marina to use them. Marina assured her that she would, but Kat knew her better than that. Marina reminded her that she also had Sara, Mike and Margot on her team as well and they have contributed significantly to her efforts.

Kat was reluctant to accept that as Marina was a lone wolf and hated to ask for help from anyone. Frustrated with her, Marina boarded her ship and departed Yord.

Marcus expressed his concern for Marina's safety but Kat assured him that she had a plan of her own, involving Kara and Ginna. She felt bad, knowing that they parted in bad spirits and might not see each other again.

CHAPTER 10

Marina was obsessed with Kronos' possible plan of attack. She knew the organization was not one to sit back and let her forces keep winning. She recalled all her recent conversations with Mike Colby and Margot, Zenith, Julian, Rebecca and Tarsus. Then she thought about her main sources of information, Korick and Kellen at Murgatroyd's Oasis on the planet Zim. That might be a good place to start so she changed course and flew to Zim.

When she approached, she decided to be secretive about her visit. She requested the last bay from the transport supervisor to perform ship maintenance. For identification, she used Margot's identification and mentioned that she was traveling alone on business. The supervisor granted her permission to dock, but he informed Stosh and Kellen about the arrival. Since the supervisor knew of Margot from her visit with Colby when Borath attacked them, he thought it strange that she would return alone.

Marina exited her ship with a hooded cloak covering her face and concealing the daggers, strapped to her thighs. Kellen arrived at the personnel hatch to the bay and intercepted Marina when she exited the bay.

"So, you are Margot today," Kellen quipped.

Marina lifted the hood enough so he could see her face. "Sorry for the secrecy. Can we talk in private?" she requested.

Kellen glanced back and forth, searching the corridor for any prying eyes, but no one was in sight. There were several empty bays between the bay with Marina's ship and the next craft so no one ventured down that end of the corridor. He led her to a service elevator which took them to the third floor.

"I didn't know you had a third floor," Marina commented.

"Few people do," he replied. "It's good for situations such as this."

Marina and Kellen left the elevator and entered a long corridor. They passed several doors that appeared to be maintenance shops. At the end of the corridor was a steel door with a sign marked 'Hazardous Materials'. Kellen mentioned that the sign gave validity to the steel door whereas the other doors were standard wooden doors and frames.

Kellen used a key to open the door and then stepped aside, allowing Marina to enter. Once inside, he secured the door and turned on the lights. The room was very elaborate with expensive carpeting and furniture. A state-of-the-art communication console was located in the corner and a well-stocked bar with glasses and accessories lined the back wall.

Marina scanned the room and was impressed. "I see the black market business is booming," she kidded.

"Thanks to your friend Colby, life has been good for me."

Kellen gestured for her to sit by his desk. The chairs were padded and covered with fine velvet material – another indication that business was good. Marina sat and commented, "Colby has been good for a lot of us. He is one of a kind."

Kellen walked to the bar, still wondering what Marina really wanted. He poured two glasses of bourbon and returned to his desk with the bottle tucked under his arm and the glasses in his hands. He handed one to Marina and then sat down. "After the incident with Borath, I thought we lost him," Kellen mentioned in a somber tone. "He's a tough son of a bitch, though."

The two raised their glasses for a toast to Mike and Margot for their bravery. They tapped glasses and sipped. "So, what can I do for you?" Kellen asked, curious.

"I'm not sure if I need advice or information," she responded, unsure of herself.

"Well, let's talk," he suggested. "Being a good listener is an important part of my business."

Marina began by detailing her thoughts on a possible Kronos attack since they were down to a single base. She explained how she was positioning her forces in anticipation of an attack. What bothered her was that it was too predictable; too easy. Kellen believed it was a good defensive strategy but agreed that something else could be in play. He inquired what else was bothering her.

Marina admitted that she was feeling the loneliness of her role. She was always a loner but it was easy when she was reclusive. Now that she was interacting with friends and allies, it was much tougher. There were too many injuries and deaths over the years by people who believed in her and were willing to die for her cause. Kellen confessed that he often felt that way as he watched friends come and go with no farewell or concern for their missions.

Then Marina admitted the one thing that surprised him. She missed the opportunity to be in love with someone. Kellen kidded that no one would take a chance on her because she would kill them, just like a black widow spider kills its mate. Marina didn't respond, which bothered him. He asked if there was someone out there that she longed for.

Marina related how she felt when she lost Britt, only to find out that he was leaving her anyway. She talked about Faust and how he made her feel alive at times, but it wasn't love. When she revealed how she and Kat became involved, Kellen was shocked. He hadn't known anyone to overcome Kat's back magic and still lead a normal life.

"You think I'm normal?" she kidded. "I'm a wreck."

"How do you feel about Kat?" he asked, curious.

Marina told him about how she treated Kat just like Kat treated her when they first met. She was surprised that Kat allowed her to abuse her in that way but it helped Kat to realize what she did to her. Now, they are like sisters. Marina was happy that Kat found Marcus but now she had no partner. At one time, she thought Margot and Jonas would be good to have as her crew, but then the mission demanded that she give them to Colby.

Kellen chuckled at the idea. "So, you were the matchmaker that tamed Major Colby, the lion of Special Forces," he teased.

"Yeah, I guess I was," she answered sadly. "I never thought Margot would fall in love with him."

"Do you have a preference for a male or female to fall in love with?" he questioned her, wary that he tread on dangerous ground.

Marina laughed at him. "For some reason, I knew that question would come up," she replied. "I don't know. I've experienced a female relationship with Kat; male relationships with Britt and Faust. I think I just want someone who can love me for who I am."

Kellen finished his drink and poured another. He noted that Marina hadn't finished hers. That was rare. "I've seen many friends here at the pub get into relationships with men and women who were from different backgrounds," he commented and sipped from his drink. "Sometimes one of the two was from a murderous group while the other was strictly the looting type. Those types of opposites in relationships usually don't last. It's more of an ideology at that point that will never change. Other things are less subtle and flexible."

Marina finally sipped from her drink and inquired, "What kind of relationships do work?"

Kellen sighed as he recalled some of his memories and experiences. He suggested that Marina find someone who has felt the same pain as her. Someone who is looking for the same feeling from their partner as she is. Marina agreed as she wondered who might fit that description. "Perhaps," she thought aloud, "I don't need romance. Perhaps I just need someone to be there for me and understand me."

Kellen raised his glass for another toast. "I think you've got it, Marina," he replied. Marina forced a smile and tapped glasses with him. They traded stories that occurred since Kronos came about over drinks until the bottle was empty. Marina announced that it was time to go. She thanked Kellen and allowed him to escort her back to her ship.

"I hope you find what you're looking for, Marina."

"So do I," she replied. "You helped me gain some understanding about myself. Thank you for that." She boarded her ship and closed the hatch.

Kellen left the bay and closed the personnel hatch. He feared that Marina was giving up on life and her purpose. Maybe all she needed was a friend. Shaking his head at the idea that anyone would take his advice, he returned to the pub.

Marina took her seat on the flight deck and thought about their conversation. Suddenly, she burst into tears. "Life really sucks!" she shouted out loud and started her ship. After requesting clearance for departure from the transport supervisor, she waited for what seemed eternity before the gates opened and she exited into space.

Darra piloted her schooner toward the Aegis asteroid field at the edge of the sector. She assumed that she would be safe there until she heard from any of her contacts. Surely someone must want to collect on Marina's bounty. Then she remembered that the bounty on her head was quite sizeable as well. "That shitbag Klingman is gonna pay for this," she grumbled to herself. "How the hell can I get my job done with a marker on my head?"

Maneuvering through the asteroid field to the other side, she noticed a significant amount of debris in the distance. "What the hell happened out here?" she exclaimed as she recognized the wreckage of several Kronos cruisers. Suddenly, she was surrounded by five Kronos cruisers that were hidden behind asteroids. Her transmitter beeped for an incoming transmission. She knew it was going to be a bad day, but she acknowledged the signal anyway.

"What?" she responded, feeling irritable.

"How did I know it was you, Darra?" asked a familiar voice.

Darra placed her hand on her forehead and she shook her head. "Well, Commander Zhi, you are the last person I expected to hear from," she replied, buying time to talk her way out of an execution. "I understand you lost a few command ships."

"Yes, especially one named the *Imperius* with a good friend of mine on board - Commander Horan. I'm sure you knew him personally," he mentioned.

"Let's cut the shit, Zhi. I'm a busy person," commented Darra. What do you want?"

"You will come aboard my ship for some quality time or you will be destroyed," he warned. "Is that a problem?"

Darra agreed to meet with him, knowing she could be killed. Unfortunately, she had no other alternative. She was transported onto the flight deck of the command ship *Chaos Reigns*. Ten sentries surrounded her with pulse rifles targeting her body.

"Disrobe," Zhi ordered her.

"What?" blurted Darra. "I'm not disrobing in front of these perverts!"

Zhi nodded to one of the men. The sentry fired a pulse into Darra's knee. She fell to the floor grasping at the knee in agony. "Why do I have to disrobe?" she asked, tears streaming down her cheeks.

"Because I can't trust you," Zhi responded. "You are responsible for the loss of several command ships and cruisers as well as all the lives that were lost on board those ships."

Darra reluctantly stripped down to her sports bra and panties. The men chuckled as they ogled her body. She shouted at them to shut up several times.

"Did you ever find Marina?" Zhi questioned her.

"What does she have to do with this?" she countered.

"It seems that you were paid handsomely for disposing of her. Unfortunately, she must have returned from the dead because she boarded my ship, killed my officers and then turned our weaponry on two other command ships; all this while we were invading Calamaar. Now, how can that be?"

Darra became desperate for a way out but there was no place to run. Zhi asked her about playing games and if she enjoyed them. "I hate games," she responded. "I'm a straight to the point kind of person."

"Good," Zhi responded. "I like that."

Zhi instructed his team of six men and four women to take Darra to the break room behind the control room and make a snack out of her. One of the men rammed the butt of his pulse rifle into the back of her head and knocked her down. The men dragged her into the break room where the women bound her wrists and tied her ankles to the vertical water pipes along the wall with thin cord. When she struggled, the cords cut into her skin and left her moaning in pain. The sentries tore off her bra and panties and then raped her over and over. The women were especially rough on her and took much more pleasure in using her than the men.

On the flight deck, Commander Zhi enjoyed the sounds of Darra grunting each time she was violated. Darra's sounds soon grew faint until she passed out. Bored, Zhi raised Carl Klingman on the monitor and informed him that Darra was being dealt with. Carl requested images of her being abused to ease his anger toward her. The two men laughed and then discussed any changes to their plans.

Zhi was pleased to hear that Tarsus would not engage his forces in the battle but questioned what other allies Marina might have. Carl mentioned that her alien allies had been disposed of and the rebel base on Ramses-3 was destroyed, prior to Marina's interference. When the transmission ended, Zhi summoned the leader of the sentries from the break room.

"I'd like you to take our little play toy to her cell and secure her in an appropriate position so that others on board may enjoy her treasures," Zhi instructed. The man assured Zhi that she would be given the care she deserves.

When the sentries dragged Darra's nude body past Zhi, he kicked her in the lower back as hard as he could. Another grunt from her indicated the pain she felt, even unconscious. Zhi then summoned his demolition officer and ordered him to rig Darra's ship to explode with a proximity sensor as a detonator. "When she passes the range of our long-range sensors, I want her to feel her freedom briefly before she joins Horan in the afterlife," Zhi informed him. The officer was eager to comply and departed the flight deck. No one ever liked Darra and everyone suspected she was screwing someone, maybe even Carl Klingman himself, to get away with the disrespect and arrogance that she did.

The *Blue Eagle* arrived on Yord and docked at the transport center. Tisch accompanied Zenith into the palace to meet with Marcus. Zenith carried a laptop computer while Tisch carried the interface components. They were met at the top of the palace steps by two militia guards who refused to admit them until Marcus came to vouch for them. Both recalled what happened to the last sentry who revealed too much to a stranger in front of Marcus and took no chances.

Marcus appeared in the lobby and invited the two women inside. "Welcome, ladies. I was told by Marina to expect a visit from you," he announced.

Zenith immediately mentioned that she needed to inspect the computer system on the class four Kronos freighter. Cheska entered the lobby and Zenith immediately sensed that she was apprehensive about sharing 'her' ship with a stranger. After Marcus did the introductions, they proceeded to the conference room.

Tisch was content to be Zenith's watchdog. She'd say little but observe Cheska and Marcus for any suspicious behavior. Zenith wanted to establish her credibility right away, knowing that Marcus was in charge of the militia forces on Yord and Cheska was the rebel leader on Ramses-3 before the

Kronos attack. Ironically, Marcus seemed to do the same, watching Tisch and Zenith carefully.

"How much do you know about the ship's control system?" Zenith questioned Cheska.

"I haven't spent much time with it, if that's what you're asking," she replied. "What is it that you are looking for?"

Zenith related how they stole the entire database off Kronos Base Three in the Nigus star system. Both Marcus and Cheska laughed at the idea that someone could do that. She continued to explain how the bases interact with their fighting ships.

"So, you think that the base can control all their fighting ships in a crisis?" questioned Cheska.

"Only within a limited range, Zenith responded. "It's a self-defense program buried in the database as a fail-safe in an emergency situation."

Now Marcus was interested. "You're telling me that you were actually on a Kronos base?" he inquired.

"I went there with Mike Colby and his partner Margot," Zenith announced confidently. "They secured the area and freed Lieutenant Tieg's men from the prison. It is now a trade station called Genesis and it's protected by the Federation."

Marcus quickly debated the fact that Tieg was a Major on Taurus and had never been to the Nigus star system. Zenith informed him that the Lieutenant was Major Tieg's younger brother and that the Major had, in fact, been to Nigus in support of the takeover of Base Three.

"I need to look at the programming on the freighter to see if we can alter its weapons systems and possibly turn the ships on each other," Zenith concluded. Marcus was impressed with the possibility and requested that Cheska take them to the ship right away. The four of them left the palace for the freighter, docked behind the transportation center.

"Forgive me if I doubt your story, Zenith," Cheska commented. "You realize how insane this sounds."

Zenith informed her that she had a test in mind to prove her theory if the ship's database held a mating program to interface with the base's program. Tisch helped her set up the lap top and interface devices. Also connected were several data drives to copy the ship's database, which was significantly smaller than the base's database that she downloaded previously. After several hours, Cheska grew impatient and left them to tend to other duties.

Marcus pulled up a chair and spoke with Tisch about her interactions with Marina. He then revealed that he was more interested in Mike Colby and his successes against Kronos for Marina. Tisch explained that Colby was an enigma, not to be understood by the sane mind. Marcus kidded that Colby sounds a lot like Marina. She, too, was an enigma of sorts.

When Zenith finally finished her analysis of the database program, she informed Marcus that they were ready to run a test. He summoned Cheska to the flight deck for test instructions from Zenith. Tisch gave Zenith a careful glance, wondering if this could work. Zenith nodded to her with a smile, eager to prove herself to them.

Cheska returned to the flight deck with her arms folded. "Is this going to take long? It's getting quite late," she complained.

Zenith requested Marcus to handle the communications between them. After packing up her gear, she and Tisch returned to the *Blue Eagle* in the transport center, leaving Cheska annoyed and impatient.

Tisch established communication with Marcus and relayed Zenith's instructions. First, Zenith instructed Cheska to pick her target on the mountain and operate the weapons system. After Cheska targeted a point on the mountain, Zenith operated and repositioned the same cannons that Cheska positioned, but from the *Blue Eagle*. Then she had Tisch send Cheska the order to reposition her cannon once more and fire on her selected target. Not only was Zenith able to block Cheska from firing, she was able to select her own target on another mountain and fire at it.

On board the Kronos freighter, Marcus was ecstatic. Cheska immediately tried to reposition another cannon but, like a game of chess, Zenith countered every move. Finally, she gave up. "The bitch did it!" she shouted excitedly. "I don't believe it!"

Marcus requested that Zenith and Tisch return to the freighter to discuss the results. Tisch and Zenith jumped up and down excitedly and then embraced. Zenith became teary-eyed and thanked Tisch for believing in her.

"You're my partner," Tisch reminded her. "If I didn't believe in you, you would still be cooking and piloting." The two women hugged again and returned to the Kronos ship.

When they boarded the class four freighter, they were surprised to see Kat standing next to Marcus and Cheska. Kat commented, "I understand we have good news to give to Marina."

Zenith was wary of being too presumptuous and explained that she still had a few more tests to run. Marcus mentioned that what she did already was incredible and was worth passing along to Marina. "What are these other tests you need to run?" questioned Kat.

Zenith detailed how the programs have other capabilities and she needed to be sure that their remote operation couldn't be over-ridden. Kat agreed but was eager to let Marina know of her progress.

Marcus suggested that they wait until morning to continue, but Zenith was anxious to learn more. She reattached her equipment to the freighter's control system and opened a notebook to record her results. Cheska warned Zenith not to screw up her ship during the night and then followed Marcus off the ship. Marcus assigned two militia sentries to stand guard at the hatch while Zenith worked. Tisch stayed with her but fatigue took over and she slept in the captain's chair.

When morning came, Zenith was still hard at work but inside the *Blue Eagle* now. With her equipment set up on the table in the center of the flight deck, she jotted down several notes. Tisch slept soundly, still on the flight deck of the Kronos freighter. Seeing the hatch open and no one watching, Marcus and Kat boarded the *Blue Eagle*.

"Good morning, Zenith," said Kat, amazed that Zenith was still working. "Have you been at this all night?"

Zenith looked perplexed and asked, "Is it morning already?"

"Sure is."

Kat and Marcus sat across from her, anxious to hear what she accomplished. Zenith held up a finger for them to wait before asking questions. She closed the notebook and powered up her laptop and interface components.

Zenith questioned Marcus about Cheska's defensive nature and her obsession that the freighter was hers. Marcus related how a friend told him that Cheska was on Ramses-3 when Kronos attacked them. He mentioned that Marina believed that a tracking device on board the ship was to blame, but it was never found.

Kat grew curious over Marcus' story and inquired who his friend was and where he heard about Ramses-3 from. Marcus, sensing that something was amiss, replied that one of Tarsus' men heard Tarsus speak of it. "Why?" he asked. "Is something wrong?"

"Very wrong," answered Kat. "There is no way Tarsus should have known about Ramses-3. Can you check with your friend and verify his information?"

Marcus promptly sent a message from his wrist transmitter. "He'll respond eventually."

Pleased with herself, Zenith faced them with a big smile on her face and planted her hands on her lap. "If this works, we will be able to control either the base's defense systems or any Kronos ship's main control system, including power distribution and environmental life support," she announced.

"What do you need from us?" questioned Marcus.

Zenith asked them to stand at the hatch and watch the freighter. Marcus stepped outside the hatch while Kat remained at the table. Zenith typed like a mad woman on the laptop with the focus of an eagle on its prey.

Marcus was unsure what to expect from the test and stared in the direction of the freighter. Suddenly, the ship ascended off the ground and hovered. "Did you do that, Zenith?" Marcus shouted from outside the ship.

"Yes, I did. Now keep watching," she instructed him.

The ship glided to the front of the palace. With the hatch open on the freighter, Tisch awoke and now stood in the entrance, horrified. "What's going on?" she shouted.

Marcus, not knowing what to say, gave her a thumbs up that all was okay. Tisch shook her head at him and stepped away. Cheska stepped out of the palace and was mortified. She rushed to the transportation center and approached Marcus. "Who's flying my ship?" she yelled.

Marcus couldn't take his eyes off the hovering ship. "I'm really not sure," he answered, still amazed.

Cheska stormed onto the *Blue Eagle* and grew frantic when she saw Zenith sitting at the table. "Who's flying the ship?"

Zenith grinned sheepishly and replied, "I am." She then brought the command ship back to its original location and shut it down. Tisch charged off the ship to the transportation center and approached the *Blue Eagle*. She wasn't sure if she should be pleased or upset with Zenith's test. All she could think was *What if it failed with her on board?* When she stepped on board her ship, Kat and Marcus embraced Zenith and the three jumped up and down like children. Cheska actually smiled for once while Tisch flopped into a chair, relieved to be back on board her own ship.

Kat stepped back with folded arms and a big smile. She inquired, "Can I tell Marina that you can take control of any Kronos ship, including its vital systems from a remote location?"

"Well, that's not exactly true," she replied. "Watch outside the hatch again."

Marcus, Kat, Tisch and Cheska stood by the open hatch of the *Blue Eagle*, eager to see what Zenith would do next. Zenith initiated the program and again typed like a mad woman. Suddenly, the *Blue Eagle's* systems came to life and ran their diagnostic checks.

"What are you doing, Zee?" asked Tisch nervously.

Zenith was oblivious to her question and continued to operate the laptop. This time, not only did the freighter rise again, but the *Blue Eagle* did as well.

"Holy shit!" blurted Marcus.

"I don't friggin' believe it," added Cheska.

Tisch was a nervous wreck over Zenith's operation of the *Blue Eagle* from a laptop. "Please set our ship down, Zee," pleaded Tisch. "I'm gonna wet myself."

Beaming, Zenith set both ships down and placed them in cold shutdown. She looked up at the others and asked, "Well? What do you think?"

Kat was wide-eyed with surprise but tried to contain her excitement. She inquired, "You can operate multiple ships from a remote location?"

"Of course, I can," answered Zee proudly. "That's what the Kronos bases do in the event of an onslaught. The program is designed to maximize the use of their forces. It takes away the human factor in controlling their ships." She further explained that when enemy ships enter the base's defense perimeter, the base takes over control of all its ships and uses them in the most efficient manner possible.

Cheska laughed and remarked, "I'll bet all those ship commanders love that."

Everyone high-fived Zenith and then hugged her once more. Cheska apologized for doubting her and promised her a drink later. Kat promptly went to the communication console on the flight deck and sent a message to Marina.

Cheska expression suddenly turned grim. Marcus noticed and asked, "What's wrong?"

"If the base can take control of the ship, then we can't use this ship to attack Base Five or any other Kronos facility that uses this program for self-defense." Everyone turned to Zenith for her response.

"Not a problem," she responded confidently. "All I have to do is remove a single circuit card from the back of the main console. That is the only point of contact the ship's control systems have with the base."

"And what about the weapons systems?" asked Marcus.

"Same thing," Zenith assured them. "With this program, we can simulate being the ship or the base."

Cheska asked Zenith to remove the circuit card immediately to prevent Kronos from taking her ship away from her. Zenith promptly complied and then hurried off the *Blue Eagle*. She was eager to fulfill her task on the freighter and get back to business on the trade routes.

Tisch thanked Marcus, Kat and Cheska for their hospitality and announced that it was time for her and Zenith to leave. When Zenith returned, she handed the circuit card to Cheska. "Here's your link to freedom," she kidded.

Marcus and Kat exited the ship but Cheska paused at the hatch. "Something wrong?" questioned Tisch.

"Yes, as a matter of fact," she replied and approached Zenith. "Is it possible you can give me a copy of that program in case I need to use it in combat?"

Zenith patted her arm and replied, "It's already installed with a backup data-pak on a shelf inside the main console. When you access it, there's a short tutorial I placed in the main menu to guide you."

Cheska placed her hand on her hips and smiled at Zenith, "You are truly an amazing young lady." With that, Cheska exited the ship.

"Time to hit the road Captain Mallory," announced Zenith.

Tisch was proud of her partner and replied, "Yes, it is. Let's head to Taurus and pick up the rest of our crew."

The *Blue Eagle* went through its startup diagnostics, fired up its engines and departed Yord. The first thing Zenith questioned Tisch about was their possible involvement in the war like Colby was involved. Tisch explained in simple terms that Zenith did her job and gave Marina's forces a valuable weapon to use against Kronos. Now, it's up to them what they do with it. Zenith was pleased to know that they were back to business as usual. Tisch informed her that they would head out to Terran for another long-distance haul of cargo after their stop on Taurus.

Kat, Marcus and Cheska ascended the steps to the palace entrance when Marcus received a response from his contact about Tarsus and Ramses-3. Marcus paused and turned somber.

"My friend confirmed that Tarsus did know that Ramses-3 was the secret staging base for the rebels and had often bragged that he knew enough to run the war without Marina."

Cheska became enraged and shouted, "That son of a bitch sold us out!"

Marcus urged her to remain calm until they speak with Marina about it. Kat suggested that he contact her immediately, knowing that Tarsus was responsible for an important part of her fighting force. While awaiting Marina's response, Marcus sent a message to General Lennox and warned her that Tarsus may have turned. He also mentioned that Tarsus might have been the leak that compromised the rebel base on Ramses-3.

Marina set her cruiser on autopilot and drifted off into a deep sleep. She had several hours to kill before reaching the Aegis asteroid field. She thought about Kellen's question to her regarding someone in particular that she should have for a partner. Britt was always resistant to her and never supported her decisions. Faust was always reserved and respectful of her because of her royal lineage, although he was accommodating. Kat will always be the bitchy sister that she loved to butt heads with. She thought about how happy she was on Terran with Margot, Sara and the others from the *Blue Eagle*. Then she recalled her conversations with Sara.

Sara seemed to understand her responsibility and shared the same thoughts on war. Sara was battle tested and paid for her loyalty with her near death experience at the hands of the mercenaries on Taurus and one less finger to go with it. Marina wondered if the two of them would be good for each other. Perhaps, after the war, she would speak with her. Maybe the two of them could enjoy retirement together as friends.

The transmitter beeped, and stirred her from her sleep. She acknowledged two signals: one from Marcus and one from Kat - both messages only. Because of the distance, she could only receive texts to read with no voice or video. She was stunned when the message revealed that Tarsus could be responsible for the attack on Ramses-3. Now she understood why the Kronos invaders didn't find the freighter hidden on Ramses-3. There was no tracker; only a mole to spill the base's location.

Then she read Kat's message about Zenith's progress and was elated. She thanked both for the updates and promised to address the issue with Tarsus at the right time. After ending her responses, she punched the console panel and shouted, "That son of a bitch! I should have known he was a coward." Marina considered how she would deal with Tarsus. Killing him would be too easy. She would humiliate him on front of his peers for being a traitor and then perhaps a public display of corporal punishment to make him beg for mercy.

Now Marina had to consider that Tarsus would likely not bring his forces to Orpheus-2, leaving them short-handed. She thought about who else she could count on for help. Golgar's forces were severely limited after Kronos' attack on them. Colby was likely on his way back to Terran in the Nigus star system on the *Blue Eagle*, in keeping with their schedule. Then she recalled that the Scrat (alien) forces committed to supporting her against Kronos. Using the signature coordinates that Colby sent to her earlier for just this kind of situation, she attempted to contact Creeg the Scrat commander several times but received no response.

Disappointed, she closed her eyes and drifted back to sleep. She soon found herself floating in the clouds, lost and disoriented. The faces of Ginna and Kara appeared in front of her, followed by Kat's face. Kara chastised her for not using them to help her. Ginna then warned her that she was heading into danger and should turn back. Marina rebuffed the girls' ability to see things based on destiny and assured them that she was fine. Now Kat grew impatient with her and informed her that they were taking control of the situation since Marina wasn't capable of it any more.

"What do you mean by that?" Marina countered, growing irritable.

"We will look after you," Kat informed her. "You are no longer able to look after yourself, so we will take charge."

"No you won't!" Marina shouted. Then she felt smothered and gasped. She opened her eyes, covered in sweat and saw the asteroid field ahead of her. "What the hell kind of dream was that?" she uttered, feeling disoriented.

Kat's voice in her head brought her to realize this wasn't a dream. "Marina, we are your reign of power," Kat reminded her. "Don't ignore us."

Marina screamed in frustration and focused on the asteroid field ahead of her. The field was dense with the smaller rocks being the more dangerous. She knew that this would take patience as the field was one of the biggest in the quadrant and also the most dangerous.

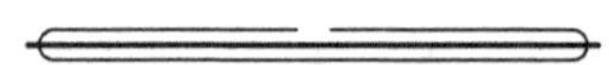

On Polaris, Carl Klingman briefed his staff of ten men and women in their conference room that no one was to send or receive any transmissions from outside the base. One of the men informed him that they just received an update from Fleet regarding their defensive capabilities. They were not aware that the drones were on the way with the upgraded soldiers.

Carl rolled his eyes and smacked his forehead. "You stupid, friggin' idiot!" he shouted. "You know why we are here!"

"But, sir, it's an authorized communication," the man attempted to plead his case.

Carl took his pulse pistol from his holster and shot the man in the face, killing him instantly. He went on to explain that one communication, if intercepted, could give away their location. "We are in battle mode!" he continued to rant. "You all know the protocol for this." Carl stormed out of the room and met Tessara in the corridor.

The two briefly discussed what happened in the conference room. Tessara suggested that they leave for a safer location as a precaution. Carl agreed as Marina and the Federation were getting too close for comfort. He and Tessara discussed consolidating their forces to take over one strategic target while relinquishing their remaining base. The two concluded that Archimedes-9 was the best target to acquire because of its location. It would cripple the long-distance trade routes and put pressure on Marina's forces to offer a truce. In addition, the Federation and rebels were unlikely to launch a full-scale attack in defense of Archimedes-9 because of the civilian population.

Tessara contacted Dr. Stylus and instructed her to direct the drones to Archimedes-9 immediately. Carl's team was assembled on board his ship and they departed Polaris for Tandenar in the Nigus star system. It would be a long journey but a safe one. Carl reminded Tessara that he had an ally there, who could provide sanctuary while they regroup. On Kronos Base Five, the drones were dispatched with the cyborgs and now the war had begun.

CHAPTER 11

Darra lay on the floor of her cell naked. She was badly beaten and violated so many times that she lost count. One thing about Kronos people: they don't like traitors. Darra's only mistake in her mind was failing to kill Marina and she paid a heavy price for it. She wondered if she should have left her revenge for her sisters' deaths alone and focused on her life working with Kronos. She had it all and now she had nothing; not even her dignity.

Two more soldiers entered her cell and violated her. In a desperation move, she grabbed the pulse pistol from one man's holster as he penetrated her over and over. Before she could fire, the second man punched her in the face and knocked her out. Her hell would continue for who knows how long.

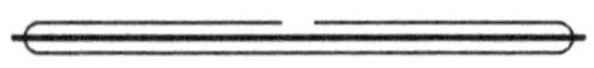

On Yord, Kat sat in the palace garden with Marcus. She felt Ginna and Kara reaching out to her from their locations. Marcus noticed that Kat's eyes changed to white and knew not to interrupt. Kat informed the girls that Marina needed allies to protect her. Then Ginna warned that Marina would be captured by her enemies in the asteroid field. Kara then revealed that their enemies would come to Archimedes-9. Kat informed them that she would make arrangements to protect Marina.

Kat's eyes returned to normal, much to Marcus' relief. She briefed him on the girls' concerns and that she needed to contact some people. She advised Marcus that Cheska needed to go to Archimedes-9. Marcus agreed with her assessment and entered the palace.

Kat pondered how Marina would be captured in an asteroid field but then realized that the field may be the hiding place for the Kronos armada. She entered the palace and went to the communication room. The officer had just come on duty and was surprised by Kat's visit. Kat instructed him to contact General Lennox, while she waited.

Kat paced as she wondered about Marina's allies. When General Lennox responded, Kat questioned her about the Scrat (alien) forces and if they would help Marina. Lennox mentioned that they had new leadership but she would request their help. Kat explained that Marina suspected something in the asteroid field and flew out to investigate. She revealed that Marina could be heading into the middle of Kronos' armada and that Archimedes-9 was likely going to be their primary target. Lennox found that to be illogical as Orpheus-2 was the more likely target, but would contact the Scrat leadership anyway, as a courtesy to Marina. The transmission ended and Kat cussed. "Why does that woman have to be so damn complicated? She's as bad as Marina!" she complained and then left the office.

Marcus met her in the lobby and inquired what her next move was. Kat revealed that she had to get in touch with Golgar on Calamaar and request his support. Marcus understood and kissed her cheek. "Please be careful, Kat," he urged. "I don't want to lose you."

Kat embraced him, hungry for his affection. "We have some time, my love," she commented. "How about we make use of it?"

Marcus smiled and escorted her up the stairs to her bedroom.

Marina carefully glided the *Reaper* through the asteroid field. While navigating her way through, she contacted General Lennox at Orpheus-2 to discuss her suspicions about a Kronos attack. Suddenly, Marina saw the wreckage of numerous Kronos ships.

"Holy shit, Sandra!" blurted Marina. "You should see this! It looks like a graveyard of Kronos vessels."

"What kind of vessels?" inquired Lennox, sensing the importance of this discovery.

Marina identified debris from command ships, cruisers, freighters, and assault craft. When she reported those to Lennox, there was a brief silence. "What is it, Sandra?"

Lennox finally replied, "Kronos attempted to steal our portal technology. We baited them into taking components that didn't work."

"And they lost a whole fleet over that?"

"Perhaps. Can you get me the names of any of those ships?" Lennox requested. "Then I can answer your question with certainty."

Marina searched until she noticed the name on one of the cruisers, the *Apocalypse*. When she relayed the name to Lennox, she heard a joyful howl through the speaker. "What the hell was that?" Marina asked, curious.

"That was a very big part of the Kronos fleet!" exclaimed Lennox. "I can't believe they fell for our trap."

Marina navigated through the last of the debris and exited the asteroid field. She was suddenly surrounded by Kronos vessels with their cannons trained on her. "Oh, shit," she muttered. "Sandra, we have a problem. There is another Kronos fleet out here and they look pissed at me."

General Lennox started to respond but then the transmission was interrupted. One of the Kronos ships jammed her communication with Marina. The transmitter beeped and Marina breathed a sigh of relief. "At least they are giving me a chance to speak with them," she uttered and acknowledged the incoming signal.

"Yes, dear," she answered cynically.

"Well, this is a pleasant surprise, Marina. It's commander Zhi."

"How are you, commander?" she asked, surprised to hear his voice. "It's been a while."

"You gave me a chance and thanks to your friend Tarsus, I am free once more," he commented.

Marina realized that Tarsus was more of a problem than she originally thought, but that was a problem for another day. "And now you have a chance to pay me back for what I did to your forces on Calamaar. Isn't that ironic?" she kidded.

"I am sending four of my men to commandeer your ship," he informed her. "You will transport on board my ship and we will discuss your payback further. Otherwise, we will destroy you and your ship." Having no other options, Marina agreed.

On the planet Terran in the Nigus star system, Sara studied the long-range sensor images and noticed a small ship heading to Tandenar, a planet not far from them. "Now, I wonder who that can be?" she muttered to herself. Suddenly, she felt a sharp pain in her head. Then she heard a conversation between three women. "I'm losing my mind," she blurted and got up from her seat.

One of the voices spoke to her and said, "Sara, this is Kat. My Seers are also channeling you."

Sara went to the balcony and leaned on the railing, looking many stories down into the valley. She feared that she lost her mind and hoped the voices would stop. Kat continued, "Marina needs your help. She has been captured in or near the Aegis asteroid field."

Now she had Sara's attention. "What can I do?" she asked, curious to hear Kat's response, if it was real.

Kat instructed her to contact the Scrat leader and request his help in rescuing Marina. Ginna added that Sara was to negotiate only and not attack the Kronos fleet. Baffled, Sara questioned the move. Now Kara joined in and explained that sometimes things aren't always what they seem. Kat expressed her confidence in Sara and the communication ended.

Sara's boss Jackson entered the office and grew concerned, seeing Sara looking down from the balcony. "Are you alright?" he asked.

Sara shook her head and related what she just experienced. Jackson urged her to sit down and relax. "What should I do?" she asked, hoping for sane advice.

"Do you believe that your experience was real?" he questioned her.

"I think so," she answered, reluctant to admit it felt real.

Jackson suggested that she contact her friend Rebecca on Archimedes-9 and verify that Marina was, in fact, taken. If so, then her experience was likely to be real. He offered to stay with her until she figured out her next move, but she needed to be alone. Marina was her friend and, if she was in danger, Sara was going to do what she could to help.

When Marina arrived on the bridge of the command ship, Commander Zhi waited with two glasses of bourbon, while seated by his console. "Welcome aboard, Marina," he greeted her calmly. "This is much better than your way."

Marina graciously accepted the drink and took a seat near Zhi. "Why the courtesy, Commander? I thought for sure you'd be anxious to kill me like everyone else, even my own people."

"You mean like Tarsus?" he asked, curious.

"Yes, like that piece of excrement," she responded. "You know, I was just about retired and out of the war business when some of your boys paid me a visit on my little planet and then blew it up."

"That must have been Darra's little coup," he commented. "Seems that she burned bridges with everyone, including Kronos since then." He finished his drink and gestured for her to follow him to the elevator. They descended several floors and then exited into a corridor.

"So, what is it you want from me?" Marina asked, wondering why the hospitality.

Commander Zhi leaned into a retinal scanner and a thick steel door unlatched, allowing them to enter. Marina recognized the section as the ship's brig, lined with solid doors on one side of the corridor and bars on the other side.

"Found me a new home?" Marina quipped.

"Hardly," responded Zhi. "I have too much respect for you."

They stopped in front of a barred door to a cell where Darra lay on the floor. She was a mere shell of her former self. Nude and dirty, her eyes displayed her hope for death to come soon. "An old acquaintance of yours, I thought you'd like to see," Zhi commented.

Marina stared at her, shocked by her condition. "That's Darra?" she asked, mortified.

"Yes, it is," he answered, savoring Darra's misery. "She is paying for what she did to my friend Commander Horan."

Darra heard her voice and struggled to look up at her. When she did, she pleaded, barely audible, "Kill me, please."

Marina inquired as to what his plans were for Darra. Zhi suggested that she decide what to do with Darra since the two were sworn enemies. Marina shook her head in disbelief and responded, "I knew her heinous sisters, but I barely knew her at all."

"Well she seemed to know you quite well," he commented. "She threw away her whole life just to get her revenge on you. For what, we never knew."

Marina explained how she killed her sisters but she felt she did them a favor, putting them out of their miserable lives. She knew there was one more sister, but never knew who it was. Marina asked to enter the cell and speak with her. Horan agreed and permitted her entry after opening the cell door, using a palm reader.

Marina knelt next to Darra and sat her up. Darra smiled and whispered, "My angel of death. You have come for me."

"I doubt that," Marina replied. "Was your hatred for me worth it?"

"Hunting and hating was my life," she responded weakly. "That's all I knew."

Marina glanced back at Zhi. He shrugged his shoulders at her and commented, "It's your call."

Marina laid her down and pressed her hands over Darra's face and nose. Darra made no attempt to resist and soon passed away. Marina wasn't sure why, but she felt sympathy for Darra. A tear streamed down her cheek as she stood and left the cell.

"You are much more compassionate than I am," Zhi mentioned as she walked past him to the brig entrance. Marina paused and looked back. "I don't like the monster that I am," she replied. "I know what she felt." Zhi opened the door and the two of them departed the brig.

When they returned to the bridge, Marina requested another drink. She felt nauseous for putting Darra out of her misery in a euthanistic manner. Zhi nodded to his first officer for two more drinks. The woman dutifully filled their glasses and set them on the console.

"Where do we go from here?" asked Marina, expecting to be treated like Darra at some point.

Zhi sighed and leaned back in his chair. "I can't let you go because you discovered our location and I liked it better when you were retired," he confessed. "So, what should I do?"

"Well, it doesn't look like I'm going anywhere so perhaps another drink would be nice," she suggested.

Commander Zhi was pleased that she was civilized about the situation and shared another drink with her. Marina considered that others would have to step up in the war against Kronos if she remained there as their prisoner. She felt as though she had given enough for her kingdom and should look after herself for a change.

As she sipped from her glass, she heard Kat's voice in her head. Kat informed her that help was on the way and that there would be no battle. Marina wondered how that would work but Kat said no more. Then Kara spoke to her and reminded her that they were there for her and would protect her.

Zhi noticed Marina's distracted look and questioned her about it. Marina responded that she imagined that there was peace in the galaxy and that she had a normal life. "Perhaps there can be peace," he commented. "We all have to want it before it can happen."

Marina nodded in agreement and requested one more drink. "You carry quite a burden," Zhi remarked. "You are only human, like the rest of us." He served Marina another glass of bourbon and suggested that it be her last. Marina agreed and savored it.

Zhi expressed his concern that Marina's forces would find the last base and destroy it. "My niece is an engineer on that base and I'd hate to see her die," he admitted.

Marina promised that she would do her best to save her if she was somehow involved in the attack. Zhi appreciated her compassion and the two tapped glasses out of respect for each other. Out of curiosity, Marina questioned Zhi about all the wreckage in the asteroid field. He explained how Klingman's ambitiousness to test a new portal system cost the lives of many ships and lives.

"The portal generator failed?" asked Marina, surprised that Lennox report was accurate.

"Of course, it did," he answered. "It placed the fleet right in the middle of this asteroid field. You know what happens when two objects try to occupy the same space."

Marina shook her head, realizing what a catastrophe that must have been. "Was your niece on that project?" she inquired.

"No, fortunately. She was working on other things like cyborg soldiers and drone technology," he revealed. "I can't tell you any more about it, so don't ask."

Zhi reminded her that she would be treated as a guest on his ship so long as she behaved. Marina gave him her word. He then instructed his first officer to show her to her quarters and informed her that the next meal would be served in a few hours. He would have someone knock up for her. Marina appreciated the hospitality, something she rarely received in her travels.

On Terran, A Scrat command ship hovered nearby and transported Sara on board. She gave coordinates and instructions to Gendry the Scrat commander to rescue Marina. The officer was impressed that Marina was able to find most of the Kronos fleet in such an unlikely area. He mentioned that they were anxious to decimate Kronos for what they did to their worlds. Sara then informed him that her instructions were to negotiate only and not to attack.

At first, Gendry was confused as to why they should pass on an opportunity to cripple the remainder of their forces. Sara explained that the message she received was that things were not as they seemed. She suggested that the fleet was deserting Kronos or perhaps there was another enemy out there that they both feared. Sara then recommended that they contact General Lennox and request a portal to speed up their journey to the asteroid field. Gendry agreed and arranged for his communications officer to contact Orpheus-2 and locate General Lennox.

Marcus and Cheska sat on the flight deck of the class four freighter and discussed how the rebel stronghold on Ramses-3 was able to be decimated by Kronos. Kat boarded the ship and informed them of Marina's capture. Marcus summoned the militia commanders and announced Marina's predicament. He ordered them to place their ships in formation and Cheska would lead them to Archimedes-9. At that time, they would assess any changes in the situation before acting. Marcus informed Kat that he was going with Cheska, drawing a chuckle from her.

"As am I," she responded. "I am your connection to Marina." Marcus groaned and agreed to allow her to join them.

On Tandenar in the Nigus star system, Carl Klingman's ship landed with just him and Tessara on board. Before shutting down, he announced to Tessara that he was moving the plans up. She grew uneasy, wondering what other options they had available to them.

"Have Kepler deliver the cyborg crews to Archimedes-9," he announced giddily. "Have them board the station and kill everyone!"

"But why not Orpheus-2?" Tessara asked, confused by his logic.

"We have no place else to go," he answered. "Looks like this is home, dear." He paced the floor while Tessara hesitated, hoping his common sense would return. Then he stunned her with his next order. "Send March and Sanchez both to Orpheus-2. I want the Federation wiped out completely!"

Tessara feared that this would be the end of Kronos if his plan failed. Carl was acting like a desperate man and that scared her more than his cold-blooded attitude. She sent the orders and then lowered her head sadly. This was one time she didn't want to know the results.

Carl noticed her sad demeanor and questioned what was wrong. She became emotional and shouted at him. "We just left our last remaining base unprotected. We left Polaris unprotected. We're risking all our ships for Orpheus-2. Who cares about Orpheus-2?" she screamed. "The Federation is only a fraction of what it once was."

Carl assured her that, at the very least, the drones with their cyborg crews would be successful and Archimedes-9 would be theirs. Still upset with him, Tessara questioned what good that would do if they lost all their ships and crews. His response stunned her.

"The ships and crews are expendable," he answered. "With the cyborg soldiers to replace them, we can run a war from Archimedes-9."

With tears streaming down her cheeks, she thought about all her friends on those ships. Many went through training with her and took pride in fighting for Kronos. No one ever expected that the leadership, Klingman being the last of them, would sell them out for cyborgs.

"Don't worry about it, Tess," he said arrogantly. "That's why you are with me and they aren't. You are valuable to me."

Tess cried out, "And they aren't? They have committed their lives to serving you and you think so little of them!"

Carl grew impatient with her and warned her to shut up and do what she's told. Tessara bit her lip and paced the floor. She wondered if there was still time to save them. Instinctively, she grabbed her pulse pistol from her belt holster and drew it. Carl sat with his back to her but he knew what she did. "You won't shoot me," he challenged her. "You need me. You are nothing without me. Kronos is nothing without me."

Tessara fired three shots into the back of his head. What she saw next really frightened her. With part of the skull and brain gone, she saw sparks from circuitry in his head. He was already some kind of cyborg. She fired four more shots into the back of his head and prayed that it would kill him.

Carl stood and turned around to face her. He smiled and attempted to speak but could only stutter. Tessara fired several more shots at his face and chest until her pistol cut out on low power. For what seemed like forever, Carl stared at her. His face was bloody with pieces of plastic and metal hanging from flesh. Tessara burst into tears and delivered a powerful kick to his head, possibly the last act she would do if it didn't kill him. With her eyes closed, her mind went blank as she felt the force of her foot striking his head and then a thud. She dropped to her knees and opened her eyes. Carl's body still stood but what was left of his head lay on the floor nearby. The eyes kept winking at her, as if mocking her.

Tessara rushed to the communication console and contacted Dr. Kepler on Base Five. She rescinded the earlier order and instructed Kepler to cancel the deployment of the drones. Kepler informed her that the launch already occurred. She attempted to call the drones back but they failed to respond to her signals. She reported to Tessara that the drones couldn't be reprogrammed for another action until they complete their assignment. In frustration, Tessara ended the transmission and attempted to contact Commander Zhi.

Commander Zhi and Marina sat together at breakfast. They continued to test each other with questions and scenarios. Then Marina asked, "Is there any way to convince you to stand down and take a neutral role in this?"

"And then what?" he countered. "Become part of your kingdom, under your rule?"

Marina laughed at him. "I don't want to rule anybody anywhere," she replied. "You can do your thing and I'll do mine. We agree to leave each other alone."

Zhi pointed out that Kronos would hunt him down for being a traitor if he failed to uphold his allegiance. Marina suggested that they could operate a commercial business on their base and interact with the other trading groups. Zhi shook his head and reminded her that he was a soldier. He could never adapt to a civilian world.

Seventeen Scrat vessels emerged from behind the asteroid field and surrounded the Kronos vessels. The first officer saw them appear on the short-range monitor and shouted, "Sir, Scrat vessels! Lots of them!"

Zhi rushed to the console and was stunned. "Where did they come from?" he shouted, angry that they were unprepared for them.

"They must have used a portal," the officer explained. "They just appeared out of nowhere."

Then they heard the transmitter ping for an incoming transmission. Zhi acknowledged it, knowing it couldn't be good. The faces of Sara and Gendry appeared, sitting on their flight deck.

"We'd like to speak with Marina," Sara requested. "Time is short for you so I suggest you do it quick."

Marina approached the console and suggested to Zhi that she could help. Zhi stepped back and warned her not to screw around. When Sara saw Marina, she was ecstatic. "Are you alright?" she asked anxiously.

"Of course," Marina replied. "My friend Commander Zhi and I just finished breakfast."

"We heard you were taken captive. I contacted our Scrat friends and they were nice enough to give me a lift out here."

Commander Zhi urged Marina to cut the chit-chat and do something about their predicament. Sara pointed out that the Scrat were still eager for revenge for what Kronos did to their worlds. She also mentioned that the Scrat General was ready to destroy every one of their ships, with or without you on board. Marina asked her to give them a few minutes to discuss their options.

Just as the transmission ended, the transmitter beeped for another incoming call. Zhi acknowledged it and was pleased to see Tessara's face. After a short greeting, he revealed their predicament. Tessara responded by relating her situation to him. When she informed him that Carl Klingman was dead, he breathed a sigh of relief.

"What do you recommend?" he asked. "The Scrat are waiting for an answer."

Tessara told him everything that Carl said about the men and women being expendable. She suggested that they settle for peace but warned that the drone squadron with the cyborg soldiers was already dispatched and they failed to recall them. Then she mentioned that the remaining two fleets that hadn't reached him yet were directed to Orpheus-2 with orders to destroy it.

Marina nudged her way in front of the monitor and inquired, "What are these cyborg soldiers you speak of?"

Tessara recognized Marina from wanted posters and was surprised to see her. "I assume you remember Borath," she commented to Marina. "Imagine a fleet of drone ships with a total of forty Boraths on board."

"Where are they headed?" Marina demanded to know.

"Archimedes-9. Carl's orders," Tessara replied. "After I killed him, I had the engineers in charge attempt to recall them but they failed. It has to do with the programming."

Zhi quickly cut in and asked, "Was Dr. Kepler one of the engineers responsible for this?"

Curious as to his interest, Tessara responded, "Yes. Why?"

"She's family. Is the base protected?" he asked.

"Negative. Carl ordered every ship to Orpheus-2."

Marina informed Zhi that they had to find a way to stop the drones before they started their attack. Zhi ended the transmission from Tessera to keep his discussion with Marina confidential to him and his crew. He agreed to keep all ships at the asteroid field and refrain from any battles as well as to reveal the location of the last base if Marina would guarantee the safety of his niece, Sianni Kepler. When Marina balked, he knew she was waiting for something else. "I'll contact the other fleets and tell them to stand down at Orpheus-2!" he exclaimed. "Now, please, help us all avoid our doomsday."

Marina promised to comply if Zhi would coordinate a truce between the remaining forces and her kingdom, otherwise the Scrat would have their day. Zhi agreed and then granted Marina her release. Another transmission came in as Sara and Gendry became impatient.

Marina instructed them to stand down as she was leaving the Kronos command ship shortly. She informed them of the pending attack on Archimedes-9 and Orpheus-2 with instructions to do whatever was necessary to defend them. Meanwhile, Zhi contacted Commander Sanchez and informed him of Klingman's demise. He instructed them to stand down but Sanchez refused. Unless he received orders from Klingman or his replacement, he would carry out his initial orders. The transmission ended with no further discussion. Zhi glanced at Marina, disappointed that Sanchez would ignore his request. He assured her the fleet assembled at the asteroid field would remain there in a neutral status until a treaty was signed later. Then he would reassign them as per the terms of their treaty.

Marina was escorted by the first officer to her ship in the transport bay and she was given clearance to depart as soon as the oxygen was removed from the bay and the gates cleared to open.

When Marina's cruiser cleared the Kronos command ship's transport bay, she contacted Sara and Gendry. She instructed them to return to Archimedes-9 and warned them about the cyborg crews inside the drones. She requested three Scrat warships to accompany her to the fifth and final Kronos base, while Sara accompanied the others to the station. The Scrat General was concerned about using only three ships, but Marina reminded him that the base was left defenseless for this desperation assault by Kronos.

Gendry inquired if she had any instructions for the Scrat ships headed to Archimedes-9. Marina ordered them to attack with extreme prejudice as these were not human crews and the ships were preprogrammed drones. Marina then requested to speak with Sara alone.

"I just want to thank you for bringing the troops with you," Marina mentioned. "When this is over, you and I need to have a chat over a drink or two."

"I'd like nothing better," Sara replied. "This shit's getting old." Both women chuckled as the transmission ended.

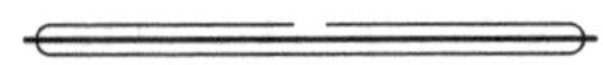

The fleet of drones appeared on the long-range sensors at Archimedes-9. Rebecca and her security team discussed what options they had to defend the station. There were few freighters docked in the station that could provide a defense against the drone fleet. Their only hope was that the Federation or Marina's militia friends arrived in time to help. The station engineer entered and informed her that the station was equipped with twenty air cannons, designed for deterrence only. They could each fire up to ten magnetic drum charges that can disrupt communications of an attacking ship or damage its hull. Rebecca instructed them to prepare to fire the cannons.

Marina was surprised when her transmitter beeped for an incoming message. She glanced at the signal and recognized it as Colby's shuttle. When she acknowledged the signal, his face appeared, smiling so innocently at her.

"What is it, Colby?" she asked, feigning disinterest. "I'm a busy woman, you know."

"Just checking in, my fearless leader," he announced playfully. "Any new information on the last Kronos base?"

"Not a word," she lied. "Don't you have a wife to worry about?"

"She's taking a nap right now. Anything important happening with the war?" he continued.

"Nope. Kronos is on the run and it looks like the fighting is over."

Mike laughed and inquired if she was drinking. She told him that there was nothing going on that he needed to know about. She did mention that Zenith's knowledge of the hidden programs on the Kronos database were very helpful. When he relented that there was nothing to be learned from Marina, he wished her well and mentioned that they should get the gang together soon for a nice dinner. "Soon enough," replied Marina and she ended the transmission.

"Oh, Margot. You disappoint me," Marina muttered to herself.

General Lennox sent her a message and informed her that a portal was set up to get her to the supposed location of the fifth base. She gave her the coordinates of the portal and reminded her to keep her in the loop if the base was really there. Marina thanked her and ended the transmission. She relayed the information to the accompanying Scrat vessels and then took advantage of the time to rest.

For some reason, this seemed all too simple. Marina was concerned about the size of the Kronos fleet on its way to Orpheus-2. Then she considered the danger that the cyborg's posed if they were able to board Archimedes-9. Rebecca's security detail wasn't armed for that kind of conflict. She had an idea about the fifth Kronos base and hoped to find a way to recall the drones to their home.

CHAPTER 12

At Kronos base five, Drs. Kepler and Stylus sat in the cafeteria and waited for news about the war. The cafeteria was eerily empty as only a handful of engineers and technicians remained on the base. The two women were edgy over the fact that the base was defenseless and that the other four bases had already been compromised and lost. Stylus questioned why Tessara would want to cancel the drone attack but Kepler was only interested in following orders. She did express concern about not having control of the drones and the cyborgs anymore.

"What do you care?" asked Stylus. "It's the Federation's problem now."

"We hope," commented Kepler sarcastically. "What if the cyborgs turn on us?" Her wrist transmitter beeped and she received a message from her uncle, Commander Zhi. He warned her that ships were coming to the base but they would not attack. He asked her to cooperate with Marina for her own safety. Dr. Stylus noticed the strange look on Dr. Kepler's face and asked what the message was.

"Beats me," she replied, while clearing the message from the transmitter. "My uncle just wanted to remind me of something but the message was cut off." She wasn't sure what was going on but there was a reason why her uncle risked contacting her with a warning. Dr. Stylus pressed her for more on the message but she shrugged her shoulders and continued eating her dinner.

Before Stylus could ask anything else, a technician barged into the cafeteria and hurried to their table. The young man blurted out, "Three alien vessels and a cruiser are approaching! What do we do?"

Dr. Kepler stood and patted the man's shoulder. "Let's make contact with them and see what they want," she instructed him calmly. Dr. Stylus went to her locker in the rear of the cafeteria and retrieved a pulse pistol. She followed them, suspicious of Kepler's intentions.

In the control room, Dr. Kepler sent out a signal to Marina's cruiser, assuming that she oversaw the force. Stylus questioned her again, wanting to know what she knew. Marina's face appeared on the monitor and greeted her. "Dr. Kepler, I presume."

"I am," Kepler replied. "Who are you?"

Marina introduced herself and related the conversation she had with Commander Zhi. She instructed Kepler to surrender the station and no one would be hurt. Kepler wanted assurance that they wouldn't be held as prisoners. Marina promised that they would be free to go where ever they wish as soon as they could be transported. Kepler agreed and granted her access to the base.

Stylus went into a rage and shouted at Kepler, "What the hell do you think you're doing?"

"I'm saving our asses," she replied. "Kronos abandoned us."

"I'm not surrendering to them," she stated and targeted Dr. Kepler with her pulse pistol.

"Put that down, you fool," chided Kepler.

Stylus walked over to the console and initiated the self-destruct sequence for the base. "I'll make sure Marina dies," boasted Stylus.

"And the rest of us, too! You fool!" shouted Kepler.

Marina docked her cruiser inside the transport bay and was escorted by a technician to the control room. She heard the announcement over the page system for the self-destruct initiation and evacuation. When they entered the control room, Stylus attempted to shoot Marina but Marina stepped behind the technician, who took the hit. Marina drew one of her daggers from her thigh belt and fired it at Stylus. Stylus targeted Marina again, but the dagger struck her in the throat before she could fire. The technician fell to the floor with a lethal wound. Stylus grasped at her throat and uttered incoherently, before falling. Marina retrieved the dagger and wiped the blood off on Stylus' blouse.

"Sianni, I presume," commented Marina.

Kepler shouted frantically, "I am, but we have to get out of here! The base is going to explode!"

Marina approached the console and manipulated the computer's system log. She found the program in the database, just as Zenith had done, and frantically searched through its menus. She couldn't find a way to terminate the self-destruct sequence which was now at five minutes and counting so she cleared the timer, thus ending the command before it executed. Sianni stared at her in disbelief, stunned by Marina's ability to access and manipulate the program.

"Damn!" Kepler exclaimed. "I didn't even know how to do that."

"Well, I don't know if it'll work," Marina complained. "We need to figure out how to stop those drones, once we're on board my ship."

Marina instructed her to assemble all the technicians and engineers in the transport bay. Dr. Kepler hurried out of the control room, leaving Marina to explore the program further. She looked pleased as she entered new coordinates into the system. Assuming the base didn't self-destruct, it would relocate to another region selected by Marina. Once she initiated the new commands in the system, she left the control room.

Marina prepared the *Reaper* for flight and initiated its startup procedure. Eight men and women entered the bay and boarded Marina's ship. The hatch closed and Marina's cruiser departed the transport bay, speeding away from the base.

Gendry contacted her about the status of the base. Marina informed him that one of the traitors placed it in self-destruct mode and they needed to leave the area. They were headed to Archimedes-9 to take on the drones and their cyborg crews. Marina then requested another portal from General Lennox to get to Archimedes-9 and, as expected, Lennox complained about the cost of generating these portals. When she inquired about Base Five for payment, Marina disappointed her, mentioning that it was about to blow and there was nothing she could do about it. She did warn her that there was a large contingent of Kronos ships headed to Orpheus-2, but reinforcements were on the way. Lennox ended the transmission, obviously pissed off, but still provided the portal for Marina.

Marina sent a message to Zenith and inquired if the hidden programs in the database could be used to control the drones and their cyborg crews. She questioned Dr. Kepler about the drones and cyborgs, hoping to learn of a weakness, but Kepler had no answers as to how she lost control of them. Kepler complained that she hadn't completed testing on the central processing units to be sure how they would respond, once activated. Dr. Kepler and her peers brainstormed for a solution but Kepler's project was always kept secret between her and Dr. Stylus, adding to their difficulties.

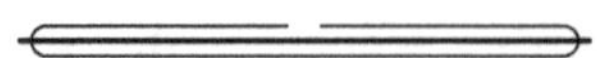

As twenty drones closed in on Archimedes-9, Rebecca's transport supervisor made several attempts to contact them but received no response. As soon as the drones were within range, Rebecca ordered her security team to open fire with the air cannons.

The cannons fired repeatedly and the magnetic outer skin of the drum charges enabled each unit to attach to the hulls of the drones. The drums detonated, damaging the hulls on several of the drones, leaving the skins severely wrinkled and some breached. After the last charge detonated, four of the drones were disabled, each stranding their cyborg crew of four.

Seven of the freighters emerged from the bay and opened fire on the drones. Oddly enough, the drones did not return fire. Their mission was to deliver the cyborgs. Cannon fire from the freighters took out two more of the drones, leaving four. But then the drones swarmed on the overmatched freighters and pummeled them with cannon fire until all of them were destroyed. The cyborgs were able to alter the drones' programming, making them all the more dangerous.

Rebeca was horrified as she watched the monitor. Their losses were already significant as they were overmatched by the drones. She instructed her security detail to move everyone to the upper levels away from the transport bay. Anyone who could carry a weapon would remain on the main level near the transport bay. Rebecca then ordered the transport supervisor to open the bay doors to allow the drones to dock and then close them immediately after to prevent a breach of the station to space.

Three drones accessed the bay while the other was in position to take out key sections of the station. The cyborgs were programmed well for this coordinated attack.

Rebecca joined her team at the first personnel hatch. The hatch exploded and five cyborgs stormed into the corridor. Rebecca's team quickly engaged the cyborgs in a shootout.

Soon seven other cyborgs entered the corridor and joined the assault. Rebecca's team was forced to retreat to the cargo area. They only inflicted a few casualties on the cyborgs while more than half of her team was already dead.

The militia vessels and the class four freighter approached the station. Marcus gave the orders for all ships to open fire on the drones. As with the earlier freighters, the drones turned on them and swarmed. The militia vessels returned fire, but took heavy damage.

On board Cheska's freighter, she informed Marcus that she would try the program Zenith gave her to control the drones and cyborgs. The drones sensed that there was no link to a command ship and fired on it as an enemy target. Marcus urged Cheska to work fast before the damage became critical.

Inside the station, the cyborgs surrounded Rebecca's team. With only a dozen of her people left, they could only buy time and hope for a miracle. One of her men lifted a manhole cover for them to escape through. Quickly, each one of them dropped down to the lower cable raceways and attempted to emerge behind their attackers. Each of the team, including Rebecca, suffered at least a flesh wound with four suffering more serious injuries.

Cheska made several attempts with the program but none had an effect on the drones in battle. Several of the militia vessels were forced to withdraw from the battle due to damage and the freighter, despite its auto-fire feature, took numerous hits.

Marina's cruiser, followed by the three Scrat vessels, appeared from the portal and joined the battle. Marina was able to outmaneuver the drones but the Scrat vessels weren't so lucky. They took numerous hits and were soon forced to retreat from the battle.

Marina finally received a response from Zenith. The message instructed her to change the parameters of one of the commands and assured her that it would work. Marina immediately contacted Cheska and relayed the instructions.

A loud bang and a jolt of the freighter warned Cheska's group of the coming danger. When a drone crashed through one of the bay doors, Cheska warned everyone to prepare for a breach to space as compartments would begin sealing off.

Kat knelt down in the middle of the room and meditated. She urgently summoned help from Ginna and Kara. Although, she didn't get a response, she felt their power surround her. Ten cyborgs ripped through the secured hatch to the flight deck and barged in. Kat raised her hands and uttered an incantation. The cyborgs suddenly slowed their motion nearly to a stop. She maintained her position to keep them under her control.

Marcus took advantage of the opportunity and circled behind them. He searched desperately for an access panel on the nearest cyborg to try and disable it. He finally found it at the base of the neck on the back of the cyborg. He crept up to the panel and removed it, using the small T-handle on it. When he opened it, he saw a series of cables, steel cords and a small control box.

Kat urged him to hurry as the power provided by the girls was weakening. Ginna was on the station and her power was still effective. Kara, because of the distance to Taurus, required more energy to project her power and it weakened her.

Marcus toggled each of the seven switches on the control box but nothing happened. Then he found a main switch on the side of the box, partially hidden by cables. He switched it off and the cyborg powered down. The remaining cyborgs moved slightly faster toward Kat, an indication of her fading influence on them. Marcus rushed to the next closest cyborg and repeated the exercise.

Cheska implemented the change to the program as Marina instructed and hurried to her console. When she initiated the program, she had to change the type of targets that the menu was set up for. She used a scanner to read one of the cyborgs and entered it into the menu. Then she took an image of a drone from the short-range sensor and inserted it into the menu. She selected each of them and ran the program. Her next option was to 'destroy' the targets or 'disarm' them. She chose 'destroy' and pressed 'run' again.

A surge of energy filled the flight deck and each of the cyborg's heads exploded, sending shrapnel in all directions. Kat fell to the floor from the impact of the blasts. Marcus and the other crewmen were badly injured and down, bleeding from several wounds each. Cheska received shrapnel in her arms and face but continued to operate the program from the main console.

With the remaining ships taking severe damage, Marina ordered them to withdraw. She would attempt to handle the remaining two drones. Dr. Kepler joined her on the flight deck and observed the battle. "Any ideas yet?" Marina inquired. "Your uncle had high praise for you for your engineering ability."

"Not yet," she replied, disappointed.

Marina maneuvered her ship between the approaching drones and, despite their cannon fire, she waited until they were nearly upon her. At the last second, she pulled out and the two drones collided, ending up in a brief fireball. The last drone exited the station and darted toward Marina's cruiser. She tried several maneuvers but couldn't shake the drone. Each time it fired at her ship, the pulses of energy passed closer. The drone had the capacity to zero in on a moving target and it was getting too close now.

Cheska redirected the targeting sensor to the remaining drone and pressed 'run'. The ship fired energy pulses at the last of the drones until it was destroyed.

"Damn," she uttered in amazement. "Will you look at that?"

Cheska searched for more targets and was disappointed to find none. She shut down the program and assisted the injured officers off the flight deck.

Rebecca and her team emerged from one of the manholes and crept toward the cargo area. It was strangely quiet and haunting in a way. When they reached the bay, they saw the cyborgs lying in pieces across the floor.

"What the hell happened?" muttered one of the men.

"I think Marina had something to do with this," she replied. "She has a way with miracles."

Marina checked in with the remaining ships but all were unserviceable for additional battle at this point.

Her thoughts for the next move were interrupted by a message from General Lennox on her wrist transmitter. She urged Marina to send any help that she could as they were outnumbered significantly.

General Lennox ordered all her military vessels out of the station to defend it. Her first officer questioned what chance they had against

Kronos' fleet. Lennox paced with her hands behind her back and replied, "Marina will find a way out of this. She humbled me many a time before we became friends. I just wish I knew how she does it."

"So, you think help is on the way?" the woman asked, hopeful.

"I don't know. She has her hands full on Archimedes-9 with the cyborgs and drones."

General Lennox instructed one of her officers to set up portals for any of Marina's allies regardless of where they were likely to be. She urged him to hurry and send the coordinates to the leaders of those allies.

On board the lead Kronos command ship, Commander Sanchez ordered his ships to begin the attack on Orpheus-2. Both groups scored early hits but the Federation ships took significantly more damage and their losses mounted.

General Lennox watched the battle on the monitor and uttered to herself, "Marina, where are you?"

Several of the Federation ships withdrew from the battle and fled the area for safety. They would attempt quick repairs and then, if successful, return to the battle. Their defenses whittled down to a mere four ships against twenty.

The first officer questioned General Lennox if she considered surrendering the station and perhaps live to fight another day. Lennox bit her lip and hesitated to answer. Surrender was not something that she would ever consider, but today was different. This was likely their final battle with Kronos, win or lose.

Two of the remaining four Federation ships were crippled and limping from the battle. The commander of one of the remaining ships requested new orders regarding their engagement from General Lennox. Now was the time to make the call: surrender or die fighting.

Seventeen Scrat vessels appeared in the distance and soon joined the battle. Then Marina's *Reaper* appeared and joined the Scrat fleet in their attack. They quickly engaged the Kronos fleet and inflicted significant damage.

General Lennox was ecstatic when she saw the Scrat vessels arrive. "Does that answer your question?" she replied to the commander in the field.

"Yes, it does! We fight!" he exclaimed and ended the transmission.

Nine more alien military vessels arrived and joined the battle. Five were Golgar's forces from Calamaar and four were Urthonian, sent from Queen Attilena.

As Marina's forces grew in number, the Kronos fleet shrank. When several of them attempted to flee, the Calamaarian and Urthonian ships hunted them down.

Cheska's freighter arrived, thanks to General Lennox's coordinates to the portal. She activated the Kronos program from the main console in the control room once more. Marcus and Kat stood nearby, both with bandages covering their injuries. Other than the three of them, the flight deck was empty, with the remainder of the officers in the infirmary.

Marcus inquired if the program would work once more. Confident, Cheska smiled at him and initiated the program's start sequence. Watching the battle, Kat marveled at the monitor. "This is beautiful," she commented proudly. "Marina's alliance has succeeded all expectations."

Cheska glanced at her and responded, "No one else could do what she has just done. Now, watch what happens out there."

Each of the remaining Kronos vessels suddenly stopped firing and shut down. Sara contacted Marina and requested further orders. Marina replied mercilessly, "Finish them off. They had their chance for peace."

Sara relayed the orders to the Scrat officers, who were more than happy to destroy the remaining Kronos fleet. Marina received an incoming message from Commander Sanchez, pleading for mercy and offering to surrender. Marina responded, "Hubris and arrogance are sins that cannot be forgiven. Would you have allowed us to surrender or would you have destroyed us?"

Sanchez hesitated to respond. Marina continued, "I thought so. At least Commander Zhi was smart enough to consider peaceful options." She ended the transmission and sighed with relief. This was the end for Kronos.

Dr. Kepler questioned if it was necessary to terminate them like that. Marina explained that there was a big difference between her uncle and commander Sanchez. Commander Zhi respected his opponents while Sanchez sought glory. Then she explained how he spared Yord to avoid losses so he could shine in the big battle.

"What will happen to my uncle?" Dr. Kepler asked, wondering how Marina would behave after victory.

Marina related that her uncle's fleet was spared and that she promised to preserve the last base so they would have a home. Then she mentioned that there was wealth in long-distance cargo hauling and that he could benefit from converting to a trade organization.

"What do you want to do with your life now that Kronos is gone?" Marina asked Dr. Kepler. When she expressed her uncertainty about her future, Marina suggested that she visit Sargassa and see Dr. Lowell, if she wanted to continue her engineering career for peaceful purposes. Kepler liked the idea and promised to consider it.

The leaders of each of Marina's allies landed on Orpheus-2. The corridors were lined with grateful crewmen and their families who cheered as the leaders passed through on their way to the conference room. When Marina arrived, the cheers were deafening. She had trouble hiding her smile and realized that her efforts were appreciated after all.

Kat and Marcus greeted her outside the conference room with a friendly embrace. Marina thanked them for everything and commented that they were quite a team. Kat reminded her that they all were her "reign of pain" and that she would never be alone.

When everyone was seated, Marina addressed and thanked each of them. She announced her plans to retire from the rebellion business and live out her life peacefully and, glancing at Sara, she hoped to do it with a good friend. She revealed her intentions for Commander Zhi's forces and, thanks to their cooperation, she would allow them to participate in commercial industry for peaceful purposes.

General Lennox questioned her about the last base and what happened. She explained that Dr. Stylus wasn't keen on the terms of surrender and set off the self-destruct sequence. Marina expressed her disappointment when she couldn't stop the program, but managed to save the engineering staff for possible employment by the Federation.

General Lennox commented to Marina that she sure cut it close in supporting her. "It's funny that you bring that up, Sandra," Marina replied, eager to address a pressing issue. "It seems that our friend Tarsus had a change of heart about whose side he was on." She then revealed that Tarsus was supposed to arrive at Orpheus-2 a while ago to support her.

"You know how I feel about traitors," Lennox replied gruffly.

"Do what you must," Marina urged. "I never liked that smug bastard anyway."

After several lesser discussions, Marina thanked everyone once more and excused herself. Sara did the same and followed her. The two returned to her ship where she informed Dr. Kepler and her staff that they were going to Archimedes-9. There they would have access to transportation to go anywhere they chose. She presented the offer to work for the Federation or to go elsewhere and start over.

Marina used the portal to reach Archimedes-9 in relatively short time. Again, she was greeted by loud cheering from many grateful people in the transport bay. The crowd split apart and Rebecca approached them with her daughter Aries in her arms. Rebecca embraced both women tightly and thanked them with tears in her eyes. Aries put her arms out for Marina to hug her. After a brief conversation about the battle, Marina informed Rebecca that she had to go. All of Kepler's staff were eager to take employment on Archimedes-9 except for Dr. Kepler. She accepted Marina's offer to meet with Dr. Lowell on Sargassa.

Rebecca could tell that this might be the last time she saw Marina. She hugged her tightly and wished her the peace that she sought her whole life. Marina became teary-eyed and thanked her for the long journey they took together, prior to leaving the black market courier business when she first rescued Rebecca from the gang of thugs. Marina walked away sadly and boarded her ship. Sara and Dr. Kepler followed her on board and the hatch closed.

"Will Marina come back?" inquired Rebecca's daughter Aries.

"No, I don't think so, Honey," Rebecca replied. "Her journey will take her elsewhere."

Once they departed Archimedes-9, Marina contacted Commander Zhi and gave him the opportunity to speak with his niece. Dr. Kepler told him of her intentions to go to Sargassa and pursue her engineering career for peace.

When Marina resumed her conversation with Zhi, she related everything that happened and gave him coordinates to a new location. He mentioned that his people expressed interest in the long-distance cargo hauling industry and would be willing to learn. Thinking of the *Blue Eagle* and its crew, Marina commented that she had just the crew to teach them.

"I have to thank you for what you've done for us," said Commander Zhi, humbled. "As much as we hated to lose the war, I think it was for the best."

"And because of you, there are a lot of people that will enjoy a new life," she replied.

"Will we have a chance to meet over drinks again some time?" he asked.

Marina chuckled and then answered, "You never know." The transmission ended. A tear streamed down her cheek and she held Sara's hand.

"What's that for?" Sara teased.

"We have a lot of healing to do."

Sara stood and embraced Marina. "We'll heal together," she replied.

Dr. Kepler was impressed by the camaraderie between the two women. She never had that with Dr. Stylus and hoped to find it on Sargassa.

The Scrat fleet returned to their home in the Nebula galaxy, while the Calamaarian and the Urthonians returned to their homes. Things returned to normal on Archimedes-9 and Orpheus-2. Repairs were made and business resumed between the stations.

Marina took Dr. Kepler to Sargassa and arranged for her to work with Dr. Lowell and Creeg, her Scrat husband. Afterward, she and Sara departed for Terran. Sara looked distracted in the copilot's seat until Marina asked what was on her mind.

"Before I left Terran, I saw a small craft on the long-range sensors," Sara revealed. "It disappeared over Tandenar. I'm just wondering who it might be."

"Well, let's find out," said Marina giddily. "This is the kind of action I still like to handle: small and grounded."

The *Reaper* did a scan of the surface and finally found the missing craft. Marina landed her ship next to it. When they exited the ship, they were greeted by Tessara.

"I wondered how long it would take for you to find me?" Tessara commented.

"And you are?" questioned Marina.

"I was Klingman's first officer. Ironically, I killed him. His corpse is on board the ship if you care to inspect it."

"So, it was you who contacted Commander Zhi and changed the plans," Marina responded.

"It was. I am ready to pay for my crimes," she confessed. "I gave many of the orders that were executed against your people." Tessara knelt down in front of her, prepared to die.

Marina glanced at Sara and shook her head. "Come on, Tessara. This was war," she reminded her. "Since you ended Klingman, how about we call it even?"

Tessara stood up and thanked Marina. She then gave her the location of Polaris and informed her that it was the last Kronos facility that she was aware of. Marina inquired about details and was pleased that it was a small base with minimal value. She would give it to Lennox to make up for not getting Base Five to her.

The two women shook hands and Tessara approached her craft. Marina called to her and suggested she contact Zhi about employment in the commercial sector. Tessara paused, looking baffled by her recommendation.

"Every good person deserves a second chance," Marina commented and then boarded the *Reaper*.

"She's a strange one," Tessara remarked to Sara and then she boarded her ship.

"Yes, she is," Sara commented to herself and followed Marina on board the *Reaper*.

When they docked on Terran in the hidden cavern on the side of the mountain, Jackson eagerly awaited them. "Miss me?" teased Sara.

"Of course, I did," replied Jackson. "I was going to send Marina a bill for taking my prized security officer." The three of them chuckled over his remark.

"You don't have to worry about Sara leaving," Marina replied. "You need to worry about me staying."

"You're kidding!" Jackson responded, stunned. "You mean you're retiring from the war to stay here?"

"War's over," announced Sara. "The good guys won."

"Then let's go celebrate!" he exclaimed, pleased by the news. "You are just in time for another gala festival, celebrating the success of the trade routes."

The women followed Jackson down a corridor and through the exit to his palace grounds. Marina was pleased to see the crew of the *Blue Eagle* there, especially Zenith. And then her favorite pain in the ass appeared with Margot.

"Marina!" Mike Colby shouted, excited. "Tell me you found it!"

"Found what?" she teased.

"The fifth base!"

Margot stood behind him and shook her head at Marina. Amused by their reactions, Marina informed him that they did, in fact, find the fifth base. And then she gave him the news he always wanted to hear. "I've arranged for you to go there in your shuttle and handle things," she announced giddily. Margot placed her hands on her hips and turned away. Marina was sure she heard her cuss. Mike was ecstatic. Meanwhile, the *Blue Eagle's* captain Tisch and her crew stared at Marina, wondering if she had lost her mind.

"Will I be joining up with a fleet?" he asked, unable to control his emotions.

"Oh, yes," replied Marina.

Sara turned away to hide her smile. Now Margot felt better, sensing that there was a catch. Zenith joined them with a tray of drinks and served everyone.

"Well?" pressed Colby, eager for details.

Marina announced that the war was over and that the Kronos fleet surrendered. She revealed that the fifth base will be used to participate in long-distance cargo hauling. Mike was baffled by her announcement.

"But…" he started. Margot covered his mouth from behind and instructed him to let Marina finish.

Marina related the terms of the treaty that she and Commander Zhi agreed to. Then she revealed that she promised to send Colby to the base to help the former Kronos members adjust to a civilian lifestyle in a commercial environment. Mike sat down in a chair, looking devastated.

Marina chastised Margot for not doing her part to keep Mike under control. Margot whispered in Marina's ear that she was pregnant and Mike didn't know yet. Marina nodded in approval and realized how Margot finally handled him.

Margot chose that moment to announce that Mike was now out of the war business and into the daddy business. Mike looked up at her and groaned, "You're not funny, Margot."

Margot kissed his cheek and stated, "My body doesn't lie. Looks like you really are retired from the war business." Mike stood up and grabbed Margot. He spun her around in his arms, howling with joy.

"Perhaps, it is better if Tisch and her crew take the *Blue Eagle* to the base and help the former Kronos people set up trade routes in that part of the galaxy," Marina commented.

Tisch was eager to take on the assignment without Mike and Margot. It was an opportunity for her and Zenith to develop their responsibilities and their roles in expanding the long-distance cargo hauling industry.

Marina approached Zenith and embraced her with an affectionate hug. She thanked her for everything she did with the Kronos database. "Without your help, we'd still be fighting the war but from a losing position," Marina emphasized to her. "You saved us all."

"But what about me?" Mike asked, feeling left out.

"What about you?" Marina countered.

"You did your duty," interjected Margot as she patted her belly. "Now stop whining." The women cheered Margot for her firm control of Mike.

"Are you really retiring here, Marina?" Tisch inquired, curious.

"I am. I have nothing left to fight about," she confessed. "The two Seers, my girls, have found their own lives. Kara has discovered boys and Ginna has discovered upper management on Taurus – with Gemini."

"That's a mistake," complained Mike.

"Maybe. And then there's Kat. She has Marcus and I've assigned her the role of ruling Yord on my behalf."

"What will you do then?" asked Margot, concerned for her friend.

Marina placed her arm around Sara's shoulders and replied, "Sara and I have sacrificed enough over the years. We both plan to have some fun around here."

"And Jackson's people make great drinks," added Sara.

"Time for a nap," Marina commented. "It's been a long war and I'm turning things over to my reign of pain – Sandra Lennox, Kat Tosci, and my Seers Kara and Ginna."

"And we need to get you situated upstairs," mentioned Sara. "You'll need an apartment with a nice view of the valley." She took Marina by the hand and led her up the stairs.

Tisch held up her drink and proposed a toast to their success. Everyone raised their glasses and cheered.

Tarsus sat at the bar in Murgatroyd's Oasis. Stosh stood across the bar from him and questioned why they didn't join the battle. Before he could speak, General Lennox and four of her soldiers entered the pub. They approached Tarsus without his knowledge.

Tarsus chugged his ale and slid the mug back to Stosh for another. "You know, I never liked that bitch Marina. And now, she's been put in her place, wherever it is."

General Lennox stood behind Tarsus and waited patiently to hear what he had to say. "Are you so sure that Kronos won the war with that battle?" asked Stosh.

"Oh, I'm sure," he boasted. "Marina was probably surprised when I didn't show."

Elspeth appeared from the office area and handed Tarsus a note. "What's this?" he asked, curious.

"It's from a friend," she replied and left. Stosh grinned as he knew what it was.

Tarsus glanced at the note which read: Sorry I couldn't be there for you, but my friend Sandra will take good care of you. He panicked as he realized he was set up. When he turned around, General Lennox punched him in the mouth and sent him to the floor.

"That's for hanging me out to dry," said Lennox with an attitude. "Kronos lost the war, thanks to Marina and now you will be tried as a traitor."

Tarsus knew he was screwed. He got up slowly and then tried to run for the exit. Lennox's soldiers grabbed him at the door and handcuffed him. Lennox noticed the interest by the pub's customers and was happy to appease them. She had Tarsus escorted to the center of the floor and announced to everyone that he was a coward and a traitor. Everyone jeered him and threw food at him. Lennox then mentioned how he and his boys lost their opportunity to inherit a Kronos base for their own purpose, but since he betrayed Marina, she blew it up instead. One of his men questioned Tarsus if that was true. He fumbled for the right words to respond but it didn't matter. His hesitation spoke for itself. The man punched him in the face, drawing another round of cheers. When he suffered enough humiliation, Lennox's soldiers took him away.

General Lennox announced to everyone that the war was over and Kronos was defeated, bringing a booming round of cheers. Lennox bowed and departed the pub. She was ready for a boring, peaceful period as much as Marina was. Then she considered how boring it would really be. "No, maybe it won't be boring," she uttered to herself. "After all, I still have Colby to deal with. Thanks, Marina." Lennox looked back at the pub once more and then boarded her ship.

www.ingramcontent.com/pod-product-compliance
Lightning Source LLC
Chambersburg PA
CBHW060315310726
48976CB00007B/2341